Chloe: Dragoon Novel #2

Evan Ratke

Cassie,

Thank you so much!

Evan Ratke

Published by Evan Ratke, 2019.

For my parents.

Printed in the United States of America

ISBN 978-1-7321156-2-0 (E-book)

ISBN 978-1-7321156-3-7 (Paperback)

First Edition 2019

10 9 8 7 6 5 4 3 2 1

Edited by Jamie Fueglein

Cover Illustration by Margaret Peyton

PHASE 1: MERENRANTA

Winter of the 55th Year after the Reform

7th Year after the Marathon Civil War

16th Year after the Marathon-Carthage War

ONE

Chloe Corday participated in her first execution that morning. Twenty-one years old with loose, bright blond hair that reached the middle of her back, Chloe walked the beach with the perpetrator and his sentencing party. She wore the typical officer's uniform, a gray winter jacket with the word "POLICE" stitched in blue letters on the back, black pants, boots, gloves, and hat. Her weapon, a standard-issue officer's pistol manufactured from an old Previous Civilization design the town still had on file, was in her hands, the safety off at the order of the sheriff, in case the perpetrator tried to fight or flee before they came to the execution spot. Chloe hoped he wouldn't do either. As a police officer she'd never killed anyone and didn't desire to.

They moved north from the town of Merenranta, boots crunching in the gray snow-covered sand, weapons clicking, heads ducking as the wind came in from the sea and crackled through the woods at the edge of the beach. White puffs flowed from their mouths, the air freezing and sharp with the smell of rot and salt. Waves crashed at the shore, the ocean choppy and gray all the way out to the horizon, so gray even the yellow light of the sun couldn't shine on the surface. Another cold winter on the coast, Chloe's sixth since she and her parents found Merenranta and settled here. As bitter as it was, however, winter in Merenranta was temperate compared to winter in Marathon, several hundred miles northwest and beneath the overcast of the Reform. Seven years after Marathon's destruction, Chloe didn't miss that city in the slightest.

One of four in the sentencing party, Chloe walked on one side of the perpetrator, her partner on the other. The sheriff and the mayor kept a wary pace in the back. Though the police kept Merenranta safe, the forests encircling the town perimeter could never be secured. With each step she trod in the snow and sand, every gray dune she passed, Chloe shifted her eyes from the perpetrator to the tree line and back again, waiting for an ambush.

The party stopped one mile up the beach, along the trees, far enough away from Merenranta the children in school wouldn't hear the shot yet close enough to retreat back to town were they attacked. Chloe and her partner faced the perpetrator, as the sheriff and the mayor circled to stand in front of him. Merenranta never executed someone from behind, no matter their crime. In his early forties, black-haired, and dressed in civilian winter gear, Mayor Amin Darabont delivered the first words of any of them since leaving town. "Martin Donnelly, by your confession, before sunrise this morning you assaulted and murdered Sarah Murphy, a citizen of Merenranta and your life partner of ten years, in your own house." Mayor Darabont was firm in his reiteration of Donnelly's crimes, official, as if he were reading from Merenranta's town charter. But there was reluctance as well. Like the person he'd murdered, Donnelly was a citizen, and Darabont wasn't one to take pleasure in killing his own people. "You've also pled guilty to hiding your status as a Second-Gen, deceiving the people of Merenranta for decades into believing you were human. Do you have any final appeals or statements you'd like to make before your sentence is carried out?"

Wrists bound with metal handcuffs that even Second-Gens would need a minute to escape from, Donnelly stood before his peers, shivering despite the winter clothes they'd given him. His head was bent, tears dripping from his eyelids, the water sparkling in the brown glow of his irises. His Second-Gen Stage was still on. It had been since Sarah's murder. That wasn't why Chloe's left arm trembled, though. It was because he had lied, like her. Chloe learned she was a Second-Gen the same day as her mother, through her mother's Awakening. From the age of five to fourteen, Chloe was a Second-Gen of Marathon, not human, seen as a danger by everyone who was. Then, upon finding Merenranta, she and her parents lied, reclaiming the false humanity lost with her mother's Awakening. The choice had been simple: hold onto this secret for the rest of their lives, or be denied citizenship and cast back into the ungoverned lands the Reform created.

No requests, no cry for forgiveness, nothing from Donnelly's chapped lips. He was either too scared or too angry to speak for himself any more than he already had. His hands were brownish-red with dried blood, his cheeks slashed during Sarah's fruitless self-defense. Maybe he didn't want to delay his punishment. Donnelly's time expired and Darabont nodded to the sheriff.

"Proceed."

Fifty-year-old Sheriff Dylan Armistead made a quick advance, pistol readied. "Look at me," Sheriff Armistead said, finger on the trigger, voice flat, unsympathetic. Armistead and Donnelly had known each other for years, but when Donnelly lifted his head, his breathing rapid, short, Armistead's response was immediate. The pistol flashed at the tip of the barrel, the report banging through the trees and across the beach to the waves. Donnelly toppled into the snow and sand. A cloud of red and pink squirted from his eye. The blood was still finding its way to the snow as Armistead brought her pistol down and put a second round in Donnelly's other glimmering eye. No one diverted their attention, all were witnesses to the town's justice.

Armistead holstered her weapon, smoke pouring from the barrel. Chloe and her partner did the same with their pistols, Chloe gripping her wrist to stop the tremors in her left arm. Bending over the departed, Armistead unlocked and removed the handcuffs before gesturing to her officers. "Woods."

Donnelly was stripped of his clothing, to be washed and reused in Merenranta, his naked body hauled ten or so yards into the forest and dumped beside a tree. Law-abiding Merenranta citizens were buried in a cemetery on the western end of town, their graves marked with stones, just as the Previous Civilization had done. Criminals were left to decay in the woods, the sight of their decomposing corpses a warning to outsiders who might try to bring harm to Merenranta.

Exiting the trees, the party split. Darabont and Armistead headed back to Merenranta while Chloe and her partner continued north, a routine patrol of the beach. Parting words were limited; neither she nor her partner had much to say about what they'd partaken in, not in front of Darabont and Armistead at least. Walking the stretches of gray beach, between the gray sea and the gray snow-drenched trees, Chloe kept her observations vigilant but her weapon holstered. When the mayor and sheriff were gone from view, the buildings of Merenranta silhouettes in the distance, Chloe rolled up her sleeve, glancing at the gash on her left forearm. Red yet fading, the cut would be healed by tomorrow, no scar, no indication it was ever there. In moments like these, Chloe wished her species didn't cure so easily.

"You were talking in your sleep, again," Chloe's partner said after a few miles. Twenty-one with long red hair tucked in her hat and freckles dotting her face, Samantha Armistead ambled at Chloe's side. Her expression was casual, though Chloe could see the concern within her demeanor.

"Probably because you were kicking me," Chloe giggled. A breeze gusted up from the waves.

"Liar," Samantha quipped. The forest swayed with the wind, branches snapping from their trunks and plummeting to the snowy floor. Unlike the barren region of Marathon where Chloe had been born and where the overcast barred adequate sunlight from the landscape, greenery was making a gradual renewal in this area. In winter, though, it was difficult to perceive.

"Then why was I hanging off the bed this morning?" A white puff respired from Chloe's mouth, glittering in the sun as it floated towards the grayish-blue sky.

"Because you still have a single bed for some reason. You know the factories will make you a bigger one, right?"

"Hey," Chloe chuckled. "That bed is giant compared to the one I had in Missio."

"Missio?" Samantha asked.

"Marathon's civilian district. That place I didn't leave until it all, uh..."

"Blew up?"

"Something like that, yeah."

"That what you were dreaming about last night?" Samantha said, seriousness inching its way into her tone.

Chloe gave an honest answer. "Marathon's pretty much all I dream about. What was I saying? When I talked in my sleep?"

"Wake up," Samantha replied.

"Wake up?" Chloe asked, her left arm beginning to vibrate again.

"Yeah, you said that a lot. I thought you were talking to me at first."

Chloe grabbed her wrist to stop the shaking, as she'd done at Donnelly's execution. "Right," she said, her voice filling with faux surprise. "I think that was when I was trying to wake my parents."

"The morning the fighting started?" Samantha asked, seeming convinced by Chloe's lie.

"The morning it got really bad. My parents never sleep well, so it's always hard to get them up in the morning. Living in Missio, I got used to hearing gunfire. The drug gangs weren't a quiet bunch. But this was something else."

"Guess nothing gets you ready for that, even if it's a long time coming."

"Oh it was. The Commanders treated their citizens and soldiers like shit. It's a wonder the civil war took nearly forty years to start. Once it got going, Marathon burning to the ground was the only way it was going to end."

Samantha shook her head. "Fuck, I knew things were bad. There wouldn't be so many bandits trying to raid Merenranta for supplies if things outside the town were okay, but I never knew the scale of it. And Carthage is..." Samantha paused, correcting herself, "...was just a couple hundred miles west of here. Marathon could've torched us like they did them."

"My dad's from there," Chloe said.

"Right. That's where he got those scars?"

"Some of them. The rest were from Serenity, when he and my mom were soldiers. That's how he lost his eye, too, and how my mom lost her arm. But considering how many Marathon soldiers died in Serenity and the Aegean Valley before the civil war, I suppose they got out all right."

"What was it?"

"Roadside bomb, I think. They don't talk about it."

"Glad my mom's a cop, not a soldier."

Chloe snickered. "I don't think I've heard you call the sheriff 'mom' before."

Samantha laughed. "She's not a soldier, but she has the mentality of one."

"She certainly kills like one," Chloe responded, before deciding if that was best to say.

If Samantha was offended, she gave no sign. "Probably why the town's happy she's sheriff. Humans, Second-Gens, she doesn't discriminate when it comes to criminals."

"Why'd she shoot Donnelly in the eyes?" Chloe had been waiting for an opportunity to ask that.

"She hates how Second-Gen eyes glow like that," Samantha told her, blunt. "Thinks it's unnatural."

Unnatural? How is evolution unnatural? "I thought you said she doesn't discriminate." Chloe tramped her boots in the snow and sand to distract Samantha from the anger in her tone.

"Yeah, when it comes to criminals. Every Second-Gen is a criminal to her."

And what're Second-Gens to you?

"What's that up ahead?" Samantha said, alert, eyes centered on the tree line, hand on her holster.

Chloe traced her partner's gaze, spotting the abnormality about fifty to a hundred meters onward, a patch of dark red snow between two trees. She leveled her right hand to her holster; her left hand quivered with her arm and shoulder. "You want to check it?"

"Yeah, watch the trees," Samantha said, drawing her pistol, moving on the dark red.

Chloe drew her own pistol and followed. Boots crunching, weapons clicking as they scanned the beach and woods, the ocean breeze nudging at their backs, they approached the trees. Fifty feet away, Chloe saw the source of the discolored snow. Her index finger curled at the trigger of her pistol, her heart rate elevating.

"Fuck," Samantha exclaimed.

"I see it too. Call it in."

Keeping her weapon level, Samantha took her radio from her belt. The size of her palm, she pressed and held a button at the top, speaking into the device. "Sheriff, this is Officer Armistead. Come in."

The body lay on its back, a meter inside the cover of the forest. Male, in his mid-thirties Chloe assessed, he was fitted in a set of winter clothes, the kind Merenranta civilians wore, but ragged and torn, the attire of nomadic civilians and bandits. A revolver sat in his hand, rusted and empty, except for two spent cartridges Chloe found when she inspected the weapon. His wounds were still fresh, red leaking from as many as ten punctures in his chest and neck. A trail of dark red snow and boot prints zigzagged from the forest, halting after about thirty feet in front of a tree, next to what appeared to be the burnt remains of a campfire. Finally, Armistead's voice came through Samantha's radio. Why she'd taken so long to respond, neither of them knew. "Go ahead."

"Officer Corday and I have a crime scene. Five miles north." If Chloe hadn't known Samantha and Sheriff Armistead were related, she wouldn't have been able to tell from their conversation, or most of their conversations.

"Copy that," Armistead said, irritation detectable in her tone, even on the radio. Two crime scenes in one day were not unheard of, but the incident at Martin Donnelly and Sarah Murphy's house had rattled the town plenty already. "Secure the site; I'll be there in approximately one hour."

Sheriff Armistead arrived just over an hour later and combed the scene for further evidence, though it soon became apparent that was of little use. There was nothing more to find. "Victim was stabbed here," Samantha proposed, as she, Chloe, and Armistead stood around the beginning of the blood trail. "Wounds look to be from a small blade, knife of some sort. Victim was stabbed four times in the neck, six times in the upper chest." Samantha rotated towards the body, her hand following the victim's dark red boot tracks, the tree stalks blowing as the wind brushed through the forest. "Victim stumbles for the beach, possibly in attempt to escape his attacker, collapses and bleeds to death before he clears the woods. That's the most we can gather."

"Where are the attacker's prints?" Armistead asked. "I'm only seeing the victim's."

"That's what we don't get," Chloe told her. "We must've circled this area a dozen times, but we never found a second set of tracks. These are the only ones. The campfire's probably his too. I'm thinking he camps here overnight, last night's snowfall buries his tracks, this morning he gets attacked, like Officer Armistead said. Doesn't explain how his attacker came and went without some marker though."

Armistead glanced down, holding the victim's revolver and two spent shells in her gloved hands. "And this is the only weapon you found on him?" Her voice was as perplexed as her expression.

"That's the only thing we found on him," Chloe answered, sharing in her sheriff's confusion.

"Lot of good it did him," Samantha commented.

Armistead sighed, disappointed.

What she was disappointed at, Chloe wasn't sure.

"So, we've got an assailant with the footprint of a ghost, who brings a knife to a gunfight, wins and makes off with everything the victim has, except the gun." Armistead turned to Chloe and Samantha. "Which of you wants to help me explain this to the mayor?" Chloe would've laughed had she not recognized the severity of what Armistead was saying. Not only was the victim's attacker capable of stealth that didn't seem possible, they were also so confident in their abilities or so well armed they didn't think they needed the victim's revolver, not even to have in case they found ammo for it later. This wasn't a nomad or a bandit. This was someone who killed nomads and bandits.

Second-Gen? No, Second-Gens are too rare for another to pop up the same day as Donnelly.

—-

TWO

They left the man as he was and returned to Merenranta, taking only his revolver. *One less gun for the bandits.* The trek back to town on the miles of gray shoreline was uneventful, even when they passed the spot of Donnelly's execution, dark red stains leftover in the snow. Chloe held her wrist to ease the shakes in her left arm, Samantha curved her head towards the waves, and Armistead strolled with no visible disruption, as if she'd merely banished Donnelly from Merenranta, not shot him twice in the eyes.

After an hour and twenty minutes they reached the community perimeter. A town of five hundred, Merenranta was an isolated speck of life, nestled between an ocean and a continent that were otherwise almost entirely devoid of it. Semi-circular in shape, Merenranta was built around a cove, the total width of the town less than half a mile end to end. There were no roads. Merenranta hadn't owned a vehicle in decades. North of the cove was home to town hall, the police station, the medical center, the school, a few other government institutions, and those institutions' employees and their children. Two hundred people in all, many who worked more than one job to keep the government staffed. West of the cove was the industrial neighborhood, in which the factories produced Merenranta's food, medicine, and other essential supplies, while the water desalination and treatment plant turned gray seawater into drinkable freshwater for the community. Although these were the tallest buildings in town, they weren't the tallest structures in Merenranta. Standing behind the industrial neighborhood were wind turbines, sixty feet high, feeding energy to the power station, lighting the town. With cities like Carthage and Marathon gone, Merenranta was the last place in the world with electricity, as far as anyone knew.

Three hundred people, the civilian employees and managers of the industrial neighborhood and their children, lived south of the cove. Like the government, some civilians held a couple job titles. The arrangement frightened Chloe's parents when they first arrived, for it bore some resemblance to Marathon's design. Government workers to the north, civilian workers to the south, divided by some body of water. However, that was where the similarities ended. Though government and civilian employees resided in separate neighborhoods, everybody's housing was the same, including Mayor Darabont's and Sheriff Armistead's. Metal shack homes, small yet equipped with insulation, lights, and running water. Besides housing, everyone had access to the same food shares and laundry service, the same education and medical care, and was free to move about the different neighborhoods as they wished, so long as they obeyed the law and performed their work duties. And, most significant to Chloe, who'd spent the first fourteen years of her life in a city of black and dark blue, there were no color restrictions in Merenranta, no sacred colors to abide by.

That afternoon, Chloe sat with Samantha, Armistead, and Darabont in a conference room on the second floor of town hall. Town hall and the police station were actually one building. Police headquarters and lockup occupied the first floor, while the mayoral staff took the second. Heated and clean, Merenranta's government office was far more comfortable than the Community Offices of Missio Chloe had been forced to endure, back in Marathon. Grouped around a table, Armistead spent a few minutes detailing the crime scene to Darabont, concluding with, "It was bizarre, that's the best I can describe it. We've had murderers who were hard to track, but not impossible."

"And there're no special methods you can use?" Darabont asked, after contemplating Armistead's account. "Something to find what you wouldn't normally see?"

Armistead shook her head. "No. If my department had more on forensics than just records from the Previous Civilization, maybe."

"What about the trees?" Darabont said.

"What about them, sir?" Armistead replied.

"Could this killer be using the tree branches to escape detection?"

Samantha glanced to Chloe and rolled her eyes. Chloe bit her lip to hold in a chuckle.

Armistead kept her answer professional, despite the absurdity of the mayor's question. "Not without making a lot of noise, and not that fast. Most of those branches are too weak and slippery to stand on anyway."

Darabont nodded. "Sounds like this is someone we don't want to take the risk of searching for, especially when they haven't killed any of our people."

"Not unless we have to," Armistead concurred. "And if that body Officer Armistead and Officer Corday found was a bandit, it might work in our favor to let this phantom keep doing what they're doing."

"Do you think there could be a connection between...?" Darabont hesitated for a moment, discomfort in his expression. "Between Martin killing Sarah and this crime scene showing up on the same day?"

This question sounded more ridiculous to Chloe than Darabont's suggestion about the killer climbing trees to avoid being tracked, but nowhere near as funny. *Why? Because Donnelly was a Second-Gen you wonder if he was scheming with someone out of town?*

"Ordinarily I'd say no," Armistead said. "But he lied about being human, so who knows what else he had going on."

Chloe stared down at her lap, so the humans wouldn't notice the scowl forming on her face.

"Hopefully, this is as far as it goes," Darabont said. "This deep into winter there's no telling what people will do. I'm sure you and your parents know all about that, Chloe." Chloe swung her head up, startled to see Samantha and her superiors looking at her now. "From Marathon?" Darabont added, when Chloe didn't respond.

"Yes," Chloe said, smiling, then frowning when she realized a smile probably wasn't what they were expecting. "Winters in Marathon were, were…" Her cheeks flushed. "We'd lose a lot of people in winter."

"Good you and your parents are here then," Darabont replied, seeming as if he didn't know what else to say. "And good job today." He shifted his head to Samantha. "Both of you."

"Thank you, sir," Chloe and Samantha said in unison.

—-

THREE

Chloe and Samantha exited town hall through the western side, stepping back into the gray snow. The sky had turned a grayish-orange-blue, the sun descending behind the darkened woods. The temperature fell with the sun, the icy air reeked with the acrid stench from the factories. Town hall was located at the border of north Merenranta and the industrial neighborhood, just across the walkway from a couple factories. Citizens were clogging the paths between buildings, heading home for dinner. Chloe and Samantha walked to the beach, just beyond the corner of town hall and the factories. The tide was low, the waters of the cove withdrawn, exposing the snowless gray seabed, empty of the plants and animals that once dwelled below the waves, according to the children of the Previous Civilization. Rounding the cove to south Merenranta, they passed the industrial facilities, most of which were shutting down for the night. Behind these buildings, the wind turbines continued their silent spinning, their blades slicing through the dimming air. "Cheng's doing a memorial for Sarah tonight," Samantha said, as the wind from the sea blew across the cove, hitting them in the side with wet sand.

"I heard," Chloe said, dipping her head away from the sand drafts. "That where you're heading now?"

"Fuck yeah. After the day we've had, I'm getting started early."

"Started on what?" Chloe asked, their boots crunching in the snow and sand. "Drinking?"

Samantha scoffed. "What'd you think a memorial at Cheng's entailed?"

Chloe nodded, apprehensive. "Are you going to eat before this memorial? I don't want to be holding your hair back again, like the other night."

"Sure you do. And it's Cheng's Bar and Restaurant, he has food there too."

"I still don't see the purpose of Cheng's place."

Samantha laughed. "How? You've been here more than six years."

Chuckling back at her partner, Chloe said, "Cheng's is the only bar or restaurant in town, and I'd never gone there till you and I became a couple."

"So you've had a month to see the purpose then," Samantha said, smirking.

"Can you please just explain it to me?"

"Only, if you promise to hold my hair back when I get sick."

Chloe had to chuckle again. "When you get sick?"

"I've had a day."

"Fuck, fine. But don't ask me for any afterwards. Watching you puke in the snow isn't exactly a turn on for me."

"That's odd," Samantha retorted, sarcasm biting at her voice. "Because you holding my hair back gets me pretty turned on."

Chloe pushed Samantha with her hand, laughing. "Fuck yourself."

"Isn't that why you're here, so I don't have to do that anymore?"

Smiling and curling her thumb and index finger as if she was about to pinch Samantha, Chloe said, "You're this fucking close to doing whatever you want in the solitary of your own house."

"All right, all right," Samantha relented. "It's more fun going to Cheng's than spending the night at home."

"What's so fun about it?" Chloe supposed that was her actual question about Cheng's Bar and Restaurant.

"Marathon never let you go out at the end of the day, did they?"

"Marathon let civilians eat dinner at the chow halls. But that wasn't for fun."

Samantha shook her head. "Shit. Sometime we're eating at Cheng's, not just drinking."

They parted at the boundary of south Merenranta and the industrial neighborhood, Samantha continuing along the beach to Cheng's, Chloe entering the rows of shack homes the majority of south Merenranta consisted of. Flooded with civilian workers returning from the factories and utility plants, the pathways through the neighborhood reminded Chloe of the barrack rows in Missio, at the end of the day when her parents and Marathon neighbors were coming home from the factories of Ignis. There was a difference with the citizens of Merenranta, however. There was exhaustion, but not on a scale a night's sleep couldn't treat. There was hunger, yet not starvation. And, even with news of Sarah's murder and Donnelly's execution, there was excitement for tomorrow, not despair for today.

No onslaught of dark blue and black clothing, no uniforms mandated by the Marathon Commanders, and no pops of Missio drug gang gunfire, Chloe navigated the walkways of Merenranta with minimal urgency. Past a group of children playing a game in the snow with a ball, stick, and four mats shaped like diamonds, the name of which Chloe had forgotten, past numerous citizens Chloe had known when she lived with her parents, who greeted her as if she'd never moved north of the cove. As long as the people of Merenranta didn't learn of Chloe's true nature, they were as welcoming as ever.

Chloe arrived at a house in the center of south Merenranta, two rows up from the beach, her first home when she and her parents found Merenranta after months as refugees moving southeast from Marathon. Turning the doorknob, stepping inside, she shut the door quick to keep the cold air out and kicked the snow and sand from her boots. "Hey."

"Hey, Chloe," her father replied, cheer in his voice. Like all houses in Merenranta, her parents' shack was comprised of three rooms, a kitchen at the front, a bedroom in the back, and a bathroom. Chloe's father stood in the kitchen, next to the stove. Thirty-nine years old with unkempt dirty blond hair, spider-webbed scars mutilating both sides of his face and the right side of his head, and a glass eye in his right socket, Sean Halley was technically Chloe's stepfather, though she couldn't remember ever calling him that.

"You're making dinner?" Chloe asked, pointing at the pan on the stove that warmed the kitchen with the scent of boiling tofu and vegetables, grown in the factories' indoor farms.

"Yep." Sean chuckled as they hugged. "At least I'm better than your mom."

"The fuck you are," Chloe's mother said, sarcastic. Three years younger than Chloe's father with long and loose dirty blond hair, Anna Corday came marching through the doorway that separated the bedroom from the kitchen. Her gloves were off, the dark blue plastic hand of her prosthetic sticking out of her right jacket sleeve. "What I tell you about bad-mouthing my cooking?" she asked her life partner of fifteen years.

"Only do it when you're making dinner?" Sean asked.

"Exactly," Anna said. "And who's making dinner tonight?"

"Me."

"And who gets to talk shit tonight?"

"You."

"Correct," Anna said, clapping her prosthetic hand with her left hand. "Now, back to it."

Sean rolled his eye. "Okay." Turning back to the stove, he teased, "You know, you shouldn't be so mean in front of your daughter. Asshole parents make asshole kids."

"That's the dream," Anna countered. "Have I succeeded yet?" she asked Chloe.

"How the fuck should I know?" Chloe said, trying to sound hostile but laughing before she could finish.

Anna groaned with mock disapproval. "Still a work-in-progress I see." She embraced Chloe with her left arm.

"Thanks, mom, that means a lot," Chloe responded, wrapping her arms around Anna, daughter and mother only fifteen years apart in age. "You two don't have to pretend to hate each other for my benefit."

"We're not pretending," Anna joked. "Conflict's the only thing that keeps it interesting when you've been together this long. The more we fight, the more we—-"

"You don't have to spell it out for me either," Chloe interrupted.

"Hey," Anna said then, her smile receding from her face with unsettling speed. "We heard you were with the group that walked Donnelly out to the beach." Worry accumulated around her mother's lips. Her father turned his head away from the stove, the same parental unease evident in his eye and between his scars. Chloe figured her parents had planned not to discuss Sarah and Donnelly until she did, but her mother had broken from that plan, unable to contain her concern.

"Yeah," Chloe muttered.

"Is it true he was a Second-Gen?" Anna asked.

Chloe nodded at her fellow Second-Gen.

"You want to talk about it?"

They ate at the table, between the stove and the wall beside the bedroom door. Three plates of tofu and vegetables on top of rice, three glasses of vegetable juice, and three forks and napkins, all crammed together. The space was tight, elbows inches apart, but it was theirs. In this private space, lit by the ceiling light as nightfall blackened the neighborhood outside the kitchen windows, Chloe told her parents about Sarah's murder and Donnelly's execution, her parents listening with sincerity. "Sam said the sheriff hates the glow Second-Gens get in their eyes. Thinks it's unnatural."

Anna nodded, understanding. "People in Marathon would say something similar. We're so rare the few humans that do meet us think we're an accident."

"Evolution made us," Chloe said, poking at the scraps on her plate with her fork. "Same way it made humanity, so we're just as much an accident as they are."

"You okay working for a boss who thinks Second-Gens are a mistake?" Chloe's mother asked.

"I like to think I work for the town, not her," Chloe replied, knowing her answer wasn't sufficient.

Sean's question was almost the same. "You okay working for a town that thinks Second-Gens are a mistake? Because most people here would agree with Dylan."

Chloe hesitated for a few seconds. She'd never gotten a complete endorsement from her parents to become a police officer. Not only was it the most dangerous job in Merenranta, it was the job with the highest chance of provoking her Second-Gen Stage at the wrong moment, revealing her family's lie to the town. Even she couldn't totally explain why she was taking the risk. But, she wasn't going to let her parents lead her into questions about her job choices. "I'm not, but I'll live. Same way you do, mom."

Anna nodded and took a bite of her dinner.

"What's Sam think?" Chloe's human father asked.

"Don't know. Couple months working together, month as a couple, guess I could've asked if I wanted. But it's not like I can request a new partner if my current one hates Second-Gens. Might as well tell Sheriff Armistead I'm a Second-Gen at that point."

"And get yourself and your parents thrown out of town," Anna responded.

Chloe scoffed. "Or shot in the eyes."

"Maybe they'd let me stay," Sean quipped with abrupt humor. "Being the human one."

Anna laughed and said, "No, I'll give you whatever stigma they don't."

"That's our whole relationship right there."

"Fucking ye," Anna jested, high-fiving her life partner.

Chloe laughed. "Maybe one of you should switch jobs. Give each other some space during the day."

"Eh," her father replied. "I accepted my fate a long time ago."

"Seriously," Chloe said. "You two work maintenance on the wind turbines all day, then you come home."

A moment passed before either of her parents spoke. With a solemn tone, her mother said, "Your dad and I have seen enough." Her father nodded in immediate agreement. "And as insufferable as he is, I'd rather keep him around than make a change."

"Are you two still having reenactment nightmares?" Chloe's question was a reflex; she must've asked it every time she came to dinner.

His expression somber, Sean said, "Always." He smiled at his life partner. "But I'd call myself lucky."

Anna chuckled. "Bet you won't be saying that in nine months."

"What?" Chloe said. "Why nine months?"

"You did it once before, and that was in fucking Missio." Sean glanced to Chloe. "How bad can this one be?" he asked, sarcasm in his voice.

"How bad can what be?"

"Have you tried sticking a knife up your ass and keeping it there for hours on end?" Anna said. "Multiply that by a hundred and maybe you'll get the same feeling."

"What the fuck are you talking about?" Chloe asked.

"I probably shouldn't talk till after it comes," Sean said, cringing.

"That would be wise," Anna responded.

"Are you fucking kidding me?" Chloe laughed, the realization hitting her like a spray of cold water in the shower. Her left arm began to shudder and she moved it underneath the table.

Her parents held hands across the table, her mother giggling as she told Chloe, "I said your dad and I have seen enough, but there's one thing we want to do again."

"Are you?" Chloe asked, grabbing her wrist below the table.

Anna looked at her stomach and nodded, "Yeah."

"Fuck, wow," Chloe heard herself say, beaming with what she assumed was delight.

"You're going to be a big sister, Chloe," her father said.

"Wow," Chloe repeated, when she couldn't think of another word. "Wow, how'd you find out?"

"Morning sickness," Anna said.

"Did you go to the medical center?" Chloe asked.

"Yep, tested and everything."

Chloe interlocked her fingers when her left hand wouldn't stop shaking, then made herself laugh. "How's it feel, dad, knowing you'll be outnumbered three Second-Gens to one human?"

Finished with dinner, they rinsed their dishes in the sink between the stove and the front door. Intending to meet Samantha at Cheng's for Sarah's memorial, Chloe prepared to leave. "So, you two are good?" she asked as they stood by the door.

"Yeah, we're good," Sean said, his eye shifting to Anna. "I don't know anything about pregnancy or childbirth, but your mom will tell me what to do."

"I'm good at that," Anna remarked.

Her father chuckled. Chloe didn't. "I meant your reenactments. Are you both okay, even though you're still having them?"

Anna was the one who answered, after an awkward few moments. "We're not, but we'll live. And it has its advantages. We haven't slept well in years, so adjusting for the baby won't be difficult."

"What're your reenactments from? Same stuff in Serenity?" Chloe doubted her inquiry was appropriate, yet her anxiety demanded it.

"Mostly," Sean said, again eyeing his life partner. "Carthage too."

"And the civil war," Anna added, glancing at Sean. "Are you having reenactments, Chloe?"

Chloe dug her left arm into her jacket pocket, so her parents wouldn't see it shake. "No, I just, was wondering. Better get over to Cheng's before Sam drinks herself onto the floor, again. Congratulations on the, the uh..."

"Thanks, dear," Anna said as the family hugged goodbye. "See you next week?"

"Yep," Chloe responded, turning for the door.

"Hey," her father said.

Chloe rotated her head back to her parents, her hand clasping the doorknob. "Yeah?"

"You know we love you."

Smiling, Chloe told her parents, "Yes, you loved me from the second I was born."

"From the second you were born to the second we die," her mother said.

Chloe stepped outside onto the dark snow-covered pathway, staring at the grayish-black sky and the half-circle of white light that shined down on the town. *From the second I was born to the second they die. Or maybe sooner than that.*

—-

FOUR

A reenactment woke Chloe in the middle of the night, as such nightmares had done to her parents for as long as she could recall. Jumping from the single bed in the backroom of her house, Chloe stumbled through pitch dark to the bedroom door. Shivering in the midnight cold, her skin soaked with freezing sweat, her long sleeve sleeping shirt and pants of no help, she banged her hands against the door, searching for the knob. Into the kitchen, the floor like ice on her bare feet, her watering eyes swerved to the bathroom door. Her chest ached, her heart jolting. Head dizzy, mouth dry, and left arm flailing like a sheet on a clothesline, she opened the door and locked herself in with the toilet, sink, and shower.

Turning on the light, Chloe sat on the toilet lid, trying to drape her arms around her chest for warmth. The tremors in her left arm prevented this. Panic brought her to the bathroom, regret kept her from going back to bed. And when the images of her guilt, images of Marathon, the Marathon Civil War, and bright red blood dripping from a black switchblade would not subside, she rose and stood at the sink, and in the mirror, above the sink, she watched the tears fall from her eyelids, one at a time rolling down her cheeks and tapping in the sink. "Stop," she whispered. The plea was ignored.

A minute passed and Chloe heard the razor calling from the cabinet, behind the mirror, its voice like a pencil scribbling in her bloodstream, attempting to write on each individual drop, an inane and vexatious task. Two minutes and the razor screamed, begging for release, as it did every night she had a reenactment. Three minutes and that urge for release became unbearable. She opened the cabinet and took the razor from its shelf. The blade was dull, long overdue for a replacement, but it would serve its purpose. She rolled up her sleeve, glaring at the gash already there on her left forearm. Healing like the rest, the relief the wound provided her was drained. A new reprieve was necessary.

"Stop," she whispered again, a final warning.

The tears still fell, her arm still quivered. Leaning over the sink, Chloe pressed her left arm against her gut, stabilizing the limb as best she could, before lowering the razor to her trembling skin. The razor blade pierced her skin, the pain welcomed. She pulled the razor across her forearm, parallel to the previous cut, forming a second red stripe of even length. Blood oozed from the wound, mixing with her tears in the sink. Chloe bled herself until her arm stopped quaking.

She cleaned her wound in the sink, washed the blade, put the razor back in the cabinet, and rolled down her sleeve, erasing evidence of her release. The act only relaxed her arm, however, not her eyes nor the remainder of her body. Tonight's reenactment was too strong to be quelled by just a cut. It required something more.

The placating sensation ignited beneath her skin, triggered by a signal from her brain she seldom permitted. To allow anybody other than her parents to see the result of this alternate sensation would lead to her exile, if not her execution. The feeling amplified throughout her body, from the crest of her head to the arches in her feet, suppressing her panicked senses like a boot stomping on a fire. Chloe waited for her irises to glow in the mirror, as they did every time she entered the Second-Gen Stage. "You all right, Chloe?" Samantha asked, knocking on the bathroom door.

"Fuck," Chloe mumbled, deactivating her alternative state before her irises could spark, and before her Second-Gen Stage could fully eliminate her turmoil. Eyes red from crying, yet human-seeming, she unlocked the door.

Samantha stood in the doorway, wearing her sleeping clothes and a worried expression. She scanned her partner from top to bottom, far more attentive than Chloe expected, especially from someone who'd gone to bed as drunk as she had. The nauseating aroma of Cheng's factory-brewed liquor was still on her breath as she asked, "You okay?" It was as if Chloe's anguish had somehow penetrated Samantha's stupor and notified her that something was wrong.

"Yeah," Chloe replied, unconvincing.

"You were crying," Samantha said, pointing at Chloe's red eyes.

"No, I..."

Samantha stepped forward. "What's wrong?"

Chloe stepped back. "Nothing I can't handle."

"Chloe," Samantha said, stern, crossing her arms, like a teacher who knew a student was misbehaving.

"I." Chloe exhaled, yielding to her partner's trepidation. "I had a nightmare."

There was a pause as Samantha pondered her next question. "You want to go for a walk?"

Chloe's shack was on the eastern border of north Merenranta, just up the beach from the cove. Flakes of gray snow fell in gentle bits, the wind cold but restrained, as Chloe and Samantha walked across the dunes to the sloshing gray waves, dressed in their police gear. The tide was high, the trek brief. To lengthen their walk, they strode along the water's slushed edge, towards the cove, in the light of their flashlights and the recurring illumination of the half-moon in the clouded sky. To their west, the shack homes of Merenranta, most of them dark, lights on in a few. To their east, the insurmountable blackness of the ocean that forever disconnected them from a whole universe that might exist on the other side. Were she not a native of Marathon, Chloe would've likely grown up believing Merenranta was the last inhabited community in the world, the only place on the planet not annihilated by the Reform.

"Was it Marathon?" Samantha said, after a minute. "The civil war, I mean."

"No," Chloe said, over the crunch of their boots, the click of their flashlights, and the rush of the waves. "The civil war was in my dream, too, but that wasn't what started it."

"What was it then?" Samantha asked, her breath yellowish-white in her flashlight.

Snowflakes flickered in the yellow beam of Chloe's flashlight as she shook her head, not wanting to recount her reenactment. Samantha tapped Chloe's arm, as if to say it was safe to tell her. "I've never talked about it. I haven't even told my parents."

"You've had this dream before?" Samantha deduced, as they neared the mouth of the cove.

Chloe nodded. "I was having it before the civil war."

"You don't have to talk about it if you don't want to." They reached the curve of the beach, where the shoreline veered into the cove, in the direction of the industrial neighborhood and the wind turbines. Standing at the curve, in a breeze of snow and salt, Samantha said, "I never told you about my dad."

Chloe looked to Samantha. "No, you didn't. What I heard, I figured it was best not to ask."

Samantha gazed at the gray and black ocean. "That's the sheriff for you. Fucking explodes on anyone who reminds her about him." She winced with what appeared to be pain, an agony of memory.

Taking Samantha's gloved hand in her own, Chloe offered a supportive grin and said, "Sheriff's not here right now."

Samantha turned to her. "You going to tell anyone?"

Chloe shook her head. "Not even under torture."

Head tilted towards the snow and sand, evading eye contact, Samantha said, "I was six. Bandit snuck past the cops on night patrol, got inside the perimeter. Probably he was looking to rob a house for food and supplies, like they do." She paused, glanced up the shore, as if about to suggest they turn around. Chloe squeezed Samantha's hand and she resumed, her eyes aimed at the cove. "My dad was coming home from night shift at the medical center. Sheriff and I were asleep. I think the shooting woke me up, but I can't remember. What I do remember is the sheriff charging out the front door with her service weapon. She left so fast she didn't see me follow her." Samantha turned her head from the cove to the ocean, her voice stuttering. "I look through the doorway and my dad's. He was. He must've stood at the door, stopped the bandit from coming in." She laughed, though it seemed more like she was gasping for breath. "I ran and hid under the bed. Was there till morning when the sheriff finally came back and found me." Samantha brushed her eyes with her arm. "Pulls me out, shakes me like a fucking spray can, says never hide like that again." Chloe kept her hand tight around her partner's. "My dad's been dead less than three hours and my mom fucking tells me to stop crying."

Chloe looked across the cove, at south Merenranta, where she was fortunate enough to have both her parents living, living and involved in her life. "Sam, I…" she said in guilt, her compassion doomed to inadequacy. "I'm sorry."

Samantha shook her head. "What the fuck is there to do about it?"

"Did you ever hide again?" Chloe asked at random, hoping to keep Samantha engaged.

"Fuck yeah I did," Samantha chuckled. "I just didn't let her catch me."

Chloe smiled, somewhat relieved by Samantha's reply. "You still do that?"

"Why the fuck you think we never stay at my place?"

Raising her flashlight to Samantha's face, as if placing a spotlight on this question, Chloe said, "You have reenactment nightmares?"

Samantha made eye contact through the yellow glare of Chloe's flashlight. "Only when I'm alone."

In that instant, Chloe wished she had the courage to tell Samantha what she was, to trust Samantha with her family's secret. But, she was a Second-Gen in a human town, with a human partner. "You want to go back?"

Backtracking on the shoreline, Chloe described parts of her reenactment to Samantha, comfortable doing so after hearing about Samantha's father. "I was a kid, about the same age you were when your dad."

She hesitated a moment. "My mom was a soldier in Serenity, my dad too, though he wasn't my dad yet. I was back in Missio."

"By yourself?" Samantha asked, wiping a snowflake from her cheek.

"With my neighbors in barrack 804," Chloe lied. Telling Samantha she'd actually lived under guarded care in her Community Office, as part of a deal enacted by her mother and the Commanders, would draw suspicion about why she received special treatment. "One night, I get news she's been killed in Serenity. It was a mistake, of course."

"She was in the hospital?"

Chloe nodded. "She and my dad both. But Marathon Hospital was in New Terra, across the Marathon River. No one bothered to let me know she was still alive."

"Fuck," Samantha said. "How long was it before you...?"

"Two months."

"Shit." Samantha patted Chloe on the shoulder. "That's what you were dreaming about?"

"Being told she was dead, yeah. And that became the civil war. Most of my reenactment nightmares end up as the civil war." The cut on Chloe's left arm stung, which she was fine with. "But my mom came home, and brought my dad with her."

"Why'd your mom join Marathon's military?" Samantha asked, a hint of what seemed like judgement in her tone. "She had a job before that, right?"

"Yeah, in the Ignis factories," Chloe replied. "They were like the industrial neighborhood, except shittier."

"Why'd she leave you if she had work?" That time the judgement in Samantha's voice was definite.

"The pay was shit too," Chloe said with slight annoyance at Samantha's criticism of her mother. "Factory jobs didn't always get you enough, especially if you were a single parent. That's how the Commanders kept getting new troops. No matter how fucked the missions got in

Serenity and the Aegean Valley, the Commanders could count on star-vation to bring in volunteers. Worked well up until seven years ago."

"Still," Samantha said, much to Chloe's growing irritation. "That's a lot for your mom to put on you, leaving you alone when you were that young."

Chloe's aggravation swelled, yet not into anger. What came to her instead was agreement: *She didn't say goodbye either, just left while I was asleep.* Fleeing this thought, she changed the subject. "My mom's pregnant."

"Really?" Samantha asked with excitement, stopping.

"Yep," Chloe said, standing beside her as they faced the waves, and the snowflakes that wafted over those waves.

"That's great. Congratulations."

"Yeah." Chloe heard the lack of enthusiasm in her own response.

Her partner heard it too. "Not so great?"

"It is. It is. I'm just." Chloe scoured her mind for the words, words she wouldn't dare let her parents hear. "I've always been their only kid, you know? And..."

"Now you're thinking they'll be too busy for you." Chloe nodded in admittance. Samantha simpered. "And, because you never go out and have no friends, you're thinking you'll be alone again, like you were af-ter your mom became a soldier."

"I have friends."

"Who? I'd like to meet them sometime."

Chuckling, Chloe pointed her flashlight at Samantha. "We're not the only cops in Merenranta."

"Those're colleagues, not friends."

"Huh," Chloe joked. "Guess I'll go wallow in loneliness." She pre-tended to walk home. Samantha grabbed her hand, keeping her at the waterline. The partners exchanged smiles. "Oh, we're friends then?"

Samantha giggled, switching off her flashlight and leaning forward. Their lips met in a kiss.

"So, not friends?"

Samantha put her hand on Chloe's hat-covered head as they kissed, Chloe reciprocating, touching tongues. "Turn off your flashlight."

"Why?" Chloe said.

"So no one will see us."

"What? Here?"

"Yeah."

"I think that's illegal."

"We're cops, Chloe. We don't have to follow the rules."

Chloe cut her light, shielding them in darkness. Samantha shoved her into the snow, pinning her on her back. Snow iced the back of her neck. Chloe didn't care. "What is it about me?" she asked with curiosity.

Samantha paused. "What is it about me?"

Chloe tugged at Samantha's jacket collar, bringing their lips back together. Samantha unbuckled Chloe's belt, unzipped her pants. As Samantha moved down her torso, Chloe's eyes made a swift scan of the beach.

A figure stood in the moonlit snowfall, its silhouette black, like a shadow.

"Fuck," Chloe yelped in alarm.

"I'm getting there," Samantha replied, unaware.

"Stop, stop!" She pushed Samantha off, zipped her pants, and clipped her belt.

Chloe flicked on her light, Samantha doing the same as they returned to their feet. The figure was stationary in the yellow beams of their flashlights, garbed in the tattered winter clothing of nomads and bandits. Short, less than five feet tall, the nomad was looking at the snow and sand, their face hidden by a hood. A backpack, as shabby as their clothes, was tied to their back.

"You okay?" Chloe said to the nomad, her hand near her holster yet not on her weapon. "We're police officers. Do you need help?" The nomad didn't respond in any way. No words. No movement.

Samantha skimmed the beach behind the nomad with her flashlight, from the ocean to the shacks, and up the coast to the woods. Nobody else.

"Where'd you come from?"

Again, no reply, as if the nomad hadn't heard Samantha at all.

Blotches of bright red emitted from wounds in the nomad's left hip and left forearm. Hurried puffs of yellowish-white flowed from the nomad's hood, as if they were struggling to breathe. The nomad raised their head. Chloe stepped back, upended by horrified fright. This nomad was a child, a girl, between eight and eleven. Her face was choked in dirt, her brunette hair long and disheveled. Her eyes stunned Chloe most. Exhaustion wasn't just present; it was chronic, consuming her eye sockets with a blankness that made Chloe wonder if the girl was sleepwalking. There was more life in her father's glass eye than either of this child's real eyes. The girl slumped to the side, eyelids shutting as she lost consciousness. "Fuck," Chloe blurted out, running to the girl as she collapsed in the snow.

PHASE 2: VOICELESS

FIVE

Chloe stumbled, her feet slipping as she ran in the gray snow, the girl slack in her arms. The child's weight was marginal, the weight of responsibility excruciating. Chloe's left arm twitched, her release sapped by her obligation to save this girl's life. Snowflakes pricked her eyes; white breaths of exertion clouded the air in front of her. The shack homes of north Merenranta passed in blurs of darkened metal, the houses indistinguishable, unified in her hazed vision. She'd lost track of what path they were on, how far from the beach they'd sprinted. Were it not for her partner, two steps ahead and leading her through the neighborhood, she would've run in circles until the child succumbed to her wounds.

"Female, between eight and eleven years of age," Samantha screamed into her radio. "Gunshot wounds to the hip and arm! Nonresponsive! Vital signs dropping! We need a trauma unit standing by in the lobby!"

"Copy that," the medical center replied over the radio.

The buildings grew around Chloe, the one-story shacks expanding into two-story government facilities as they reached the western side of north Merenranta. "Where'd she come from?" asked a night patrol officer, his late teens' voice squeaking on the radio.

"You tell me," Samantha snapped. "You fuckers are supposed to be watching the perimeter! How'd she get by?"

Chloe's Second-Gen Stage hovered within her subconscious, disabled yet knocking at the door to her active mind, demanding to know why it wasn't allowed in. *Your Second-Gen Stage will get you there faster. And get me and my parents thrown out of town immediately after.*

"The fuck do we do, Sam?" another night patrol officer said through the radio.

And if the kid dies when you could've gotten her help quicker?

"We left her pack at the beach, one of you get it and bring it to the station," Samantha instructed. She and Chloe quickened their stride.

Chloe looked down at the girl in her arms. Her face seemed distant, indistinct, as if death was already dragging her away from the living world. "What?" the officer responded in confusion.

"Her pack, her fucking backpack! She had a pack with her and we left it at the beach! One of you dumb fucks get it and bring it to the station! Check it for weapons too!"

"Roger that."

The medical center materialized in Chloe's sight, its arrival sudden, as if the building had teleported to them so they didn't have to make the full dash across north Merenranta. Three floors tall and adjacent to town hall on the border of north Merenranta and the industrial neighborhood, the medical center was wide awake, windows lit. The lobby was at the center of the structure, running from the east side to the west. Muffling her Second-Gen Stage, Chloe followed Samantha through the eastern entrance, into the bright and heated lobby. The room was vacant, except for the clerks at their desks and the trauma team waiting with a gurney.

Chloe placed the girl on the gurney, the nurses wheeling the child to the side and through a set of double doors. The trauma and surgical operations wing of the medical center occupied half of the first floor, the other half dedicated to less dangerous procedures. Down a hall that intersected with other hallways, Chloe and Samantha trailed the gurney as a doctor examined the girl. With each announcement, the doctor's tone became graver. "One entry wound, left hip. No exit. One entry wound, left forearm. No exit. Get the on-call surgeon."

"She's on her way down," one of the nurses said.

"Room 12, let's get her prepped."

The on-call surgeon and her team got started in the operating room. Chloe and Samantha hung in the hall, pacing the floor to work off heightened adrenaline. They didn't stay long, however. "Sam, come in," an officer said on the radio, ten minutes later.

"Go," she told him.

"I've got the kid's bag, taking it back to the station."

"Copy that. Wake up the sheriff, we'll meet you there. Rest of you on the perimeter, watch yourselves."

—-

SIX

"She's a nomad, best we can tell," Samantha said, as she, Chloe, Sheriff Armistead, and the officer who fetched the girl's pack stood around a table in the main room of the police station, under the dim yellow of the ceiling lamps. The child's pack sat on the table, brownish-red with dry blood and wet from the snow. "She didn't say anything before she passed out."

Armistead nodded, her eyes drooping with weary black circles, her grayish-red hair as messy as her uniform. "And she approached the two of you? On the beach?"

"Yes," Samantha said, nervousness creeping into her demeanor, just as it did to Chloe. The sheriff knew Chloe and Samantha were a couple, everyone did. There wasn't a law against coworker relationships. But there was a law against sex in community spaces, such as on the beach, a violation Samantha's mother would not ignore, not when her own officers were the offenders and not when the witness was a child.

"What were you doing?" the sheriff said, shifting from Samantha to Chloe and back, not accusatory though getting there. "You're not night patrol."

Eyes widening, Samantha began to speak. "We were..." If she had a cover story, her brain was still writing it.

"Ma'am," Chloe interjected, her left arm ticking behind the table. "We were on a walk."

Armistead focused on Chloe. "You were on a walk?"

Chloe nodded, taking solace in the fact that what she was saying wasn't technically a lie. "I was having trouble sleeping, so Officer

Armistead suggested we go for a walk. We were on our way back when we ran into her."

"It's really by accident we were there when the kid showed up," Samantha said, joining the narrative. "We're still not sure how she got past the perimeter without one of the night cops spotting her."

If Armistead wasn't satisfied with their story, she gave no indication. Her attention turned to the girl's pack. "She had this with her?"

"Yeah," Samantha said. "We left it at the beach, didn't want the extra weight when we ran her to the med center."

The officer who'd gone to the beach chimed in. "Didn't seem like there was much in it at first." He unzipped the pack and dumped its contents on the table. "Couple canned foods, empty water bottle, matchbox with no matches, typical nomad stuff. None of it surprised me, till I looked in here." The officer opened one of the side pockets and removed an object.

The floor seemed to bend, as if the building was sliding into the cove. Chloe clutched the table for balance with her right hand, her left hand shaking too hard to grip anything. Her tongue dried as it had when she woke from her reenactment, her pulse beating in her neck and wrist. Armistead thanked the officer and told him to return to his post, which he did, leaving the object on the table. It was a knife, a switchblade, black, and tainted with brownish-red blood from the tip of the blade to the bottom of the handle.

Armistead spoke first. She sounded as if she were outside, talking through the window. "How many times was that dead guy stabbed yesterday morning?"

"Ten," Samantha replied. "Six in the chest, four in the neck." She too sounded as if she was talking from out of the room.

The switchblade in Chloe's head was back. It appeared in her reenactment earlier that night, as it often had for the past seven years, always black and dripping with bright red. Now, the image of this black and red knife was choking her mind again, preventing her from concentrating on the real black and red knife lying in front of her. "How many times was the girl shot?" Armistead asked.

"Twice, arm and hip."

"What caliber rounds were they?"

"We won't know till she gets out of surgery. But they didn't look any bigger than pistol shots."

"Or revolver shots. That dead man's revolver had two shells in it, two spent shells."

"Fuck me," Samantha said, her voice alternating between a shout and a whisper as the possibility hit her. "How the fuck?"

"We can't be certain if it's her yet," Armistead rejoined. "If she survives, we'll find out."

"You okay, Officer Corday?" Samantha asked, yanking Chloe back into focus, the memory of the switchblade disappearing, for now.

"That's from Marathon," Chloe said, apprehension in her tone.

"The knife?" her partner responded, bemused.

Chloe nodded, tucking her left hand in her jacket pocket. "It's a Marathon military switchblade, standard-issue."

"How do you know?" Armistead queried.

"Marathon soldiers carried them." Chloe balled her left hand into a fist. "Used them in the civil war, a lot."

Armistead nodded. "And how do you figure this kid came to possess one, and potentially kill someone with it, someone two feet taller, a hundred pounds heavier, who may've shot her twice?"

"Marathon's been a pile of rubble for seven years, scavenger's paradise," Chloe answered. "And I have no idea how she could've done this. Frankly, it makes no sense to me."

"So there could be a bunch of bandits running around with weapons they looted from Marathon?" Samantha said, her voice anxious at the suggestion.

"One problem at a time," Armistead said. Samantha tipped her head. "The priority right now is the girl. Did she kill that man? If so, how, why, and how the fuck did she turn herself into a ghost when she did it? Most of that we're not going to learn unless she survives, and gets well enough to talk."

"Officer Armistead and I can head back to the med center," Chloe said. "Whether the girl pulls through or not." Her gloved fingers prodded at her left palm as she hoped for the child's survival. "They'll have the bullets from her arm and hip. We'll bring them back here, see if they match the revolver cartridges."

Nodding in approval, Armistead moved for the station exit. "Good, do that. Call me on the radio when you know."

"Where're you going, Sheriff?" Samantha asked.

"I'm going to sleep," Armistead said as she walked through the doorway, into the dark building lobby. "You know what time it is?"

"Shouldn't the mayor know what's going on?"

"I'm not waking him up," Armistead replied, already around the corner and out of view, her boots tapping for the east exit.

"Fuck," Samantha moaned, the lobby doors screeching as the sheriff left her and Chloe with their investigation.

"What?" Chloe asked.

"I forgot to ask for overtime."

The orange-yellow light of dawn was rising from the ocean by the time the on-call surgeon met with Chloe and Samantha. They'd been sitting in the lobby of the medical center for hours, except for the sixty minutes Chloe took in the bathroom to wash the girl's blood out of her clothes with borrowed cleaning supplies, her left arm crying for a razor throughout the entire effort. Chloe was drifting somewhere between sleep and dazed consciousness. Samantha was asleep, using Chloe's shoulder as a pillow. "Morning, officers," the surgeon greeted, still wearing her scrubs as she came out of the trauma and surgical operations wing.

"Morning," Chloe mumbled, rubbing her eyes as she stood, Samantha slow to do the same.

"You two had a rough night, I'm guessing."

"At least we weren't in surgery," Chloe responded, noting the surgeon's fatigued expression.

The surgeon chuckled, a tired, reflective laugh. "Yeah, kid made it hard on us for a while. Her amount of blood loss was no fucking joke." She grinned. "But nomads must be tougher than us, because she's on her way up to recovery."

"She's alive?" Samantha asked with a level of astonishment that told Chloe her partner had written the girl off hours ago.

"It would appear so."

The respite Chloe felt was more than she'd anticipated. She didn't know the child and there was a strong chance she was a murderer. And yet, hearing the girl would survive made Chloe recognize how fearful she'd been for the child's life, even after their discovery at the police station. "How is she?" Chloe asked, trying not to smile or seem too happy.

"Asleep, she'll be that way for most of the day with the meds we're putting her on. What she came in with, I wouldn't mind if she slept clear through to tomorrow."

"Do you have the bullets?" Samantha said.

The surgeon pulled a sealed plastic bag from her pants pocket. Two iron slugs sat at the bottom of the bag. "Two rounds. Mangled, but not bad for how long they were in there." Samantha took the bag, her fingers caressing the bullets through the plastic.

The question surfaced in Chloe's mind, the question she, Samantha, and Sheriff Armistead failed to ask each other at the police station. They'd been too distracted, wondering if and how the girl killed the man, instead of asking how she stayed alive. Chloe and Samantha found the man's body well before noon. The child didn't approach them until after midnight. If the man and the girl had the confrontation Chloe, Samantha, and Armistead were thinking they did, then there was a twelve-hour-plus gap where this child, no more than eleven years old, endured two bullet wounds, wounds she'd taken five miles away, and managed to walk to Merenranta, on her own. "How long were those rounds in there?" Chloe asked, both amazed and scared by what this girl might've accomplished.

Gasping, as if still struggling to accept it, the surgeon said, "Twelve, fifteen hours, and that's before you two brought her in."

"How did she not bleed out?" Samantha asked, picking up on Chloe's perplexity.

The surgeon shook her head. "You're probably the tenth person to ask that in the last hour. To be honest we're at a loss. We found burn marks on the skin around her wounds, and on the wounds themselves."

"Burn marks?" Chloe said.

"Kid tried to cauterize," the surgeon said, her tone grim. Chloe remembered the matchbox from the girl's pack, the matchbox with no matches. "Several times it looks like. That's not what's fucking with me though."

"What is?" Samantha asked.

The surgeon's eyes went from the walls of the lobby to the floor and ceiling, as if she was afraid to answer. "It's like the kid had fucking body armor, on the inside. The damage internally, it's bad but nowhere near as bad as it should be. No nerve damage, no broken bones, I can't believe I'm saying this, she just got out of surgery for fuck's sake, but this kid could be up and walking in a week, no chair, no crutches, fucking standing on two legs and walking right out those doors."

Chloe and Samantha looked to one another, as if either of them had an explanation.

Second-Gen? No, it's impossible for a kid this young to have Awakened Second-Gen abilities.

Evidence storage was in the backroom of the police station. Here, amongst the shelves of cardboard boxes, Chloe retrieved the two spent cartridges from the dead man's revolver, holding them in her hand as Samantha donned a pair of disposable gloves and opened the plastic bag from the medical center. Mangled as the on-call surgeon said, the two slugs were nevertheless identifiable as bullets. The bullets and cartridges were set side by side in Samantha's palm; the match was probable. "Fuck," Samantha said, her voice low, sorrowful.

"Should we call the sheriff?" Chloe asked, her left arm quavering, a lump in her chest.

Samantha stalled, her face frozen on the proof of the child's guilt. It occurred to Chloe that although Samantha resigned the girl to death when she was in surgery, her partner was also hoping she wasn't the murderer, that she was an innocent child, shot by someone less deserving of life. At least then, the girl's arrival would make a little more sense. "Not yet, there's something else."

"What?"

"How'd she get inside the perimeter, past night patrol?"

"I don't know." Chloe had a thought. "But I might know how we can find out."

—-

SEVEN

It took fifteen minutes to retrace their midnight walk, but they soon found the mesh of boot prints, theirs, their fellow officer's, and the child's, all partly buried by last night's snowfall, yet still visible. Following the girl's tracks up the beach, towards the edge of the Merenranta police department's security perimeter, they trudged through the ocean's morning breeze, the air frosted with salt and decay though warming with the sun. "Why'd she come to us?" Chloe pondered aloud, their boots crunching in the gray snow.

"How do you mean?" Samantha asked, looking down at the snow and up at the terrain ahead of them.

"Why'd she dodge the night patrol cops, just to walk up to us?" Chloe said, squinting in the yellow flare of the sun. Irritating as the sun could be, she would be fine if she never saw another cloud for the rest of her life.

"Maybe we didn't look as threatening to her," her partner theorized. "Night patrol cops keep weapons drawn all night, with their own personal shoot-on-sight policy. I'd take a couple people fooling around on the beach over that. She probably didn't realize we were cops."

"Hopefully she didn't realize what we were doing."

"Yeah, bad enough if the sheriff finds out. Worse, if she finds out from the youngest murderer in Merenranta's history."

"Maybe the man shot her first."

"Doesn't matter who did what first, still doesn't make any fucking sense we found the man in the snow and not her."

The boot prints led to the woods, to a snow-laden trunk at the front of the tree line. And that was where the trail ended; not dissipated, ended. It was as if the girl had killed the man and vanished from existence, only to then return from whatever alternate universe she'd traveled to, reappearing in the snow beneath this tree. "What the fuck?" Chloe said for the both of them.

They circled the tree and the surrounding area, nothing, no more tracks. The snow was completely undisturbed. Even if the child paused after each step to cover her prints, only a blizzard could hide them this well, and last night's snowfall had been anything but. Chloe was checking the snow around a set of close-by trees for the third or fourth time when Samantha called to her, confounded. "Chloe." Her partner was standing at the tree, over the last pair of prints before the girl's trail concluded.

"What?" Chloe asked as she joined her.

Samantha pointed. "These tracks are different from the rest. The others have a normal depth to them, like you would see from a kid her size walking a slow pace. These prints here are too deep and..."

"Too far apart," Chloe said. The boot prints were spread wide, as if the child stepped in the snow with her legs stretched to each side. Tiny splotches of dark red stained the snow next to the girl's left boot print. "That blood looks like it splattered from her wounds when..."

"She landed." Samantha and Chloe looked at each other, and then up at the tree. Above the girl's boot prints was a branch, bent with snow, though large enough for a child's feet to fit and flat enough at the base for a child to stand. A streak of dark red colored the trunk, beside the branch's stump, as if the girl had bumped her bleeding hip or arm against the tree, before jumping twenty feet into the snow without breaking a single bone.

Chloe and Samantha stepped around to the stalk directly behind the first tree. This trunk was red as well, the branches between the two trees intertwining, enough for the girl to hop from tree to tree, assuming the girl could do any of this. The same was true of the third and fourth tree; they didn't go farther than that; they knew what the child had done, not how she did it, but what.

"She's been using the trees, like you said, sir," Samantha told Mayor Darabont as they, Chloe, and Sheriff Armistead sat at the table in the town hall conference room. It was almost noon. The officers had to wait most of the morning for the mayor's meeting with factory managers in the industrial neighborhood to finish before briefing him on the investigation. "We still don't know who attacked who first or how she got the upper hand, we won't till she wakes up, but we're starting to form an account from the evidence we do have. Girl and man fight, man shoots girl, girl stabs man, or vice versa, girl climbs tree and leaps from tree to tree to not leave any tracks, takes backpack with her; either it was hers to begin with or she stole it from the man, man moves towards beach, dies, girl makes her way towards Merenranta while attempting to cauterize wounds with matches from pack until she runs out, climbs trees again to avoid night patrol, jumps down inside the perimeter, walks along the beach and finds Officer Corday and me."

"A lot of holes in that account," Darabont said, befuddled.

"Holes big enough to walk through," Samantha agreed, confessing their evidence was lacking. Compared to police investigations conducted in the Previous Civilization, the records of which Chloe skimmed a couple times during slow days at the police station, her and Samantha's investigation was inadequate for several reasons, not just the poor quality of their evidence. However, considering the Merenranta police department might be the last police department in the world, their shoddy police work would have to do. Samantha snickered. "If this kid was an adult or a teenager I'd bet she was a Second-Gen, Awakened and everything."

Chloe flinched.

"She's too young to be Awakened," Armistead said, with an angered tone, as if Samantha had infuriated her with that mere jest about Second-Gens. "Even if she was a Second-Gen, minimum age for an Awakening is—-"

"Thirteen, I know," Samantha interrupted, annoyance in her voice. "This girl's a couple years younger than that at least, so no. Still, we aren't going to be able to, to...fill these gaps without interrogating, without interviewing her, and even then I doubt it'll all make sense."

"Why wasn't there more at the crime scene?" Armistead asked. "Even if she came and went using the trees, there should've been more from her, a few boot prints she made while she was stabbing a man to death, blood from being shot, something."

"I'll be sure to ask her when she's awake," Samantha replied, snarky enough to make Chloe, Armistead, and Darabont raise their eyebrows.

"And you're confident she's alone?" Darabont asked.

"Based on the evidence we have, yes," Chloe said, knowing how little that meant.

"Based on the evidence we have," Armistead retorted. "We've got an expert killer who also specializes in stealth. The fact she's a kid makes it more likely there's someone else involved, someone who taught her."

"I want an officer outside her room, twenty-four seven," Darabont ordered. His obligation to show leadership battled the agitation in his eyes and on his face.

"Yes, sir," Armistead said.

Darabont turned to Chloe and Samantha. "I want you two in her room as soon as she's awake. However long it takes, find out what she knows and report to us when she talks."

Chloe was surprised by the mayor's sternness. *Do you want us to question the girl or torture her?* "Yes, sir," she and Samantha said in unison.

Chloe and Samantha exited town hall at noon, their investigation stalled until the girl regained consciousness. Yawning as they walked to the beach in the chemical exhaust of the factories, Chloe said, "You hungry?"

"Fucking starving," Samantha answered.

"How can you be starving?" Chloe asked. "You ate last night."

"I'm not actually starving, I'm just really hungry."

"Why didn't you say you were really hungry then? Why'd you pretend you were starving?"

"I wasn't, it's just. Yes I'm hungry. You going home to eat?"

"Yeah, I guess," Chloe said, yawning again. "I'm fucking tired."

"Too tired to cook?" Samantha asked, excitement replacing exhaustion.

"Why're you smiling like that?"

Cheng's Bar and Restaurant was at the mouth of the cove on the south side. A one-story structure, small though not as small as the town's shack homes and built at the curve of the beach, Chloe had only visited the place at night, when the bar was packed with off-duty workers, civilian and government alike. And even then, she never stayed more than an hour. She'd certainly never eaten a meal at Cheng's.

The building was split into three sections, the kitchen in the back, the rows of tables in the front, and the bar in the center. Aside from a couple staff in the kitchen, the place was empty. The nighttime bar crowds were where the establishment's real income came from. Though the air was sour with the scent of salt, as if the place flooded with seawater and couldn't get the smell out, the floor and walls could've been polished five minutes ago, the furniture unchipped, ageless. Chloe and Samantha sat at a table along the front wall, beside a window, the unblemished glass providing a view of the cove and the ocean. In the daylight, Chloe could see her home, across the cove to the north. "Here," Samantha said, handing Chloe a piece of paper from the table. "Menu."

Chloe scanned the menu, finding food options of an absurd and unnecessary quantity. "What're we having?" she asked, the choices overwhelming her before she got a quarter of the way down the page.

"You decide. It's your ration slips, and your stomach."

The prospect of selecting a meal from a list long enough to require a whole sheet of paper was so daunting Chloe's left arm vibrated, the menu jiggling in her hand. She slid the paper back to Samantha and hid her left arm under the table. "You choose."

"No, you," Samantha responded, grinning as she sat back in her chair.

"Why?" Chloe said, irritated. "You always decide what drinks to get when we're at the bar."

Samantha laughed in enjoyment. "That's because I'm still not certain you know what alcohol is. Food you've got some experience with, so I shouldn't have to baby you."

"Can I ask Cheng to pick something for me?"

"That's not how a restaurant works."

"Can Cheng recommend something?"

"Sure."

"Why's he not allowed to choose for me if he can suggest something?"

"I heard my name," Cheng said as he came to their table. Supposedly afflicted with a type of constructive insomnia as early as his teens, Cheng was the founder, owner, and operator of Cheng's Bar and Restaurant. In his late thirties, his black hair was cut above his ears and even around his skull, except for the longer strands in the back. He wore his establishment's uniform, a long sleeve shirt, green, like some of the trees in summer, and a pair of winter pants and boots. They might've been the only clothes he kept. "Afternoon, officers, I'm not in trouble, am I?" Cheng joked.

"Give me a free drink tonight and we'll drop the charges," Samantha replied, shifting in her chair to face him.

"How about one right now? Seeing how you're here early, even for you." Cheng laughed, Samantha laughing with him. "Not that that's a bad thing. High-functioning alcoholism's been my forte since I opened. Universe forbid you and your cop friends get your drinking under control."

"Not a chance," Samantha assured. "But I'm going to have to pass on the drink for now. Still on the clock."

Cheng nodded. "I heard you two brought in a nomad last night. Some kid. What's the story there?"

"Still confidential," Chloe said, her left arm refusing to relax.

"So the investigation's ongoing then?" Cheng said, smiling.

"You'll hear plenty about it from the cops who can't keep their fucking mouths shut," Samantha quipped. "Can we order?"

"What do you want to drink?"

"Drink?" Chloe asked, baffled. "I thought we were ordering food?"

Samantha smacked her face with her hand, chortling. "We order drinks first, Chloe."

"Why?"

"I don't know why, that's just what people do in a restaurant."

"And I have to pick my own drink?"

"Yes."

"I can come back," Cheng said, mystified by their conversation.

"I'll have water," Samantha told him, before he could walk back to the kitchen.

"Same," Chloe said. "It's okay for me to pick the same thing as you, right?"

Samantha lifted her hand, as if she was about to smack her face again. She stopped herself though and said, "Yes."

"So, two waters?" Cheng asked.

"Leave," Samantha said. Cheng left them be, returning to the kitchen.

"What do we do now?" Chloe said.

"Wait for him to bring us our drinks. Decide what to eat. Talk."

Chloe didn't want to look at the menu again. "Talk about what?"

Samantha shrugged. "I don't know. What'd you and your parents talk about when you ate in Marathon, at the uh..."

"Chow hall?"

"Yeah."

Chloe shook her head. "Nothing."

"Nothing?"

"Nothing I can remember. Meals at the chow hall were always take the food they give you, no matter how shitty it looks, eat as fast as you can so you can get to school and your parents can get to work before their supervisor fucks them over for being late. My family did all our talking before bed."

"What was school like in Marathon?" Samantha asked, attempting to keep the discussion afloat.

"Fucking sucked," Chloe said.

"Why's that?"

Let's see, half the shit they taught us was lies the Commanders made every kid in Missio learn. The school was in the Community Office, which was cold as fuck and smelled like a sewer. And, everybody knew I'm a Second-Gen. "Did you like school?" Chloe asked.

"No kid does."

"Now imagine being a kid in Marathon and going to school, in Marathon."

"Was Marathon still making you go to school while the civil war was getting started?"

Chloe nodded. "I would've gone to school that last day, if Marathon hadn't erupted like it did. It was like the Commanders had no clue there was a war happening in their own city, until it killed them."

"At least the Commanders are dead."

"Fucking ye." Chloe heard a clinking noise from the kitchen and saw Cheng approaching their table with a tray and two glasses of water. The shakes in her left arm surged, the appeals for release howled in her mind. She and Samantha's investigation so far had been a diversion, a way to placate her urges for a razor. But now, with the girl still unconscious and Cheng about to take their food orders from a list of options so long it was impossible for her to choose, Chloe couldn't ignore her need for relief. "Order for me," she said as she rose from her chair, her voice fluttering.

"What?"

"Order for me. I'm going to the bathroom." Chloe darted between the tables, her eyes on the floor to elude Samantha and Cheng. The bathroom was around the bar to the right, a tiny closet-sized room with a floor somehow cleaner than the rest of the building, a mirror without a smudge, and a toilet that was never clogged. Door shut, locked, she leaned against the wall, in front of the sink and mirror, and rolled up her sleeve.

The first gash was gone, the skin repaired. The second gash was already healing, like the first cut before it. Chloe didn't have her razor. She would have to improvise. Removing her glove, she wedged her left arm between her stomach and the sink. "Stop," she said, bringing her fingernails to the healing cut. The quivering continued.

Chloe dug her fingernails into the gash, curling her fingertips back and forth, her nails clawing at her skin. Blood trickled from the cut, pain yelling at her nerves. She closed her eyes, breathing deep as she savored the ache in her arm, relished in her reprieve.

That girl could've died.

Chloe opened her eyes, pressed her nails in farther.

That girl could've died, because you didn't use your Second-Gen Stage.

Red swamped her digits, drowned her fingertips as it seeped across her arm.

You could've run faster with your Second-Gen Stage, got to the med center quicker.

She ripped her fingers out of her arm, speared them back in, yanked them out again, gouged her arm again.

But you didn't, because you put your own life ahead of that girl, even when she was dying in your fucking arms!

Again and again, Chloe pierced her arm with her nails, grunting, agony spiking up to her shoulder and down to her fingers, blood splashing in the sink.

You almost killed her! You almost murdered someone, again!

Chloe hoped her nails would tear through her flesh, through her veins, all the way to the bone.

The tremors ceased before she could get that far, her release fulfilled for the time being, without the need of her Second-Gen Stage. She used toilet paper to clean the blood from her arm and the sink, flushed the red-sodden tissue in the toilet. Her arm sat under the faucet till the bleeding subsided. If she were human, she'd have to worry about infection. But an Awakened Second-Gen was immune to infected wounds and physical disease. What she wasn't immune to, was her partner's mounting dread.

"Something wrong?" Samantha asked as Chloe returned to her seat, having been gone long enough that Cheng was already coming back with their food. Samantha's expression was the same as it'd been when she accidentally intervened in Chloe's release last night, likely driven by a throbbing suspicion her partner was in distress.

"No," Chloe answered, summoning every avenue of her mind to make her tone sound casual, as if she didn't know why Samantha would ask her that. She glimpsed her right hand, her glove hiding her finger-nails, still red with her own blood.

They ate, paid, and were heading back to north Merenranta when the call came on Samantha's radio. "Sam, come in," said the officer stationed outside the girl's recovery room at the medical center.

"Go."

"The kid's awake. Not talking, but she's awake."

The recovery wing made up the entire second floor of the medical center, a lone extended hallway of patient rooms and staff areas. The girl's room was in the middle of the hall, overlooking the western lobby entrance and facing the industrial neighborhood and the wind turbines. Like the others, her room was composed of a bed, a bathroom, and a couple chairs for visitors. Heated, illuminated by ceiling lights, the brightness of which could be adjusted, a week in this room might've been a relaxing stay for the girl, if the machines next to her bed weren't constantly chirping as they monitored her vitals and managed her pain medicine.

The girl was in bed, garbed in a patient gown, with her left arm in a cast and sling, and her left hip resting on cushions. Her skin had been bathed, her hair rinsed and combed. Chloe wouldn't have been able to say for certain if this was the same child she and Samantha met last night, were it not for her eyes. Still just as depleted and vacant as they'd been when the girl showed her face to Chloe's flashlight, her eyes were like the eyes of a corpse, emotionless and seemingly unaffected by the environment around them. Yet the child was nowhere close to dead. Before entering, a nurse explained to Chloe and Samantha that not only had the girl woken far sooner than anticipated, the amount of energy she possessed was not anywhere in keeping with a gunshot victim, especially someone her age and with the medication she was on. The staff's only lingering concern was that her heartbeat was higher than normal. Now, as the officers positioned themselves in the room, the child sat up in her bed, following them with her undead eyes, her heart rate rising on the monitor. This girl knew she was being flanked.

"Hi," Samantha greeted, her tone calm like her expression, as if she had no knowledge of what the child did. She sat in a chair between the bed and the bathroom wall, Chloe taking the chair between the bed and the window. The girl was silent, as she'd been the night before. "I'm Officer Armistead." Samantha gestured across the bed to Chloe. "This is Officer Corday. We're here to ask you a couple questions, okay?"

"You gave us a scare last night. Happy to see you're doing better," Chloe said, trying to sound sincere in her relief. She was, but the discomfort she felt was intolerable.

The child's reaction was nominal, her body immobile, except for her eyes, which rotated without sentiment to Samantha, Chloe, and down to the weapons in their holsters. Her heart rate jumped a couple beats. "Is that okay, if we ask you some questions?" Samantha asked, glancing to Chloe when the girl didn't reply.

"It's okay, uh." Chloe leaned forward in her chair. "It's okay, dear." The word sounded wrong somehow, as if its usage was reserved for an adult who'd earned a child's trust. Chloe definitely did not have this child's trust. "You're safe. You don't have to be scared." She made this statement, not knowing if it was a lie. Mayor Darabont could discontinue the girl's treatment and exile her if he came to believe the child posed a threat to the town. Lie or not, it got the girl's attention.

Twisting her body towards Chloe, her eyes ditched Samantha as if she wasn't in the room anymore. The child glared at Chloe, shivering in her chair, unable to escape the girl. It was as if the child was the one holding the flashlights now, and was shining them both in Chloe's face. The gash on Chloe's left arm still ached with release, but less than she preferred. The enhanced pain tolerance that came with her species was uncooperative.

"Can you talk to us?" Chloe asked.

The child shook her head. Samantha gasped in what Chloe first thought was disappointment, before recognizing her partner was surprised the girl responded, even if it was something as simple as head movement.

"Why not?" Chloe said next, attempting to lead the child into conversation without her realizing.

The girl didn't speak but pointed, at her neck.

"What? Is something wrong with your throat?" Chloe turned to Samantha, who looked back at her with mutual puzzlement. The staff had said nothing about the girl being sick. There were no signs of fever on her health monitor.

The child shook her head again, raised her index finger to her mouth.

Chloe got the hint that time. "You can't talk at all?"

The girl nodded.

"Because you're mute?"

Another nod from the child.

The officers stared at each other with the same expression. *What do we do now?* "Can you write?" Chloe inquired.

The girl's head didn't nod or shake. Chloe guessed she didn't understand the question.

Chloe put out her hand and pretended to scribble with her fingers. "You know, write letters, words."

"Sentences," Samantha muttered, almost getting a laugh from Chloe.

The child nodded.

"Go ask one of the nurses for a pen and paper," Chloe said to her partner, comprehending then that she'd taken Samantha's place as the girl's lead interrogator. "And tell someone she's, you know, mute."

Samantha stood and left the room, shutting the door behind her. She was gone no more than three minutes, three minutes that expanded to half an hour with the silence that dropped between Chloe and the girl. One of them couldn't talk; the other didn't know what to say. Their quiet was not inactive, though. Two pairs of eyes moved about, gazes crisscrossing as the officer and the child assessed one another, as if they believed they could learn whatever they wanted from each other's presence alone. Chloe didn't know if the girl was learning anything from her appearance, but she was gathering something from the child's. The girl was skinny, far skinnier than she should've been, her ribs visible through her patient gown, her cheekbones too pronounced. This wasn't unusual for nomads and bandits. What were strange to Chloe, however, were the child's arms. Twigs of skin and bone would've been consistent with the rest of the girl's frame, yet her arms were muscular. The development in the girl's arms, and legs too, was extensive, well beyond the fitness standards for children at the school. "You get those muscles climbing trees?" It was a stupid question; one Chloe didn't hear herself ask until the girl replied.

She snapped her fingers, the noise jolting Chloe back in her chair. The girl's chapped lips curved, creating what must've been a smile. It didn't have the feel of a smile though. There was emotion, yet none of the cheer or joy or silliness that children's smiles were grown from. This wasn't the grin of a child. This was the smirk of a killer who'd learned something from Chloe after all. The girl now knew these officers were on to her.

Samantha came back with a pen and notebook, setting them on the bed for the girl. Chloe gave her an anxious look as she sat down, trying to be discreet yet knowing it probably didn't help. The child was as smart as she was resilient. Resuming her questioning, Chloe pondered where and when the girl would attempt to outmaneuver them. Perhaps, she already had. "What's your name? My name's Chloe. What's yours?" She almost said "dear" again.

The girl's heart rate restarted its climb on the monitor; Chloe's did the same. The child opened the notebook, took the pen in her free hand, and connected pen to paper. When she was done writing, she spun the book around and slid it to Chloe's side of the bed. The letters were large on the paper, easy to read. "ADDIE."

"Addie?" Chloe asked, both for confirmation's sake and to let Samantha know what the girl had written.

The child nodded.

"Okay, Addie. Chloe, Addie. Our names sound alike, a little." She chuckled. Addie and Samantha didn't. Chloe turned the notebook, slid it back to the girl. "How old are you, Addie?"

Addie replicated the process, writing and displaying her answer for Chloe to read. "10."

You're only ten fucking years old and you're doing all this? "You're ten?"

Addie nodded.

Chloe glanced to Samantha and pushed the book back to Addie. "How long have you been...when did you lose your voice?"

"NEVER HAS ONE."

"You never had one? You were born without a voice?"

"CORDS BAD."

"Cords bad?" Chloe didn't grasp what the girl's written words meant.

"Vocal cords?" Samantha said.

Addie nodded without acknowledging Samantha.

"Your vocal cords were damaged, before you were born?" Chloe asked.

The child dipped her head.

"I'm sorry to hear, I mean, learn that," Chloe said. She found Samantha in the periphery of her eye. *The med center can test that, see if she's actually mute.*

Addie shrugged. If she truly had been mute since birth, then speaking wasn't something she missed.

"Who shot you, Addie? Who hurt you this way?"

The girl's reply was swift and not at all what Chloe anticipated. She was expecting a lie. "MAN I KILL."

Chloe hesitated a few seconds before repeating Addie's answer, waiting to see if the child would change her mind and write something else. The girl didn't even change her expression. "The man you killed?"

Addie nodded, without the slightest trace of guilt or apparent awareness of what she'd admitted to. It looked as if she was about to smile again.

"Fuck," Chloe heard Samantha mumble, dismay in her voice. Addie wasn't just confessing to murder, she was confessing with no care for what she'd done, no regard for the potential consequences.

The follow-up question came from Addie. Chloe was too stunned to talk for the moment. It was as if the girl's muteness was contagious. "WHY HERE RIGHT? FIND BODY? WANT TO KNOW?"

"Yes," Chloe murmured, afraid to speak louder than that. "Can you?" She took a breath. "Tell me what happened?"

Addie gave a single nod, as if to say no problem, and got to writing. "HUNGRY. MAN HAS FOOD IN BAG. TOOK IT WHEN HE SLEEP. MAN WAKE. POINT GUN."

"You were hungry and tried to steal the man's pack while he was asleep? But he woke up and drew his gun, his revolver, on you?"

The girl lowered and raised her head.

"Okay. What happened after he drew his gun?"

"STAB HIM."

"What'd you stab him with?"

"YOU KNOW. IN MY BAG."

"You mean the man's bag?"

"WHATEVER. MINE NOW."

"Was it a switchblade? A black one?"

Addie nodded and wrote. "FROM MARATHON."

"How'd this happen? He had a gun, how'd you..."

The girl was already scribbling. "CLIMB TREE. HANG FROM BRANCH. GRAB BAG. CLIMB UP. MAN WAKE. POINT GUN. JUMP ON HIM. STAB. JUMP BACK TREE. CLIMB AWAY."

"You never touched the ground?" Chloe said in amazement.

The child shook her head.

"When did he shoot you?"

"WHEN I JUMP ON HIM."

"He shot you as you fell on him?"

Addie nodded, wrote. "HE FAST. ME FASTER."

He shot her in mid-air. The initial blood from her wounds must've separated too much to be seen, or mixed with the man's. "Why didn't you ask the man to share his food with you?"

"LESS FOR ME."

"When did you eat last? Before you stole this man's pack and killed him, when was the last time you'd eaten something?"

"2 WEEK."

"Two weeks?" Chloe and Samantha exchanged a look of disbelief. "You mean two days?"

The girl shook her head and wrote again, "2 WEEK."

The officers shared another glance that lasted several moments. *A human who doesn't eat for two weeks can barely move.* "Okay," Chloe said, deciding to bypass the child's outrageous claim, though everything involving this child was outrageous. "You killed the man and climbed away, then what?"

"TRY FIX CUTS. CANT MAKE FIRE BIG. RAN OUT MATCHES."

"You tried to cauterize your wounds, until the matches from the man's pack ran out?"

The child nodded.

"And because they ran out you came to Merenranta, for help?"

The girl nodded.

"Using the trees to evade the officers on night patrol?"

"THEY HAS GUNS," Addie penned.

"So did we, but you walked up to us."

Addie sneered as she wrote on a new page. "SEE YOU 2 FUCKN."

—-

EIGHT

"Fuck me," Mayor Darabont said, shaking his head as he and Sheriff Armistead read from Addie's notebook, a few hours later. Chloe and Samantha sat on the opposite side of the table, back in the town hall conference room, waiting for their superiors to finish the transcript. Questions were asked by the mayor and sheriff, to bridge the gaps in Addie's writing. "This part where she wrote, don't know, don't remember, what's that in reference to?" Darabont asked, once he'd collected himself after reading the child's confession and description of her crime.

"Her last name," Chloe answered, through the numbness she felt from hearing the girl's responses read back to her. "Apparently she doesn't remember what her last name is." Darabont didn't reply, his dumbfounded expression was sufficient. "She's a ghost, ma'am," Chloe told Armistead. "Like you said."

There was skepticism on Armistead's face as she looked across the table. "That's assuming what she's written here is true, that she doesn't know her last name, that her first name is really Addie, and that she's actually mute."

Chloe was quiet, counting on her partner to question the sheriff's thinking. Samantha didn't disappoint. "Why would she lie? What's the point?"

"I don't know," Armistead admitted. "But the way she writes, she doesn't sound like someone who's one hundred percent there."

"She's a nomad kid," Samantha retorted. "She probably doesn't know how to write any better. And considering how we found her, or how she found us, her writing's not that bad."

"Is there a page missing?" Darabont asked Chloe, amid Samantha and Armistead's debate. "She writes 'they has guns,' and then her next answer is about her last name."

"The way you and Chloe described this kid's behavior, she seems highly disturbed," Armistead diverted. "Clearly, she's fucking with us."

"Thought it was odd she gave us her confession but not her last name, that was the next thing I asked about," Chloe said, gripping her left wrist beneath the table in case her left arm started quavering. It didn't. Darabont nodded, accepting her lie.

"Of course she's disturbed," Samantha said. "That just means she's fucked up, not that she's fucking with us."

Darabont closed the notebook. "What would you recommend?" he asked, turning to the sheriff.

Armistead's response was quick, as if she'd known the question would be asked and prepared an answer before the meeting began. "She's a liability, to community resources and safety. Send her on her way."

The abrasiveness of the sheriff's tone brought the room to a standstill for a solid thirty seconds.

Samantha was the first to speak, firm in her reply. "You want to exile her?"

"You can't be exiled unless you're a citizen," Armistead said, unwavering. "I'm talking about not letting her in."

"Results are the same whatever you call it," her daughter rejoined.

"She's a risk we have no use in taking. We've already lost a citizen this week. Let's not make a habit of it."

"She's under guard, twenty-four seven, like the mayor ordered."

"It's not just her I'm worried about. Whether she's fucking with us or not, someone had to teach her. Writing, stabbing, hiding, there was someone else in her life at some point." Armistead pointed at the window, facing the forest to the north. "That person could be out there right now."

"Ma'am," Samantha said, trying to stay professional despite the frustration in her voice. "Forgive me, but that doesn't seem plausible."

"What about this seems plausible to you?"

"None of it, but there's evidence to support the kid's story. There's no evidence this hypothetical mentor of hers is still in the picture. And how could she and some other person plan all of this? How could they know she'd get shot and need our help?"

"I'm not saying they planned it, but now they have an opportunity. All this kid has to do is get better, which according to the med center she'll do in record time. Then, she can head out, link up with whoever she was with, and tell them everything she knows about this place. She's already demonstrated her skill for getting inside our perimeter."

"All the more reason to let her stay. If this other person's really out there, why not keep the girl here?"

"The longer she's here the more she learns, about Merenranta, about the people who live here, about its police." Armistead looked to Darabont, tapping the notebook with her finger. "We need to cut her visit short, before she can get a full read on us."

The officers sat in silence as Darabont pondered the sheriff's advice. Curving his head to Chloe and Samantha, he said, "You two are the leads on this investigation. What do you think?"

Shock reverberated around the table. A mayor asking any police officer other than the sheriff for counsel was unprecedented, enough, Chloe feared, Armistead might retaliate against her and Samantha in some way if either of them answered. Samantha did not share that dread apparently. "We need more time."

"More time?" Darabont asked, not noticing Armistead's discontented expression.

Samantha nodded, her eyes acquiring and at the same time disregarding her mother. "More time to get a read on her. We still don't know where she's from, how she can do what she does, how she can kill someone and not care."

"You think we should let her stay?"

"For now," Samantha said, modest. "While she's recovering. Keep her in her room, even when she gets well enough to walk by herself. The med center's doing tests tomorrow morning to see if she's really mute. That'll begin to tell us how honest she's being. I'd rather not throw her back into the woods when we know so little about her."

"And you agree?" Darabont said, focusing on Chloe. The combined glares from the mayor, the sheriff, and Samantha restricted Chloe to a nod.

Darabont nodded in response. "Okay, she stays for now. But she better be completely forthcoming over the next couple days. Otherwise, her stay won't last. You two are back in her room tomorrow, after her tests are done. This is your only assignment. You don't go back on patrol until I make a final decision."

"Yes, sir," the officers replied.

Chloe saw the dissatisfaction on Armistead's face as the four of them rose from their seats at the end of the meeting, her eyes flashing between Darabont and Samantha. *That's the second time today Mayor Darabont gave us orders directly instead of delegating to the sheriff.*

It was after dark when Chloe and Samantha left the police station. Hungry and plagued by weariness, Chloe almost didn't hear Samantha as she said, "Where you heading?"

"Home," Chloe said, as they stood in the town hall lobby.

"Going to make yourself dinner?" Samantha asked, a pesky smile on her face.

"Yep, and take a shower. You?"

Samantha's smile widened, her head shifting to the west lobby exit, towards the route to south Merenranta and Cheng's.

Chloe grimaced, knowing. "You've had a day?"

"Fuck yeah," Samantha said. "You sure you don't want to come?" There was a hopeful expression around her grin, a genuine desire for Chloe to join her for a round of drinks, and several more after that.

"No, I'm good," Chloe told her nonetheless. "See you later?"

"Yeah," Samantha replied, her smile diminishing.

"Don't get sick," Chloe said, as the partners separated.

"I've had a day," Samantha half-jested.

The moon was behind the clouds, the night dominating in its blackness, the icy salted cold pushing down on Chloe's shoulders as she plodded through the snowy pathways of north Merenranta, back to the beach and her shack. She was still on the western side of the neighborhood, white breath puffing above her head, when one of the buildings caught her attention: the school. Enrolling students from ages five to eighteen, the school was in that sense like Chloe's Community Office school back in Missio, yet vastly superior to Missio's schools in every other sense.

Chloe was walking to the school before she'd instructed her legs to do so. Most of the windows were dark. School hours were from 9:00 to 4:00, and it was well past 5:00. A couple windows were still lit though, the main entrance unlocked for after-school activities, arranged for children whose parents were working late and didn't have anyone else to watch them. Chloe hoped the teachers supervising these activities were paid overtime.

Jealousy flared as she entered the halls of the school, her boots tapping and squeaking as she sought out the after-school classrooms. While not spotless, the floors were decently clean, the building warmed to an adequate degree. The hallways of her Community Office had been layered with grime, the interior air bitter and rancid with decay and sewage, the walls bare and black, as every structure in Marathon was. The walls of this school were draped in students' artwork, illustrations, paintings, and other creative efforts, all fashioned together in a seemingly endless assortment of colors. Dark blue and black were just two choices among many. The children of Merenranta could draw with whatever color they wanted.

She heard the after-school activities before she found them. The children were singing, their young yet emphatic voices rounding the corner as Chloe came to it. "Ring around the rosie!" Chloe turned the corner. "A pocket full of posies!" She saw yellow light coming from a classroom window, illuminating the darkened hall. "Ashes, ashes!" She came to the classroom and stood by the door, looking in the window. "We all fall down!" The children sang the last line at a yell. Chloe's eardrums tingled with the noise.

They were grouped on a carpet at the front of the classroom, none of them a day over seven years old. Most were lying on the carpet in a circle. One child was standing in the middle, cackling with glee. A teacher was outside the circle at the edge of the carpet, clapping his hands. "All right, you all did awesome." Beaming, he pointed at one of the children in the circle and told him he was the last to fall down, meaning he would have to stand in the circle now. The boy denied this at first, but soon switched places with the child in the center, the others rising from the carpet and linking hands, forming a ring around the boy. "Everybody ready?" the teacher asked, the children shouting that they were. "Let's go again."

The circle of children revolved around the boy, singing, "Ring around the rosie!" Chloe smiled at the game, wishing there'd been games like it in Marathon. "A pocket full of posies!" She didn't know what that line meant, though her amusement persisted. "Ashes, ashes!" Chloe chuckled, covering her mouth with her hand so she wouldn't disrupt the game. "We all fall down!" The children crumbled to the carpet, Chloe's smile crumbling with them.

The children decorated their expressions with childishly dramatic faces of death, as Chloe rolled up her sleeve and rubbed the gash on her left arm. Although they were playing dead, Chloe couldn't detach herself from the circumstances that surrounded Merenranta like a ring, waiting for one of these children to wander too far from their parent's eye, too far from the town perimeter. Because even the best parents couldn't determine what became of their children. Some children, like many of Chloe's neighbors in Missio, died before they reached adulthood, or even puberty. Other children vanished, their whereabouts never resolved. A few children, however, lived to become someone like her. There wasn't a violent impulse in either of Chloe's parents, yet the daughter of Anna Corday and Sean Halley was a murderer. Chloe had more in common with Addie and Martin Donnelly than she did with her own mother and father, or with her own partner.

"Can I help you, officer?"

Chloe rolled down her sleeve, turning as a second teacher approached from the hallway bathroom. "Uh," she said, stumbling with an answer she didn't really have. Then, she realized what brought her to the school, why she'd searched for an after-school class. Addie may've been a killer, and one who lacked remorse for the person she'd killed, but she was still a child. "Yes actually."

Box of colored pencils and sketchbook in hand, courtesy of the teachers at the school, Chloe returned to the medical center, well against her better judgement. Arriving at the girl's room, she gave the officer on guard a break to get something to eat from the center's kitchen. Addie was where Chloe and Samantha left her, three empty meal trays stacked on the floor beside her bed. "Hi, uh, again," Chloe said as she came in and closed the door. Addie didn't offer any kind of non-verbal reply. Her heart rate didn't even change on the monitor. Chloe was familiar now, no longer a threat in the child's lifeless eyes. Whether that was good or bad, Chloe had yet to discover. "How're you doing?"

Addie gave a thumbs-up, without lifting her head from the pillow.

"Good, that's good," Chloe responded, sitting in the chair between Addie's bed and the bathroom wall. She set the sketchbook and pencil box at the foot of the bed. "Thought you might get bored, I brought you some..."

The girl sat up, tossing her blankets aside as she moved towards Chloe. The officer lurched back in her chair; hand at her side, close to her weapon. Addie took the sketchbook in her hand, flipped through its blank white pages. Chloe put her hand on her leg, breathing through her nose to calm herself. Opening the pencil box, Addie's eyes browsed the numerous colors for a full minute. If she was confused or curious as to why there were so many, her demeanor didn't show it. She chose the black pencil, probably because it was the same color as the pen she'd used earlier. Addie sat cross-legged, the book in her lap as she wrote. Her pain medicine must've been working better on her than on any patient before her, because there was no external sign of discomfort, not so much as a wince. This would've surprised Chloe, were it not for everything else she'd learned about this child in the past fifteen or so hours.

Addie twirled the book around in her lap for Chloe to read. "MINE?"

"Yep," Chloe said, intertwining her hands in her lap and leaning forward. "In case you get bored." She smiled, but Addie was already looking down, turning the sketchbook and writing more.

"WHAT THESE FOR?" The child gestured at the multitude of colored pencils.

"Drawing," Chloe told her.

"DRAING?" Addie asked in her writing.

"Yeah, pictures. Something to do while you're here."

"PICURES?"

"You know, pictures, I mean uh, drawings." Chloe lifted a pencil from the box and moved her hand back and forth across the bed, pretending to sketch.

Addie studied Chloe's demonstration and wrote, "FUCK YOU DOING?"

Chloe paused, stared at the girl. "Drawing, do you really not know what that is?"

The child shook her head.

"Fuck me," Chloe blurted out, too horrified to stop herself.

Addie nodded, as if in agreement. Putting down the sketchbook and pencil, she hung her legs over the side of the bed, facing Chloe, her heart rate ticking up on the monitor.

Chloe sat up in her chair. "What're you?" Addie leaned over, planting her hand on Chloe's leg. It dawned on Chloe then, why Addie was comfortable approaching her and Samantha when she saw them about to have sex on the beach, why she commented on it in her interview, forcing Chloe to tamper with police evidence by tearing the page from the notebook. A ten-year-old shouldn't have been accustomed to sex, unless they had experience with it, enough to start having sex with someone they thought was asking for it. Addie slid her hand towards Chloe's crotch. "No, no." Chloe pushed the girl's hand away, sweating with sudden nausea. "That's not what I." Addie lowered her hand to Chloe's belt buckle, trying again as her heartbeat continued to rise. "No, stop." Chloe seized Addie's wrist, her strength overpowering the child's as she held her arm back. That didn't last.

The girl's heart rate exploded on the monitor, only to plummet a second later, below what it was when Chloe came in. She watched in paralyzing incomprehension as a resurrection occurred in Addie's eyelids, her eyes returning to life in a storm of rage and something Chloe couldn't identify. Violet light glowed from the ten-year-old's irises. Addie wasn't in Chloe's grip anymore, Chloe was in Addie's. The child flung the adult from the chair, slamming Chloe on her back, next to the bed. Addie dropped on Chloe's chest, her movement noiseless, without as much as a grunt of exertion. The girl clamped her hand down on Chloe's neck, sealing her windpipe.

Her oxygen depleting, her nerves pulsating, Chloe tried to roll out from under the child, grabbed Addie's wrist with both hands and tried to free her neck. Both attempts failed. They failed because Addie was a Second-Gen, an Awakened Second-Gen. Ever since the first Second-

Gen was discovered and the species investigated, more than half a century ago in the last years of the Previous Civilization, the analyzed rules of Second-Gen evolution stipulated an Awakening couldn't take place until a Second-Gen was at least thirteen years of age, when they'd matured enough to make the transition. As with most Previous Civilization knowledge on Second-Gens, those rules were frozen in the cold that followed the day of the Reform, their eternalness undisputed, trusted by Chloe, her parents, Merenranta, Marathon, and more. Fifty-five years after the Reform, however, those rules were no longer current apparently. At just ten years old, Addie had complete access to the enhanced abilities of her species, abilities that enabled her to move after two weeks without food, kill people twice her size, climb trees, walk for miles and survive for hours with two gunshot wounds, and heal from those wounds at inhuman speed. Chloe was also capable of these feats.

The signal broke from Chloe's brain, activating the process throughout her body. The panic of suffocation, the fear of this lethal child, and the question of how Addie was Awakened at such a young age, all repressed by the concentrated and calming feeling of her alternate state. Energy spiked from these initial sensations, this energy becoming strength. Her Second-Gen Stage igniting, Chloe saw the surprise materialize on Addie's face. Chloe's irises would be shining now, the child realizing this officer was a Second-Gen, just like her.

Releasing her hold on Chloe's neck, Addie moved to the side, sitting on her knees. The child's IV wrapped around her head as Chloe coughed her way back to normal breaths, her throat and neck sore, like they used to get before her Awakening, when she could still get sick. Recovering, she untangled the girl's IV and sat up on the floor, next to Addie.

The two Second-Gens held their shimmering eyes on each other, Chloe coming to understand it wasn't just anger that provoked Addie into attacking her. Amidst the violet of Addie's irises, the stretches of her expression, fright was poking through. Addie was a murderer, a

Second-Gen, and a terrified child. Wherever she came from, whoever taught her the skills she knew had made her so scared she was limited to two primary responses, confrontation and submission. Sex brought about submission. She'd been trained, manipulated, harmed, to react that way. Having a revolver drawn on her, or her wrist being grabbed, elicited violence. There was an absence of empathy in her actions because fear filled her cognizance to capacity. Addie was too busy being afraid to feel sorry for others. Now though, the girl didn't know how to respond in the face of another Second-Gen, quite possibly the first she'd ever met.

Chloe held her index finger to her mouth, aware of the crime she was committing against her town. Her sympathy for this Second-Gen child was too substantial to ignore, even at the risk of being deemed a traitor. She and her parents had been living with that threat since their first day as citizens of Merenranta. "Don't tell anybody, Addie."

Addie nodded.

Withdrawing her Second-Gen Stage, Chloe uttered a sentence she'd heard her parents say to each other over the years, when reenactments found them. "You're safe, you and I are safe and everything is going to be all right." Chloe didn't know if she believed those words, yet she repeated them till the glow left the girl's irises, their secret hidden beneath the two of them.

PHASE 3: DRAWING

NINE

3:00 in the morning by her police wristwatch and Chloe was still awake. She and Samantha went to bed in her shack just after 11:00, beginning four hours of agitated tossing and turning while her partner lay next to her in peaceful, drunken slumber. Chloe informed Sheriff Armistead and Mayor Darabont of Addie's sexual behavior upon leaving the medical center, suggesting the girl was at one time a sex slave, perhaps quite recently. The sheriff and mayor agreed this was a possibility, yet no scars or lasting injuries were found on Addie's body that would indicate she was sexually assaulted. Thus, no one except Chloe was certain, because no one except Chloe knew the child wasn't human. There were no physical signs, because the girl's healing abilities mended even the most damaging assaults. An Awakened Second-Gen could be raped a thousand times without crippling effect. This likely meant the child had her Awakening before her assaults, and she was a slave to more than one person. One assaulter wasn't enough to restrain a Second-Gen, especially not Addie.

An Awakened Second-Gen at ten years old, three years shy of the maturing age for an Awakening: this reality had Chloe rolling in her blankets, twisting her head on her pillow, shivering from a cold sweat underneath her sleeping clothes. Addie was the first of her kind, among humans and Second-Gens both, at least as far as Chloe knew. The fact this girl happened to wander into Merenranta made it possible she wasn't the only premature Awakened Second-Gen in existence. Whether she was the first or one in a population, she was the third Second-Gen Chloe had met in her lifetime, after her mother and Martin Donnelly. The guilt of withholding this secret, from her parents, from Samantha, from Merenranta, was churning in her stomach, as if the truth was preparing to vomit out of her. The child was stable for now, but if her Second-Gen Stage was triggered again, any harm she brought to the town or herself was on Chloe.

"You awake?"

"Yeah," Chloe said, tucking her trembling left arm under her torso. She shifted to face Samantha so that they were practically on top of each other, their bodies tangled together on the tiny mattress. Samantha's eyelids were open; when she'd woken and why, Chloe didn't know. White moonlight gleamed through the window behind Chloe's head, reflecting off Samantha's glassy eyes and dilated pupils in the blackened bedroom.

"Thinking about kids?" Samantha slurred, Cheng's liquor still present in her speech and on her breath. "The kid?"

Chloe nodded her head against the pillow. "Yep." She yawned into her hand. "You?"

Samantha didn't answer. Instead she asked another question. "Why did, didn't you call me when, when?" She looked past Chloe, as if there was someone else in the room. "When you went back to..."

"Back to Addie's room?" Chloe said, finishing Samantha's query.

"Why didn't, you ask me to goes with you?" Samantha asked, concern sounding between her slurs.

Samantha's worry was received with exasperation from Chloe. To her, her partner should've already known why she hadn't gotten a call to join her at the medical center. "I assumed you were busy."

"Nots if you'd calls me," Samantha said.

Chloe thought about lunch at Cheng's the previous day, centering on a moment that unsettled her. "What'd Cheng mean when he called you a..." She paused, recalling the term from her wearied memory. "A high-functioning alcoholic?"

Intoxication wasn't enough to hide Samantha's anxiety. "It means it's a problem, not a problem."

Even if Samantha were sober, Chloe wouldn't have been convinced by her response. "Drug addicts in Missio used to say the same thing. Marathon didn't have drinking, but we had a lot of other addictive shit."

Samantha shook her head, giving a coherent reply. "They're not the same."

"You were at Cheng's a lot later than you were the other night," Chloe said, voice rising with allegation.

"I had a day."

"When was the last time you didn't have a day?"

"I don't, I'm not going to talk about this."

"Fine." Chloe rotated away from Samantha, towards the window.

Caressing Chloe's arm a few seconds later, Samantha said, "Do you want to?"

Chloe shook her head without looking back at her partner. "No."

"Right, I just, thought I'd ask."

Lying on her quivering left arm, Chloe shut her eyes to the moonlight, wondering if she'd fall asleep before sunlight. She didn't.

Chloe went about her morning in a trance of oppressive enervation, too tired to yawn, so tired she couldn't tell if she and Samantha were actually getting dressed, eating breakfast, and clocking in to the police station, or if she was dreaming. Only when she and Samantha entered Addie's room at the medical center did she know she was conscious, her alertness rousing to meet the challenge of interacting with this inexplicable child. Addie's tests were done, the damage to her vocal cords and her resulting muteness confirmed. The girl was in her patient gown, sitting cross-legged on the bed, with as little visible ache from her wounds as she'd had the night before. Her Second-Gen pain suppression plus the medicine from her IV must've removed any enduring agony. The pencil box was open in front of her, the mini pencil sharpener that came with the box beside it, the sketchbook in her lap. Left arm still in its cast and sling, she was holding the black pencil in her right hand and scribbling in the book, in a manner that told Chloe she was drawing.

"I thought you didn't know what drawing was," Chloe said in confusion, as she took her seat between the bed and the window, while Samantha sat between the bed and the bathroom wall.

The child raised her head from her sketchbook, her attention concentrating on Chloe, ignoring Samantha, though the increased heartbeat on the health monitor showed she knew the second officer was there. Chloe and Addie were allied, not by friendship but the need for secrecy. Samantha and Addie had no such relationship. To the girl, Chloe's partner was still a threat. Turning the page in her book, the child wrote a response and put the book on the bed for Chloe to see. "WHAT DRAING?"

Chloe pointed at the sketchbook and the black pencil in Addie's hand. "The drawing you were doing just now." A notion came to her. "Do you not call it 'drawing'?"

Addie shook her head.

"What do you call it then?" Chloe asked, recognizing the child knew how to draw, yet the skill had never been defined for her with words like "drawing" and "pictures."

"REWARD," the girl wrote in reply.

"Reward?" Chloe glanced at Samantha, as if that would help. "A reward for what?"

"BE GOOD."

"You got to draw as a reward for being good?"

The child nodded without expression.

Chloe shoved her left hand in her jacket pocket to hide the shaking, but Addie's inert eyes scanned her shoulder and moved down her arm, taking note of the unsteady limb. "We're here to ask you a few more questions," Chloe said, before the child could comment on her arm. "Can you tell us...?" She hesitated, adjusting her question to make the girl more comfortable. "Me, can you tell me where you're from?"

It didn't help.

Addie shook her head.

"Why not?" Chloe said, thinking on Darabont's demand that Addie cooperate or be subject to exile.

The girl shrugged, her eyes glimpsing Samantha for a split-second.

Chloe nodded, understanding. "Okay, we'll try an easier one. Where were you living before you killed, before you came to Merenranta?"

"OTHER PLACE."

"Obviously. The last few days before you came to town, where were you living?"

"FOREST."

Chloe moaned in annoyance. "Where in the forest?"

"CAVE."

"In a cave, you were living in a cave?"

Addie bowed her head.

"Was this cave beside a creek?" Samantha asked before Chloe could.

The girl nodded, without looking at Samantha.

The partners made eye contact. "North Creek," Samantha said, referring to a creek that flowed through the woods, eight miles north of Merenranta, from someplace farther inland. It wasn't the most inspired name. The sides of North Creek were fissured with several small caves, often used for shelter by nomads and bandits.

Chloe nodded to her partner in agreement and asked Addie, "How long were you living in this cave beside the creek?"

"1 NIGHT."

The sheriff's voice crackled on Samantha's radio. "Officer Armistead, come in."

Flinching, Samantha rose from her chair and responded into the radio. "Copy, standby." She stepped into the hallway, closing the door so the child wouldn't hear whatever Armistead was going to say.

The moment the door clicked shut, Addie flipped through the pages of her sketchbook, back to the drawing. She tore the page from the book, folded it in half and held it out for Chloe to take. "What's that for?" Chloe asked. Paper in hand, the girl brought her index finger to her mouth, her eyes shifting to the door. Chloe nodded, bringing her index finger to her own mouth as she comprehended Addie didn't want Samantha or anybody, except her, to see this drawing. Accepting the paper, Chloe was about to unfold it when the door squeaked open. She stuffed the drawing in her jacket pocket and the child turned the book back to the page she was on, as Samantha returned.

"Sheriff wants to meet with us," Samantha said in a less than excited tone.

"Why?"

"Fuck if I know. She just said meet her at the station when we're done here."

"WHO SHAREIF?"

"Don't ask."

They met Sheriff Armistead in her private office at the police station—-not Armistead and Mayor Darabont, Chloe was quick to notice—-just Armistead. Part of her was tempted to ask if the mayor knew about this meeting, but not the part that wanted to keep her job.

"And she was alone the entire time, she claims?" the sheriff asked from behind her desk, as spotless and organized as her office, cleaner than Cheng's Bar and Restaurant, the cleanest room in Merenranta.

"Yes," Samantha told her mother as she and Chloe stood in front of the desk. There were no chairs, visitors had to stand, Darabont included. The lights were off, the room lit in the natural yellow of the mid-morning sun, which glared through the window behind Armistead. Outside the building, the gray water was low in the cove, refusing the sun's rays. Black smog billowed over the industrial neighborhood, the civilians of Merenranta at work keeping the town awake.

Armistead took a moment to collect her thoughts on Samantha and Chloe's report from the interrogation. "How long did she say she's been following the beach?"

"Months," Samantha said, turning to Chloe, who nodded in reaffirmation.

"How many months?"

Chloe spoke. "She doesn't know."

Armistead's expression grew skeptical. She may've laughed if humor didn't contradict everything about her personality. "How could she not know?"

"She probably lost track," Chloe said. "My parents and I did, till we got here."

The sheriff's doubt didn't abate. "And you think she's been moving south all these months, by herself? You think that's something a kid her age could survive, even with her skillset?"

Well, she's a Second-Gen, so yeah. "I think she's desperate enough she could, yes," Chloe stated, left arm vibrating behind her back.

"Desperate?"

"To get away from whomever she was enslaved to."

Armistead tilted her head towards her desk, sighing with disappointment. Chloe's sex slave theory was still just conjecture to her.

"You still think the girl was with someone?" Samantha said, her tone more inquisitive than confrontational. Either she was trying to avoid another debate with her mother or she too was uncertain of Chloe's theory.

"Yes," Armistead said in blunt reply, not afraid to say what she believed. "And that's what we're going to prove."

"Ma'am?" Samantha asked, as she and Chloe traded glances of surprise.

"The girl said she stayed in a cave at North Creek."

"I don't get what that's supposed to prove," Samantha said.

"There could be evidence of another person, an associate, in that cave."

"You want us to go to North Creek?" Samantha asked, a stunned anger gathering in her voice and expression.

"I'm sending you to North Creek." Armistead was stern. To decline this assignment meant being written up for insubordination. "Find the cave the kid spent the night in."

"Creek's a two-hour walk," Samantha protested. "That's a ways to go with no backup."

"Call me on the radio when you find the cave," Armistead said, unaffected by the potential danger she was putting her daughter in.

"Yes, ma'am," Chloe and Samantha chimed. It was clear to Chloe now why they had this meeting without the mayor. Darabont had his own meetings with the school principal and the head of food share distribution this morning, but he'd given the officers permission last night to interrupt with updates pertaining to the Addie investigation at any time. The mayor wasn't absent because he was unavailable, Armistead just didn't want him present. The sheriff was looking to show the mayor that the girl was conspiring with somebody else, to pressure Darabont to follow her advice and exile the child. Even if Chloe and Samantha hadn't come to her with news of North Creek, Armistead would've found some way to guide their investigation in the direction of her choice. Left arm shaking all the more, Chloe exited the office with her partner.

—-

TEN

An hour later, she and Samantha were four miles north of Merenranta, walking the gray-snowed beach. The sun was blocked by a mountain of clouds, the gray surf frenzied with rough waves, the air howling off the ocean and blasting Chloe and Samantha with frigid wind. Snow had been falling since the second mile of their trek, the flakes riding the breeze, hitting Chloe and Samantha sideways and from above simultaneously. Such was the consequence of living by the sea. Winters weren't as brutal as they were in Marathon, but the weather could change at an instant. Shivering in the cold, the officers alternated between bending their heads to shield their eyes from the squall, snow, seawater, and sand, and holding their numb faces to the beachfront and tree line to watch for hostile activity.

"Is something wrong with your arm?" Samantha asked, lowering her hat as close to her eyelids as she could without obstructing her vision. The question came after an hour of fleeting casual conversations to pass the freezing time, with another hour of glacial marching to go. There was nowhere Chloe could run.

"What?" Chloe replied with false ignorance, a puff of white air exhaling from her mouth and blowing across Samantha's face.

"Your arm," Samantha said, motioning to Chloe's left arm. "Is something wrong with it?"

"What do you mean?" Chloe asked, knowing full well what her partner meant.

"I've seen it shaking a bunch. You have a tick or something?" A white puff respired from Samantha's mouth and carried into the forest.

In that moment, Chloe was thankful for the cold. The rest of her body shook as much as her left arm, hiding the exact tick Samantha had discovered. "No," she said, unable to conjure up anything else. It was only after she continued her lie that she realized it would've been easier to claim she did have a tick, yet didn't know why it was there. "You think I have a tick?"

"I don't know," Samantha said with abrupt uncertainty, as if she was concerned, though not enough to defend her concern. "I was just...I thought it might be a problem."

"It's not," Chloe responded, her left arm quieting with relief. Samantha's worries about her partner were growing, but so far she hadn't tied them together. The exchange collapsed there, as fast as their prior discussions, leaving them with another bout of uncomfortable silence, aside from the noise of the snowstorm. Chloe could only bear this for a few minutes before she asked a random question she'd been meaning to ask for the last couple days. "What's that sport where someone whacks a ball with a stick and runs around the bases? I saw some kids playing it the other day and couldn't remember the name."

"Baseball?" Samantha said, happy to be talking again as well.

"Yeah that's it." Chloe made a scan of the woods. "How is it? I've never played."

Samantha shrugged her shoulders, facing the beach ahead of them. "Fun to play, boring as fuck to watch."

"Not your favorite?" Chloe asked, tilting her head to lessen the blow from a gust of snow and sand.

"I always liked lacrosse more," Samantha said, ducking her head behind Chloe to dodge the same draft.

"Is that the one where you get to hit people?" Chloe asked with genuine interest.

"Body check," Samantha corrected. "You can't actually hit people in sports, unless it's boxing or something like that."

Chloe chuckled to herself. "You can in pentagon."

"What?" Samantha said, oblivious to the sport.

"Pentagon, you can hit people in that," Chloe replied, grinning. "That's all the game is really."

"You making this up?"

"No it was real," Chloe laughed. "In Marathon."

"Oh," Samantha nodded. "That explains the stupid fucking name. You said you could hit people?"

"Yep. There was a ball you had to score on some goals, but mostly people just beat down on each other."

"That must've been fun."

"Wouldn't know, never played."

Eight miles north of Merenranta, Chloe and Samantha veered off the beach, into the thickets. Amidst the creak of trees swaying with the airstream, the crack of branches breaking under the falling snow, and the thump of snow piles plopping to the ground, the officers located the lowest point of North Creek. Twenty meters back from the beach and surrounded by grayish-brown trunks, lay a sinkhole, a dark circle in the gray snow. Trickling and splashing, the waters of North Creek drained into the hole, down beneath the ground, on course to meet the saltwater below the sand. This close to its end, the creek was only a couple feet wide and an inch deep, yet so gray Chloe couldn't see the bottom. Even fifty-five years later, the Reform still polluted North Creek, as it polluted the ocean.

They moved inland, Chloe keeping to the north edge of the water, Samantha to the south. The creek expanded, the sides elevating into muddy rock-strewn bluffs, some eight to ten feet high, a natural trench with water at its base. A quarter mile into a forest as barren as the sea, they found the first caves. Formed by erosion, these caves peppered the slopes of the creek, a few of them large enough for an adult to crouch in, or a child to stand in. Descending and ascending the hillsides, their boots tapping on the rocks and squishing in the grayish-brown mud, they checked each cave, the ones that weren't flooded, at least. When a cave yielded no results, no evidence of Addie's stay or anybody else's, the officers continued on. Whilst traversing the winding waterway, the zigzagging mounds, Chloe skimmed the woods, the incessant barrage of trees and branches that congested the horizon in every direction. Though they fluttered with the breeze, it seemed as if the trees were reacting to the officers' presence, watching their movements.

Half a mile up the creek with no success, Samantha decided they would each inspect one more cave then head back. Standing ten feet apart from her partner on the other side of the creek, Chloe nodded without speaking. Like the snow and wind that chased them into the forest, tiredness from nearly two days without sleep had found her again, the monotony of searching caves to support Sheriff Armistead's personal mission having weakened her brain's defense. On top of that, her stomach grumbled. It was past noon. She and Samantha hadn't eaten since breakfast. Rounding a turn in the creek, however, Chloe's energy returned, her hands drawing her pistol as the water in North Creek turned dark red.

"What the fuck?" Samantha said, wielding her pistol as she too noticed the slick of dark red in the gray water, near Chloe's side of the creek. The streak extended up the creek, around another turn, disappearing behind a slope. Boots stamping in the snow and mud, the officers followed the red line, negotiating the curve. Their pistols clicked, rising with their hands and arms, index fingers curling at the triggers when they saw the bodies.

There were two, lying just beyond the curve, on the north side of the creek at the water's edge. Pistol scanning the hillsides, the trees behind those hillsides, and the branches above, Chloe advanced on the corpses, Samantha using rocks embedded in the creek to cross and join Chloe on the north side. The bodies lay headfirst beside the creek, their hair soaking in the water, their feet aimed up the mound. Dark red and pink splattered the snow around their shoulders and heads, or what was left of their heads. One body lay with its face in the snow, the back of its skull broken in a soup of blood and brain. The second body lay face up, except without a face. Like the sinkhole at the end of the creek, a hole consumed this person's eyes, nose, and upper lip. The lower lip and chin were the only surviving features of this person's individuality, though there wasn't much to gauge from either of those.

The ragged winter gear they wore told Chloe and Samantha the corpses were nomads or bandits, the lack of supplies or weapons indicating they'd been ambushed, murdered, and robbed of those things. These factors were predictable, yet the officers were left confused. "This must've just happened," Chloe observed, brandishing her pistol at the blood stains in the snow. "Snowfall still hasn't covered the splatter. Wounds are still bleeding."

"How long do you figure?" Samantha asked, standing opposite the bodies from Chloe.

"Half-hour, if that." Chloe made another scan of the creek, woods, and overhead branches, her answer making her nervous.

"How can that be?" Unease in her tone, Samantha mimicked her partner. "We've been following the creek longer than that. We should've heard the shots."

"Maybe they were drowned out by the storm," Chloe suggested.

"Not with these wounds," Samantha countered. "They're high-caliber shots. They should've rang out for miles, even in this weather."

"Unless they're low-caliber, but were fired point-blank."

Samantha shook her head. "Tracks don't show that." With her hand, she drew Chloe's attention to two pairs of boot prints that frayed the snow along the creek. "Victims came down the creek, moving east towards the beach." She pointed at the snow between her and Chloe. "Stopped here, why I don't know, maybe they were taking a break." Turning her arm to a third set of boot prints that came down the bluff and went back up, Samantha said, "Shooter came from this hill, separate from the victims. No chance the shooter could get to point-blank range without being seen. Shooter hangs back in the trees, gets the drop on the victims, walks over when they're down, takes what they've got, and moves back uphill. Judging by the wounds, I'd bet shooter used a rifle."

Chloe traced the shooter's tracks, her eyes following them away from the creek, into the trees until she lost sight. A thought brewed in her mind, her nerves swelling into fright as she gazed through the snow and stalks, the forest and its unseen inhabitants blurred in a darkness of gray. Chloe raised her pistol and kept it that way. "Let's head back," she said, voice quiet, her tongue dry with fear.

"You fucking read my mind," Samantha said, lifting her pistol as Chloe did, her body tensing.

The officers trekked back down the creek, the scraping, screeching trees pursuing them to the beach, and down the beach, all the way back to Merenranta. It wasn't till they were sitting in the warmth of the town hall conference room, mud and snow cleansed from their boots, the storm passed, late afternoon sunlight dimming in the window, that Chloe felt safe. This sense of safety didn't last.

"So, you didn't find the kid's cave?" Sheriff Armistead asked, sighing, dissatisfaction verging on rage. She and Mayor Darabont sat across the table as Chloe and Samantha finished recounting their investigation of North Creek.

Chloe looked at the table, her left arm shuddering at her side as she braced for Armistead's ire, letting Samantha speak for both of them. "No, we found the bodies before we could find her cave. Given the circumstances, it didn't seem worth the risk to keep going."

"Understandable," Darabont replied, his tone sympathetic to the officers. "I'm not sure what good it would've done even if you'd found the cave."

Raising her head, Chloe saw Armistead turn to her superior, her face clenching. "It could've provided evidence."

"Evidence of what?" Darabont asked, sympathy draining from his expression.

"Evidence the kid is lying, that she's not here by herself like she's been saying," Armistead said, undeterred. "But the trip wasn't a complete loss."

"How so?" Samantha asked, combative as she'd been yesterday.

Armistead appeared to grind her teeth as she looked to Samantha, as if she had to stop herself from screaming at her. "The stiffs you found, with at least one shooter still active."

There was a pause as Samantha's eyes enlarged. "You're saying those gunshot victims, the kind of victims we find in the woods all year round but especially now with the winter as it is, were killed by someone linked to the girl?"

"We have to consider that possibility," Armistead declared, continuing her effort to drive the investigation towards her objective, the exile of Addie.

"I have to say, Dylan, I think you're reaching," Darabont said, stern yet lacking the poise of Armistead's angered posture. "And I wish you'd come to me about this assignment before you sent them out. I think it took away a lot of time they could've spent questioning Addie."

"We've gotten nowhere talking to this kid. She's just going to keep saying she was alone, until she gets well enough to walk out of the med center and reconnect with her accomplice."

"She talks to Chloe," Samantha interjected.

Chloe scowled at her partner, as if she'd shared a secret she'd promised not to tell.

"Everything we've learned from her she's told Chloe, not me. She pretends I'm not there most of the time. She's slow with Chloe's questions, but she's answering them. We give her time and she'll tell Chloe enough for you to make a decision, sir."

The twitching worsened in Chloe's left arm. *Fucking thanks, partner.* She was afraid to respond with any more than an incensed expression.

Darabont nodded. "Thank you, Sam. You and Chloe can go."

"Sir?" Samantha said, taken aback.

"The sheriff and I will meet with you tomorrow morning to discuss next steps."

The officers hesitated, shifting their heads to Armistead. "Go on, both of you," she snapped.

"Thank you, ma'am," Samantha muttered.

"Thank you, sir, ma'am," Chloe stammered, as she and Samantha rose from their chairs and fled the room, their superiors turning to face each other. Chloe shut the door behind them and she and Samantha started down the hallway of mayoral offices, heading for the stairs.

Darabont's voice carried into the hall, heavy with accusation.

"Is there something going on, Dylan?"

"How do you mean, sir?" Armistead replied, sounding unfazed.

"Do you think there's a problem with the investigation?" Chloe and Samantha entered the stairwell, out of earshot of the mayor and sheriff's squabble.

"How long do you think they'll be going at it?" Chloe asked, a few minutes later, when she and Samantha left the police station, the sky grayish-orange outside the lobby doors.

"Fuck if I know," Samantha said with a shrug, as they walked to the west lobby exit. "Depends on how long it takes the mayor to realize he's wasting his time. Sheriff's never going to admit to anything."

"How fucked does this make us?" Chloe said, the lobby doors squeaking as they went through, into the cold of sunset.

"No more fucked than we already are," Samantha replied, their boots crunching in the fresh layer of snow.

"That's promising," Chloe quipped, as they joined the evening foot traffic, heading for the beach.

A smirk crossed Samantha's face and Chloe got an idea of what she was going to say. "You know what always makes me feel better?"

"I'm not going to Cheng's," Chloe said, last night's conversation still glued to her memory.

Samantha laughed, to Chloe's anger. Either Samantha couldn't remember their discussion because of how drunk she'd been, or it was a joke to her. "Come on, you don't have to drink, just get dinner."

Chloe's left arm juddered at the thought of having to pick from the menu. "That's worse than drinking."

"I'll pick for you, you can just hang out till you're done eating." Samantha's voice was casual, yet her expression was stiff, as if she was begging.

"I don't know," Chloe said, wondering if she should go tonight, giving herself an excuse not to go the next night.

"You know, if you think about it, you being there makes me less likely to drink too much."

Chloe was the one who laughed that time. "We both know that's not true."

Chuckling, Samantha said, "At least you'll be there to hold my hair back."

Shaking her head in a mixture of anxiety and amusement, Chloe decided being with her partner was better than waiting and worrying until Samantha came home. "Okay."

Chloe was quick to regret her choice. It was dark by the time she and Samantha arrived at the south end of the cove, the moon behind the clouds, the freezing wind surging from the sea. With the day over, the tiny structure of Cheng's Bar and Restaurant was packed with civilian and government workers, three dozen patrons at minimum, crowding the luminous bar and tables, a crescendo of noise and smell, the scent of seawater combined with the chemical aroma of the industrial neighborhood. Chloe and Samantha managed to get a table at the same window they'd eaten at yesterday. The racket of intoxicated chats, laughs and shouts, drinks being requested, was such that the waiter who took Samantha's food orders could hardly hear her, just as Samantha and Chloe could hardly hear each other. Samantha ordered some sort of alcoholic drink Chloe didn't know, as if she knew any of their names. No sooner had Samantha drank her glass dry was she called over to the bar for shots with a few friends. Chloe declined Samantha's offer to join and watched as her partner stood at the bar, banging a shot glass on the countertop and downing the contents with her friends, each of them emerging a little more rowdy, a little more unsteady. They coaxed one another to do more and Cheng refilled their glasses. Chloe turned away after the third go-round.

Sitting alone at their table, Chloe ate her food when it finally came, almost forty-five minutes after Samantha ordered. She thought to tell Samantha their dinner was here, but her partner was in the midst of conversation at one of the tables on the other side of the room, her face bright and flushed, a glass in hand as she told some story to a couple of factory workers. Chloe didn't eat her meal in silence, though. Nearly two full days after the girl's arrival, Addie was a popular topic. And like Addie, word had spread that Chloe and Samantha were the officers tasked with her investigation.

"I heard she can't talk, like she's mute or something," a woman said, stopping at Chloe's table on the way back to her own.

"Yep," Chloe replied, trying to minimize eye contact so the woman would assess she didn't want to talk.

The woman got the hint. Others didn't.

"Is she by herself?"

"Is it true she killed a guy?"

"Is the mayor letting her stay?"

Chloe's answers dwelled in a pattern of vagueness. "The investigation is ongoing…That's still confidential…We don't know yet." Her responses would've been unsatisfying to anybody. To Merenranta's prying, suspicious, citizens, Chloe's refusal to divulge was enough to bring about noticeable resentment, even if they didn't act on it. People in this town were incredibly trusting, of those granted citizenship. Beyond the permitted residents of Merenranta, however, everybody, including a child, was seen as a possible threat. In their defense, Addie had the capacity to be a threat. Then again, so did the citizens.

The last question wasn't meddling, yet it impacted Chloe the most. "She enjoying her sketchbook and pencils?" asked the teacher Chloe met in the school hallway last night, sitting one table over from her.

"Yeah she is, thank you," Chloe told him, unable to decide if that was a lie or not.

"Good," the teacher said with a smile and nod, resuming his meal and drink with his life partner.

Remembering Addie's drawing, Chloe dug her hand into her jacket pocket, having placed the picture there hours ago and forgotten about it. Retrieving the paper and holding it in her lap beneath the table, she checked to be sure no one was paying attention, and then unfolded the sheet.

The drawing was of a room, the floor black, the walls black, the ceiling unfinished but black as well. Four black stick figures were standing in a circle, their bodies featureless, except for one whose head was marked with a purple dot where their right eye should've been, a red line where their left eye should've been, and long grayish-brown lines at the back of the head, hair. Aside from this purple-dotted, red-lined, grayish-brown-haired figure, whose hands were empty, the other three black stick figures were holding jagged black objects in their arms, in a stance that told Chloe the objects were guns. Two more black stick figures were crouched on their knees at the center of the circle. Though drawn without weapons, these two figures held something between them. Another stick figure lay on the floor, significantly smaller than the other six figures, legs black, torso and arms dark blue, two purple dots for eyes, their hair long and brown.

It was Addie, Chloe understood, her stomach roiling and her left arm quavering with such violence she held the paper in her right hand so she didn't tear it with her left. Addie was lying on the floor, her arms and legs seized by the two stick figures sitting around her. Her Second-Gen Stage was active, her violet eyes glowing, yet the three figures with guns kept her from fighting back, forcing her into obedience. The scene was taking place under the apparent supervision of the purple-dotted, red-lined, grayish-brown-haired figure. These were the people Addie had been enslaved to, who'd taught her the skills she knew, and whom she'd escaped from. That wasn't the sole reason Chloe's senses called for release, however. The black floor, the black walls, the black ceiling, Addie's black legs, dark blue torso and arms, a room of all black and a girl dressed in dark blue and black clothing. There was only one place in the world that built rooms like that, made clothes in just those colors.

Addie's picture went back into Chloe's jacket pocket. She took a couple ration slips from a case on her belt and left them on the table, payment for her dinner. Rising from her chair, Chloe moved down the row of tables, through the drunken crowd, to the exit. Opening the door, Chloe glanced back and saw Samantha making her way towards their table, wobbling like a desk with a broken leg. Samantha didn't see Chloe standing at the doorway, and Chloe made no attempt to signal her. She walked out and closed the door behind her, hoping Samantha wouldn't follow.

Chloe was walking up the beach, the icy breeze at her back, her eyes directed across the blackened cove to north Merenranta, when she heard boots crunching behind her. "Where, where's, where're you going, Chloe?" Samantha asked with a slur, approaching in the white light of the now visible crescent moon.

"Home," Chloe lied, turning in the snow to meet her partner, her left arm stretched behind her back, shakes hidden.

"Why?" Samantha said, blinking, as if trying to focus through the haze of alcohol.

With a white-puffed sigh of irritation, Chloe said, "You said I only had to stay for dinner."

Samantha shifted her head to the shack homes of south Merenranta, then the blackish-gray waters of the cove, as though she didn't want to look at Chloe when she asked this next question. "Why, whys can you stay longer, long?"

"No," Chloe told her, strict.

A white cloud respired from Samantha's mouth, sparkled in the moonlight as she said, "I's was." A dispirited expression covered her face. "I thought we could hang out, talk."

Chloe scoffed, looked past Samantha at the bar. "You've got plenty of company for that, Sam. They're certainly keeping you occupied."

Drunk as she was, insult registered with Samantha. "That's because, because they act likes they want to be here."

"I don't want to be here, Sam," Chloe said, listening as her voice rose to an infuriated shout. "I wouldn't have come if you hadn't begged me to!" She asked a question when Samantha didn't reply, fury commandeering her tone. "Why do you keep trying to drag me over here? Every fucking night it's, let's go to Cheng's, let's go to the bar! What, am I just here to have sex with you after Cheng cuts you off for the night?"

Samantha shook her head. "No, no, I just want to, to, know."

"Know what?" Chloe snapped.

Staring at the snow and sand, Samantha hesitated before speaking. "Marathon, yours, your nightmares, Addie, your arm."

Alarm joined Chloe's anger. "What about my arm?"

Samantha lifted her head and pointed. "I sees it shaking, Chloe."

Chloe's reaction was less about anger and more about preventing Samantha from linking her various concerns together, stopping her from getting a clear view of her partner. "You want to know what's wrong with me? How about you figure out what's wrong with yourself first!"

Rage transferred from Chloe to Samantha. "The fuck you talking about?"

Even before she spoke, Chloe was dizzied with shame for what she was saying. "You think I have a problem because I don't hang out with a bunch of fucking drunks every night? Maybe I like taking time for myself! You're the one who can't be alone, Sam!"

Samantha's response was free of slurs, as if she was making a concerted effort to prove Chloe wrong. "I'm not staying at your place tonight."

Fuck. "Fine, hold your own hair back then!"

They parted, Samantha stomping back to Cheng's, Chloe around the cove to north Merenranta. A short walk, made often if not several times daily, yet now for Chloe it morphed into a miserable slog. The pain of exhaustion from the last two nights and the guilt of their argument bound to her legs, pulling her back one step for each she took. The urge to go back and apologize to Samantha was as immediate and as crushing as her need for release, if not fueling her need for release.

Fear of worsening their dispute kept Chloe on the path to the medical center. It was better, she determined, to try and say sorry to Samantha when her partner was sober. Entering the lobby and climbing the stairs to the recovery floor, she patted the piece of paper in her jacket pocket; refocusing on why she left Cheng's and came to the medical center.

Addie was lying awake in bed, the on-call nurse leaving with her finished meal trays as Chloe arrived at her room. Blankets up to her chin, left arm above the covers in its cast and sling, Addie looked as if she was about to go to sleep. But when she saw Chloe come in and shut the door, the girl rose from the blankets and crawled to the foot of the bed, where her sketchbook and pencil box sat. Taking a seat between the bed and the bathroom wall, Chloe asked her question, the words slicing at her tongue as they left her mouth, as if they felt it was best to stay buried in her brain. "You're from Marathon?"

Legs crossed, sketchbook open in her lap, black pencil in her hand, Addie nodded and wrote, flipping the book for Chloe to see. "HOW KNOW?"

Right arm trembling with her left, Chloe withdrew the drawing from her pocket and held it up for Addie to see. "Dark blue and black."

Addie's undead eyes widened and she wrote, "YOU FROM MARATHON 2?"

PHASE 4: AWAKENING

ELEVEN

"HOW HERE IF YOU FROM MARATHON?" Addie asked in her sketchbook, confusion surrounding her listless eyes.

"Same way you are, I walked," Chloe told her. "My parents and I left Marathon seven years ago, after the civil war destroyed..." She paused, correcting herself. "...after we thought the civil war destroyed the city."

Addie wrote a reply and turned her book for Chloe to read. "WHAT YOU MEAN THUGHT?"

Drawing in hand, Chloe said, "This is Marathon, right? That's where you were before you came here? You were living in a part of Marathon the civil war didn't destroy?"

"NO. MARATHON ALL GONE."

Chloe looked at Addie's picture, examining the room of black-colored pencil for clarification. "This isn't Marathon?"

Addie shook her head.

"But you are from Marathon?"

Addie nodded.

"Where's this then?" Chloe asked, perplexed.

The child was slow to write, as if she preferred not to talk about the location in her drawing. "SERENITY STATION."

The name was at once familiar and unfamiliar to Chloe. "Serenity? You mean the city from the Previous Civilization?"

The girl nodded, heart rate rising on the monitor.

"What's Serenity Station?"

Addie cringed as she scribbled. "MARATHON SOLDIER BASE. UNDERGRUND SERENITY."

Chloe grasped what the child was saying. "I didn't know Marathon had a military base in Serenity."

"SECRET."

"And that's where you lived before you found Merenranta? This Serenity Station?"

Addie's heartbeat continued its uptick, her expression grim. "FUCKING SUCKS."

"I'm sorry, Addie," Chloe said. "I can't begin to imagine." Her words of support seemed to bounce off the girl, yielding no perceptible response. Not only had this child's enslavement made her incapable of feeling sympathy for others, she couldn't receive it in return. "How long were you there, before you escaped?"

Addie blinked as she wrote, as if she didn't want to see her own answer. "CIVIL WAR."

Fuck, you were there almost seven years? Chloe put the picture away and asked a different question. "Do you remember the civil war? You must've been three at the time."

"1ST THING REMEMBER. DAY I SECOND-GEN."

"The last day of the civil war...was the day of your Awakening?" Chloe said in surprised comprehension.

The child nodded.

"You had your Awakening when you were three?" Chloe knew what Addie was, yet the girl's existence still left her in a place of disbelief.

"SOLDIER ATTACK ME. AWAKENING. KILL HIM."

The black switchblade reappeared in Chloe's consciousness, drenched in its usual stains of bright red. Left arm quivering in her chair, heartbeat elevating with Addie's, Chloe tilted her head towards her feet, taking a breath as she contemplated what Addie was telling her. This child's life in its entirety, from her earliest memories to now, was a sequence of violent events, some committed by her, some against her. To Addie, murder wasn't just rudimentary, it was ingrained in her childhood, a skill as ordinary as learning to write or draw. Looking up, Chloe found a question written for her. "WAS YOU AWAKENING SAMEDAY?"

Left arm and body shuddering at the thought of the black and red knife, Chloe responded at a whisper. "Yeah."

"HOW?"

Chloe shook her head. "I don't know. Second-Gens are so rare, the chances of you and I both Awakening on the same day in the same city is even less likely than both of us turning up in the same town seven years later. But, those things happened."

Addie shook her head back. "HOW YOURS HAPPEN?"

"Is the civil war all you remember from Marathon?" Chloe asked, ignoring Addie's query.

The girl tapped her written question, asking again. "HOW YOURS HAPPEN?"

"You don't remember your parents or where you lived in the city?" Chloe said, clutching her left arm with her right hand, though it did little to hide or help her tick.

"NO PARENTS," Addie wrote, shaking her head before tapping the question again. "HOW YOURS HAPPEN?"

"Who'd you leave Marathon with?" Chloe asked, averting her eyes from the sketchbook.

Addie pounded the book with her hand, demanding to learn something from Chloe after writing so much about herself.

Chloe lifted her twitching index finger to her mouth, shaking her head. Addie raised her index finger to her own mouth, nodding her head. The standoff lasted almost twenty seconds, then, with a sigh, Chloe relented. "My Awakening happened the same way yours did." There was plenty of truth to her answer, yet it didn't feel honest.

It seemed sufficient for Addie, who wrote, "WHAT SIDE SOLDIER ON?"

"What side was the soldier on? You mean in the war?"

Addie nodded. "COMANDRS OR TERERISTS?"

"I don't know." This reply was fully true. "Everybody was shooting at everybody. I doubt the soldier knew what side she was on either. What side was yours on?"

The girl shook her head. "NO ASK."

"You called them terrorists instead of rebels. Guess the people you left Marathon with, who took you from Marathon, were on the Commanders' side."

Addie didn't just nod her head; she threw it downwards, as if to emphasize how loyal to the Commanders the people in question were, or her annoyance that Chloe hadn't figured that sooner.

"Who were they?"

The child's heart rate soared on the monitor. "BLACK DRAGOONS."

Unlike the Serenity Station, this name was totally unfamiliar to Chloe. "Who is...? What is a Black Dragoon?"

Addie shook her head, impatience mounting. "MARATHON AS-SASSINS."

Chloe nodded, starting to understand. "Marathon had an assassination unit?"

"KILL TERERISTS PEEPLE COMANDRS TELL THEM KILL."

"These assassins were military?"

"SECRET."

The child's claim wasn't difficult for Chloe to believe. The Commanders of Marathon certainly wouldn't have been above using clandestine death squads. Recalling the six black stick figures in Addie's picture, but not wanting to take the drawing out again and distress the girl any more than she already was, Chloe asked, "How many were there? Six?"

The girl nodded and wrote, "CIVIL WAR KILL MOST. SIX LEFT."

So just those six in the picture. "Those six left Marathon for the Serenity Station, and have been surviving there since the civil war?"

"KILL. SURVIVE."

"What about the soldiers already at the station?"

"KILL THEM."

"Not enough supplies to go around." Chloe was hesitant to ask her next question, fearing it could trigger an outburst in Addie. However, she had to know. "Why'd they take you with them?" It was only after she asked that the reason became obvious.

Addie's heart rate elevated again. "MAKE ME DRAGOON."

The tug of nausea had bothered Chloe at different points over the last couple days. As it invaded her stomach now though, she wished she could vomit. "They made you an assassin?"

The Black Dragoon nodded.

Chloe's queasiness became fury. "Because you're a Second-Gen?"

"SPECIAL SECOND-GEN. BETTER THAN BEFORE."

"Better than before?"

The girl rolled her vacant eyes, scribbled harder, as if telling Chloe to pay closer attention. "BETTER THAN DRAGOON SECOND-GENS BEFORE ME."

Chloe sat forward in her chair. "There were other Second-Gens in the Black Dragoons?"

"2."

Heartbeat kicking inside her chest, Chloe said, "Are these two Second-Gens still Dragoons?"

"1. COMANDR."

"This commander of the Black Dragoons is a Second-Gen?" Chloe asked, thinking of the purple-dotted, red-lined, grayish-brown-haired figure.

Addie nodded and began to write something.

"What about the other one?" Chloe said, before Addie could finish.

Crossing out what she'd begun to write, Addie wrote, "DRAGOON BEFORE CIVIL WAR. COMANDR TELL ABOUT HER. FAILURE."

Left arm quaking so bad it broke loose from her own grip, Chloe asked, "Did the commander tell you this Second-Gen's name?"

The child nodded. "CANT REMEMBER. A SOMTHNG. LOST HER ARM ON MISSION."

Whether Chloe was silent a whole minute or just imagined she was, the quiet that followed Addie's answer rushed over all of Merenranta, and even the wind from the ocean hushed at the presence of those words in the girl's sketchbook.

"I have to go."

She was out the door before Addie could write a response. Down the stairs, her left hand refusing to grip the rail, out the lobby doors, her body immune to the cold, she found herself running through the snow to the beach, as if she'd slept plenty her whole life and had all the energy she would ever need. Around the cove, past the industrial neighborhood, into the shack rows of south Merenranta, she bolted down the path, not stopping till she was stomping through the door to her parents' home without a knock.

"Chloe?" her mother said, standing at the sink, bare feet swelling from pregnancy. Anna's surprise made a swift turn to apprehension when she saw the state her daughter was in. Leaving the glass she'd been holding on the counter, she approached Chloe, extending her left hand for her daughter to take. "What's wrong?"

Boots and pants saturated with snow and sand, skin damp and shivering with sweat, left arm flapping at her side for her parents to see, Chloe tried to muster an explanation but couldn't. The rush that carried her to her parents' shack hadn't dwindled. She was standing at the doorway, yet felt as if she was still sprinting. Anything she said would be lost in her exertion, and what she'd come here to say, she only wanted to say once.

Anna wrapped her hand around Chloe's right hand, eyeing her left. "What's wrong with your arm?" she asked, voice pitching as if she thought Chloe was injured.

"Chloe?" Sean said, entering the kitchen from the bedroom, his scarred expression stirring with concern as he scanned his life partner and daughter. "What's going on?"

"Come here, sit down," Anna instructed, tugging Chloe forward, putting her hand behind her daughter's back. "Get her some water, Sean."

"Right." Chloe's father closed the door and filled a glass in the sink.

Chloe's mother led her to the table, rubbing her back as they sat down. "Can you tell us what's wrong?"

Chloe looked at her arm as it fluttered in her lap, knowing what was wrong though not knowing how to begin.

"Here." Her father set the glass on the table in front of Chloe, taking a seat across from Anna. "What's wrong with your arm, Chloe?" he asked, noting the unhinged limb.

"Chloe?" her mother said when she didn't respond. Anna took Chloe's left hand in her own, gripping it tight as it shook and lifting Chloe's arm up to the table. Chloe's eye line rose with her arm. "What is this?" her mother asked, beseeching her daughter for an answer as the arm banged on the table.

"Is it hurt?" Sean asked. Chloe looked up at him, his eye staring back at her. She shook her head, her first real response since barging into her parents' shack. Doubt filed through the scars on her father's face. Fright tailed his skepticism as he studied Chloe's left arm, and then Anna's left arm, as if the two limbs seemed similar to him. "Can you roll up your sleeve, Chloe?"

Chloe might've refused, but she could see the notion developing in her father. Refusing would just strengthen his inkling. And plus, compared to what she'd come here for, showing them what was under her sleeve now felt insignificant, despite how long she'd hidden it. Without a word, she rolled her sleeve back, let her parents look, let them see the gash. The cut was faded, almost healed, yet the tremor that moved through both her parents told her it was clear to them where it'd come from.

"Did you?" Her father coughed, as if his words were choking him. "Did you do that to yourself, Chloe?"

She nodded.

Her mother had to inhale before she spoke. "How long has this been going on?" she said, as if the concept of self-inflicted arm wounds was familiar to her.

Chloe shrugged, still holding her tongue. *Not long, six, seven years.*

"Chloe," Anna said, stern with worry. "You need to tell us, dear. You need to tell us, so we can help you."

The whirlwind in Chloe's mind finally abated, her thoughts collecting around the kitchen table, focusing on her parents with a rage she never believed she could feel towards them, a discomforted searing that halted the shaking in her left arm, as if the limb was afraid of her. "Why don't you tell me instead?" she snapped, pulling her left hand away from her mother's.

"Tell you what, dear?" Anna said, seeming more confused by her daughter's sudden anger than the question she was asking.

"Tell me why you lied to me," Chloe heard herself say, ire driving her interrogation forward.

Her parents turned to each other, swapping puzzled glances. Yet, within their exchange, their expressions seemed to hold an unspoken note of comprehension, as if they both had an idea of what lie their daughter might be talking about but didn't actually think it could be that. "When did we lie to you, Chloe?" Sean asked, more sympathetic than defensive, as if he thought Chloe was accusing them as part of some psychological breakdown.

Chloe had to pause before she said it. Once she did, there would be no way to retreat. "Fifteen years ago." She turned to her mother. "You told me you went away because you made a deal with the Commanders. You became a soldier, so I would be taken care of." Chloe shook her head, and even though the light in the kitchen was on and stayed on, the light around Anna's face appeared to darken, as if her mother was both inside and outside at the same time. Talking at a furious whisper, Chloe said, "But you weren't a soldier, were you?"

Her mother sat motionless, as if hit by a stroke that would leave her still and speechless for hours. Her father was looking at the table, hand on his mouth, as if fighting the need to vomit, or scream, or both. The terror in his eye and amongst his scars told Chloe what she'd already suspected about him. "You too?" she asked.

Sean took his hand off his mouth and lifted his disfigured face to his daughter. His cheeks twitched, like they did whenever his scars burned, yet he didn't rub them, didn't try to treat his pain. "How'd you find out?" he asked, voice quavering with frightened acceptance. Perhaps he'd known from the moment he met Chloe that this conversation would happen, and now that it was here he wasn't about to flee from it.

"You two were Black Dragoons? Assassins?" Chloe replied, disregarding her father's question. This wasn't his investigation.

Her father blinked his eyelid like there was something stuck in it. "Yes, Dragoons. We were partnered together, your mom and I. That's how we met."

"That's right," her mother interjected, her voice uneven as her life partner's was, acknowledging what her daughter had found out about them. "I made a deal with the Commanders, like you said." Her expression ticked, as if she too had mutilations stinging her face. "Became a Dragoon, not a soldier."

Her parents' frankness didn't lessen her anger. "So everything you said about Serenity? The roadside bomb? Those were lies too?"

"Most of them," Sean said. "We were in Serenity. Our first mission was there."

"How many missions?" Chloe stuttered as she asked. "Did you..."

"Two," Anna said. "Lost my arm on the second. Sean lost his eye, got the rest of his scars. That's what sent us home."

"Where was your second mission?" Chloe asked, and then gaged what the answer was. There was only one place it could've been, if not Carthage or Serenity. "The Aegean Valley?" Her parents nodded and waited for Chloe's next question. Even in her rage, she was reluctant to ask. A second nod from her mother and father nudged her onward, as if now that she was learning the truth about them they wanted her to know everything, "Did you, did you two kill anyone?"

Anna sighed through her nostrils. "We were assassins, Chloe."

Chloe shut her eyes for a second, hoping this whole night, her fight with Samantha, her meeting with Addie, and this discussion with her parents, was some overlong dream, a fabricated reenactment. She'd wake up in her single bed with Samantha at her side and her left arm trembling. She didn't, but her arm started shaking again. "How many?"

"I killed nine," her father replied quick, as if wanting to get the number out fast before he lost his nerve.

"Eighteen," her mother said, a millisecond later. Anna turned to Sean. "More, if you count Jason and the people in Athens we didn't help."

Chloe put her arm back in her lap so it didn't beat against the table. "Who were they, the people you killed? Were they all terrorists?"

Tears dripped from her mother's eyes; her father's face ticked as if the scars were about to peel from his cheeks. Gritting his mutilated jaw, Sean shook his head and said, "No."

The tears were in her eyes too. Chloe blinked them away. "Who were they then?"

Anna wiped her eyes with her hand, and told her daughter, "Kids." She stammered as more tears came. "Two in Serenity, one in Athens. No older than twelve, any of them." She moaned, as if in pain. "You were six, and everything we did was classified under threat of treason. I thought if I told you we were soldiers, then when you got older and could keep things to yourself, we'd tell you what we really were. But then everything with the civil war happened and we found Merenranta and..."

"You thought you'd leave it in Marathon," Chloe growled. "Like we did when we told Merenranta we aren't Second-Gens."

Her mother nodded and covered her wetted eyes with her hand, so she didn't have to see her daughter's face. "Yes."

Chloe's ire graduated to disgust, not just at her parents but herself as well. For fifteen years she'd felt it, slight yet always there, like a buzz in her ears, sounding at random, without explanation, a hunch that her parents hadn't told her the entire story about their service in the military. However, she didn't want to ask them anything that might change her view of them, especially when she lived in Missio as a known Second-Gen and her parents were her only friends. Now, with knowledge of her parents' deceit, Chloe recognized that her parents' lies were what taught her how to lie. To Anna, to Sean, to the sheriff, to the mayor, to Merenranta, and to Samantha, she lied to everybody she knew. Like her parents, she was a liar. Like her parents, she was a killer.

"Chloe," her father said, tears in his eye.

"Don't," Chloe barked, and rose from the table. Looking at both parents, she said, "I wish you never came home." She turned and ran for the door.

"Chloe," her mother whimpered.

Chloe didn't turn around, didn't stop. She was out the door and sprinting before either Dragoon could chase her.

She ran all the way home, ran to the bathroom, ran to the razor. "Stop." Her sleeve was rolled up, the blade drawn, her left arm jammed between her body and the sink. "Stop." Dragging the razor through her arm, she reopened the cut that was already there, delighting in the pain it gave her. Blood sprinkled off her skin, staining the sink, the floor, and her jacket with drops of bright red, her arm continuing to shake, even with the release. She thought to call on her Second-Gen Stage, but chose another method.

"Your mother isn't coming back, Chloe. She's dead," she heard one of her guardians at the Missio Community Office tell her six-year-old self. "She died in Serenity. You can't stay here anymore."

Chloe jabbed her skin, cutting a second line of bright red on her forearm aside the first.

"Mommy," she heard her six-year-old self shout when she saw her mother alive, two months later, embracing her without knowing who her mother had become or what she'd done while she was gone. A third gash was made, bright red oozing from three holes in her arm, melding together. Still, her arm didn't stop, didn't slow.

"Listen to me, Chloe. This was not your fault," she heard her mother tell her six-year-old self when she asked if her mother left because she was mad at her. "This was not your fault. It's mine, it was all my fault, no one's but mine. Okay?" Chloe made the fourth cut along the side of her arm. Bright red dribbled on her boot.

"Nice to meet you too, Chloe," she heard her father say to her six-year-old self when they met for the first time. "Your mom's told me a lot about you. She missed you very much." The fifth gash went on the other side of her arm, painting the sink bright red.

"I was a soldier, Sean and I both," she heard her mother lie, a lie her six-year-old self trusted. "That's why I was gone for so long." She made the sixth cut close to her elbow, pressing the blade deeper than the previous five.

Her arm relaxed, soothed by agony, yet Chloe wasn't finished. She sat on the floor, between the door and the toilet, back braced against the wall. "Chloe, get up," she heard her father say to her fourteen-year-old self, yelling over the sound of automatic gunfire and explosions coming from outside barrack 804, a morning of thunder on the last day of the civil war. "Get up, we have to go!" Blood wetted her lap from the seventh gash.

"Mom! Dad?" her fourteen-year-old self cried when she lost her parents in the crowd on Broad Street, between Ignis and Missio, smoke from the building fires clouding her eyes, gunfire deafening her ears. Tears fled from her eyes, joining the eighth cut.

"Give me that fucking bag," the soldier demanded, pointing a T-05 rifle at Chloe's fourteen-year-old self as she lay in the snow, beside the Inner Fence. "I'll fucking kill you, give it to me!" With Chloe's tears and the ninth gash to her arm came the understanding that these releases weren't enough, would never be enough.

"Wake up," the boy shrieked. "Wake up!"

He sobbed over the soldier's body as Chloe's fourteen-year-old self looked on in guilt-filled horror, the bright red switchblade still in her shuddering left hand. The tenth cut was made with an awareness that she couldn't keep lying, couldn't keep hiding who she'd become or what she'd done. It was possible she'd chosen to be a police officer for that purpose, an unconscious selection in hopes her Second-Gen Stage would be revealed to the town. Arm carved and glazed bright red, she stood and put the razor in the sink, leaving her bathroom spattered with blood. One person in Merenranta deserved to hear the truth before everybody else.

Samantha's door was unlocked. Chloe knocked twice and entered. The kitchen light was on, the bedroom door open to the darkened room and double bed in the back of the shack. Chloe noted a set of boot prints on the floor, heading for the bedroom, as if someone had come in, turned on the kitchen light, and gone to the bedroom without bothering to clean the snow and sand off their boots. "Sam?" she said, mouth dry, voice vibrating, as she kicked the snow and sand off her own boots.

"What the fuck's?" Samantha shouted from somewhere in the bedroom Chloe couldn't see, tone incensed, still slurring from Cheng's.

Chloe crossed the kitchen, blood running down her jacket sleeve, moistening her glove, tapping on the floor in drops of red. "It's Chloe," she said, standing in the bedroom doorway.

"Fuck off," Samantha ordered.

The bedroom was empty, apparently, no one in the corners or along the walls and windows beside the bed. Chloe worried she might be hallucinating. "Sam?"

"What? Fuck, fucking told you." Samantha crawled out from underneath the bed, fully clothed, as if she'd just come home a minute ago. Head veered away from the door and Chloe, she said, "I fucking told you to fuck off."

"What were you?" Chloe began to ask; ignoring her partner's drunken bitterness. She recalled their conversation on the beach, how Samantha hid under her bed the night her father was murdered, how she continued to do so whenever she was alone. *You were hiding? What from?*

"Fuck you want?" Samantha asked; eyes on the floor as she stumbled to stand up.

Chloe turned from the bedroom and sat at the kitchen table, rotating her chair so she faced the doorway. Hands in her blood-tarnished lap, heart racing, and eyes sore from crying, she waited.

"Fuck you want?" Samantha asked again, using the wall for balance as she stepped from the bedroom. Snow soaked her pants and boots. Her eyelids were red, like Chloe's certainly were. They enlarged when they saw the blood. "Fuck!" Samantha rushed to the table, standing over Chloe. "Fuck happened, Chloe?"

Chloe took a breath of preparation and said, "Sit down, Sam," gesturing to the chair next to Samantha.

"Fuck is this, Chloe?" Samantha said, bending over to search her partner for injury.

"Sit down and I'll tell you," Chloe retorted, sniffing the liquor on Samantha's breath and clothes.

Perplexed, Samantha sat. When she was situated, Chloe drew her pistol, triple-checked that the safety was on, and placed the weapon on the table between them, barrel pointed at the bathroom door. Then, Chloe held out her arm and rolled up her sleeve. "Fuck me," Samantha exclaimed, reaching over the table, as if she was going to use her hand to try and clamp the lacerations in Chloe's skin, use her glove to wipe the blood from her partner's limb. "Fuck, I call the med center!" Samantha grabbed her radio from her belt.

Chloe pulled her left arm back and gripped Samantha's wrist with her right hand. "Don't."

"Why? The fuck did this to you?"

"I did," Chloe said, firm in her statement.

Samantha's mouth hung open, brushing Chloe with a waft of liquor. "Why?"

Tipping her head down, Chloe closed her eyes and made the call to her alternate state. Her heart burst with panic, then relaxed as the calm of her Second-Gen Stage roused beneath her skin. Energy arrived to treat her sleep deprived mind and body, strengthen her arm until it was as if those ten bleeding gashes weren't there. Before her better judgement could persuade her not to, Chloe lifted her head and opened her eyelids, watching as Samantha's face stiffened and sobered with shock. Blue light shined in Samantha's eyeballs. Chloe knew that was the glow from her own irises, reflecting off her partner's eyes. "Is it unnatural to you, Sam?"

Samantha didn't answer. Even if she never drank a sip of alcohol in her life, she probably couldn't have answered. Samantha's gaze drifted from Chloe's glistening eyes to the pistol on the table, considering it.

Chloe wasn't angry. She'd anticipated this. Letting go of Samantha's wrist, she nodded at the radio in her partner's hand. "Call it in, shoot me, whichever works."

"You're, you're a Second-Gen?" Samantha mumbled, sitting back in her chair and looking at Chloe, as if her partner's glowing irises weren't enough evidence.

"Afraid so," Chloe said, almost smiling with the respite of her confession.

"How long have you been one, been a Second-Gen?" her partner asked, attention shifting again to the pistol on the table and the pistol in her holster, but only for a couple seconds.

Chloe might've laughed if the situation wasn't what it was. "Since I was born, Sam. That's how it works."

Samantha nodded, seeming to process the fact she'd been in a relationship with a Second-Gen, had sex with a Second-Gen. "How long have you known? When was your...Awakening?"

"I've known since I was five," Chloe told her, surprised Samantha hadn't picked up the pistol or made the call on her radio yet. "My mom had her Awakening when she was twenty, that's how I found out. Had mine when I was fourteen."

Thoughts coupled in Samantha's stunned expression and she spoke with heightened coherence. "Your Awakening was during the civil war. Wasn't it?"

Chloe glanced at the pistol, as if doing so would incite Samantha to take it. "That's right."

But her partner seemed to forget the weapon was there, forget the radio she held. "How'd it happen?"

Chloe sat in astonishment for a few moments, her left arm bleeding on the table. She hadn't expected to get this far with Samantha. She'd assumed Samantha would shoot her or arrest her the second she saw her irises glow. Like her parents, though, she couldn't stop now that she was telling the truth. "It was the last day of the war. Fighting was blowing up all over the city, every district. Even a child could figure out Marathon wouldn't be standing the next day. My parents and I looted this supply warehouse in Ignis, stole as much food and gear as we could carry on our backs." Her left arm didn't shake, yet Chloe yearned for a razor. "We got stuck in this crowd on the way out, separated. All the shooting and smoke, I couldn't hear or see a fucking thing. I ended up moving along this fence, the Inner Fence, trying to follow it down Broad Street to South Gate. Then..." Chloe waited to see if Samantha would grab the pistol, hoped she would.

"Then?" Samantha asked, attentive, as if Chloe had never drawn her pistol to begin with.

"Then, this soldier comes out of the smoke," Chloe resumed, voice tottering, fright surfacing despite her Second-Gen Stage. "She puts me in the snow. Aims a T-05, a rifle, at my face. Tells me to give her my pack or she'll kill me." She held up her right hand. "I take the bag off. Soldier crouches down to take it. I'd felt it coming, pretty much that whole morning, my Awakening. Wasn't till then it finally broke." Chloe put her right hand down and raised her left. Blood tapped on the table. "Soldier sees my eyes glowing. I see her about to shoot me. Or maybe not. I don't know. I take the switchblade off her belt. Get her." The switchblade returned to Chloe's head, black and dripping with bright red. "I don't know how many times, until she doesn't have a neck anymore."

"Self-defense," Samantha said, as if that absolved Chloe of any wrongdoing.

Chloe stared at the floor, so she didn't have to look at Samantha. "I crawl out from under the soldier's body and her fucking kid comes running over. A boy, maybe five at the oldest. He tries to wake his mom up and I..." The tears Chloe withheld came flowing now. "I just left, dropped the knife in the snow, took my bag and fucking ran. Every gun in the city's being fired and I can still hear that fucking kid crying till I get to South Gate. Found my parents, headed south, watched the city burn behind us." She lowered her left arm to her side. "My arm started shaking that day, hasn't quit since."

"And you never told them what happened?" Samantha inferred.

Chloe shook her head. "They know I had my Awakening. A lot of people were shot around me, so I told them that's what brought it about, where the blood came from." Tears seemed to weigh Chloe's face down as she looked up at Samantha. "I lied. I didn't want them to think I'd become." Tears choked her.

"A killer?" Samantha said, tilted forward, regarding Chloe with the utmost concentration, as if all of Merenranta was just that table and the two of them.

"That I'd become exactly what everybody in Missio said I would be."

"How do you mean?"

Chloe twisted her head from side to side. "People in Missio found out my mom and I are Second-Gens when we did. It wasn't like Merenranta. Marathon let us live there openly. But that didn't mean we were the same. One day I'm a fucking five-year-old kid, the next I'm a killer, always a killer to them. My mom and I didn't get to be anything else, not in Marathon and not here. What's worse is you all might be right. Martin Donnelly kills his life partner over some argument. I kill a boy's mother." Chloe dabbed her cheeks and eyes with her glove and pushed her pistol towards Samantha. "Maybe it's best for your mom to shoot as many of us as she can find." She dipped her head again, shut her eyes, and awaited her punishment. Death or exile, for her and her parents. Both would suffice, though Chloe favored death. "We should've died in the civil war, with the rest of Marathon."

The chair creaked as Samantha stood, moving away from the table before she fired or called for backup, Chloe presumed. She tensed her body, listening for the click of a pistol or radio. Neither resounded. Rather, she heard the squeak of Samantha's boots, closing. Then they stopped, leaving Chloe in her personal darkness, both quiet and blaring at the same time.

"Look at me," Samantha said in the black.

"Get on with it," Chloe sputtered. She felt the liquid breaching her eyelids.

"Look at me, Chloe," Samantha implored, as if she needed to see Chloe's glowing irises one last time, one final verification before she executed her partner.

Just a flash, a flash and it'll be done. Arms and legs vibrating, disregarding the calls for stability from her Second-Gen Stage, Chloe opened her eyes, glared through the tears at her release.

Chloe's pistol was on the table, untouched. Samantha was crouched on the floor in front of Chloe, her pistol in her holster and her radio clipped to her belt. Cheeks soaking as tears rained down from her eyes, Samantha's lips bent in what Chloe thought, yet couldn't believe, was a smile. Samantha rose, curled her hand around Chloe's head and connected their lips, kissing Chloe with enough force she pushed her back in her chair. Chloe sat still in bafflement as Samantha's tongue moved about her mouth, as if searching for something. Parting, Samantha held her face before Chloe's, her eyeballs blue with Chloe's glow, her smile growing. "Feels the same to me," she said to her Second-Gen partner.

A laugh croaked from Chloe's vocal cords, her stream of tears becoming a torrent, except now they were tears of relief, a cry of acceptance. She planted her face on Samantha's shoulder, weeping with a foreign sensation she determined to be joy. Samantha's arms enveloped her, welcomed her. Her partner kissed her hat-covered head, rubbed her back. The stench of liquor was still there, but that didn't change what Samantha was giving her. "I'm sorry," Chloe cried.

"It's okay," Samantha told her, voice soft, soothing.

"I'm sorry," Chloe said again. She would say it a hundred times if Samantha let her.

"I'm sorry too," Samantha wept. "I'm sorry. It's going to be okay, it's all going to be okay."

Chloe didn't know how it would be, yet she nodded into Samantha's shoulder, trusting her partner.

"Let's get your arm fixed. Okay?"

"Okay."

There was a medical kit in Samantha's bathroom, behind the mirror. Samantha washed the blood from Chloe's arm, bandaged each of her cuts, and wrapped her arm in gauze. Then, she scrubbed the dark red blotches from the table and floor, rinsed Chloe's jacket, pants, and gloves in the shower, whilst Chloe told her everything she'd discovered, everything she'd kept from Merenranta. The Black Dragoons and her parents' history with them, Addie's enslavement and flight from what little remained of the Dragoons and their Second-Gen commander, and, most important, that Addie was an Awakened Second-Gen, who had her Awakening at the age of three, on the same day as Chloe, in the same city as Chloe, and now had found her way to the same coastal town as Chloe. It was this news of Addie's premature Awakening that made Samantha sit down. Sharing it was liberating for Chloe, disorienting for Samantha, so much so she didn't have the energy to contemplate the questions it raised. Nor did Chloe, who turned off her Second-Gen Stage and practically collapsed from exhaustion. Samantha suggested they go to bed and they did, though they didn't go right to sleep. A kiss goodnight led to several kisses, which led to them ditching their clothes at the bedsides.

When they were done they lay in Samantha's bed, Chloe on her back, Samantha on top of her. "What're we going to do?" Chloe asked, her right arm around Samantha's back, her left arm at her side, her wounds aching.

"We'll think of something," Samantha said, twiddling Chloe's hair in her finger. "We can't tell anyone else, not while the sheriff's like she's been. Pretty sure she still thinks the bandit who shot my dad wasn't alone, so fuck knows if she'll simmer down."

"Is your mom the reason you drink?" Chloe said, easing her tone, trying not to sound judgmental.

Samantha nodded against Chloe's chest. "She's as good a reason as any. Had my first drink behind the school when I was sixteen. Nearly went deaf from all the yelling my mom did when she found out. Kept doing it just to fuck with her, but eventually it wasn't about her anymore." She snickered. "Safe to say you were right, I was wrong."

Chloe grinned, relieved by her partner's admission. "You were right about something."

"Yeah, I knew there was something about you," Samantha said, chuckling. "A little more time and I bet I could've guessed you're a Second-Gen."

"Actually, I meant your bed," Chloe laughed, glancing at the wider double mattress. "It's much more comfortable, like you said."

"Get the factories to make you one then."

An idea gathered in Chloe's mind. She would've kept it to herself, but after everything in the kitchen, it didn't scare her. "Or maybe you can bring this one to my place."

PHASE 5: COHABITATION

TWELVE

Four days after Chloe's confession to Samantha, they sat in the town hall conference room, awaiting Mayor Darabont's decision. The yellow of the morning sun gleamed through the window, reflecting off the table, unoccupied except for the two officers. Whether the sheriff would arrive with the mayor or beforehand, Chloe didn't know.

Rested as they were, Chloe and Samantha's wait was uncomfortable. Healed without a single scar, Chloe's left arm twitched at her side, jolting her shoulder. At least now, she wasn't alone in her shaking. Samantha trembled in her chair, her shakes slight yet noticeable, the chair squeaking. Chloe was sure Samantha could hear the alcohol at Cheng's shouting from across the cove, just as she could hear her razor, all the way from home. Neither of them had released in the last four days. However tense they already were for this meeting, withdrawal made it worse.

"What do you think he'll say?" Samantha asked, when quiet threatened to chop both their skulls in half.

"Probably something like." Chloe surveyed her partner and joked, "You feeling all right, Sam?"

"What?"

"That's what he'll say if you keep shaking like that," Chloe tittered. "You need to hide it better."

"Yeah, because you did such a good job hiding yours," Samantha retorted.

The door screeched open behind them. Chloe put her arm behind her back, stuffing it between her back and the chair. Samantha clasped the sides of her chair, using her arms to steady herself as Mayor Darabont shut the door and walked around the table. "Morning, officers," he greeted, sitting across from them.

"Morning, sir," the officers replied.

"Busy here as always, thanks for waiting."

Chloe and Samantha both saw it, the empty chair next to Darabont that went unfilled. Samantha was the one who asked. "Where's the sheriff?"

"In her office, I presume," Darabont said, with a tone that seemed to be trying to say he didn't know or care. His expression was rigid though, as if he both knew and cared, and was glad Armistead wasn't here. "Unless she's walking patrol."

"She's not joining us?" Chloe asked, grinning to mask her surprise.

"No," Darabont told them, his respite too obvious to ignore.

"Oh," Chloe said, thinking of Darabont and Armistead's argument four days ago, and every disagreement they'd had since. *Guess Merenranta's parents are taking a break.*

"So, I've made my decision," Darabont said, jumping away from talk about the sheriff. Happy to move on as well, Chloe and Samantha sat in wordless anticipation. "Now that Addie's recovered, in a timeframe that's frankly nothing short of miraculous."

Samantha coughed.

"The med center's going to be discharging her later today. If she were an adult, with the crime she's committed, I'd have her escorted to the edge of town and exiled. But given she's a child and given her history with the..." He paused, bringing his hand to his chin. "What'd she call them again?"

"Black Dragoons," Chloe said, clenching her back as her left arm poked her spine. Darabont and Armistead had read the notes from Chloe and Addie's conversation about the Black Dragoons—-albeit, those Chloe and Addie had rewritten after destroying the originals. As far as Darabont and Armistead knew, Addie was a human child, kidnapped by the Black Dragoons and their Second-Gen commander on the last day of the Marathon Civil War, enslaved for almost seven years before escaping the Serenity Station and fleeing southeast.

"Marathon's military assassination unit," Samantha added. Chloe glanced to her partner, still not understanding why Samantha agreed to this plan. She'd broken the law already by keeping Chloe's secret, but betraying her native-town for a child she barely knew was something more.

"Black Dragoons," Darabont repeated. "Given Addie's history with these Black Dragoons, I've chosen to grant her provisional citizenship."

"Provisional citizenship, sir?" Chloe said.

"She'll be allowed to remain in Merenranta on a monthly basis. I'll reassess at the end of each month to renew her citizenship, based on how well she's adjusting."

"So she can stay?" Chloe asked, as if she hadn't heard the mayor.

"For now, yes," he replied.

Chloe's arm settled a bit, the cries of her razor decreasing to a more manageable volume. She shared her moment of relief with Samantha, who relaxed in her chair, smiling as Chloe was.

"There's a complication," Darabont continued, his expression shifting. "We don't have anywhere for her to stay. Staff at the med center already have kids of their own or are too scared of her to take her in. Same with your department." The mayor hesitated, as if Chloe and Samantha were his superiors. "I know you two just moved in together and space in your shack is cramped at best, but—-"

"You're asking if we can take her?" Chloe interrupted.

"If you think you can handle her," Darabont said. "You're the only ones she's comfortable around, and you're the ones who brought her off the beach in the first place." He looked at the table, face flustering with what appeared to be sorrow. "Speaking from experience, though, this isn't something I want you both agreeing to lightly."

"Experience?" Samantha inquired.

Darabont raised his head. Chloe forgot about her arm for a second. She'd never seen her mayor so grim, doubted many people had. "You think the worst is behind you. You've found a community that'll take you in, that's safe, relative to where you've been. You're living with a couple that can't have kids of their own." His words scraped against the table. What he was telling Chloe and Samantha, he probably didn't tell often. "It all fits together like it should, until you look at the other kids in your neighborhood, in your class, and remember, they didn't let their parents and twin brother get raped and shot by a gang of bandits while you watched behind a tree because you were ten years old and didn't know what the fuck else to do."

Chloe heard Samantha cough, though that might've been her.

"You remember that and this refuge you've made starts to unravel, for you and the people trying to help you. Some kids crawl back from that, some kids stay lost in the woods, no matter how long they live here. Addie's been with us a week, but she's still in the woods, and you two have to decide if you're the ones to lead her out of them."

If Chloe and Samantha chose to be Addie's provisional guardians, Darabont went on to tell them, the town government would provide assistance, which included allowing Chloe and Samantha to forgo their regular patrol duties, until Addie reached a point where she didn't need constant supervision. The Addie investigation may be over, but the child would still be Chloe and Samantha's sole assignment. The mayor then left them alone to decide, what he'd said about himself restricted to this room at his order.

When the door clicked shut, the officers turned to each other. "You think we can manage this?" Samantha asked.

"We can hardly manage ourselves," Chloe said, spasms increasing as her arm hung at her side.

"Maybe it'll help us as much as it helps her, distract us."

"Could also make us worse."

"Yeah."

Chloe held her left wrist in her right hand, pondering. "But if we don't take her and someone else does, someone she doesn't know, she could panic and..." She lowered her voice to a whisper. "Throw on her Second-Gen Stage and..."

"Out she goes," Samantha said. "And the sheriff and the mayor start asking us how we didn't know."

Why'd you agree to help if you knew it could fuck us both? "Mayor's wrong about us having to decide, we don't have a choice. Do we?"

"Guess not. You want to tell him, or should I?"

Together, they told Darabont they would be Addie's provisional guardians. The prospect of this should've terrified Chloe, yet she was less scared for herself and Samantha than she was for Addie.

The supplies arrived at Chloe's shack, now Chloe and Samantha's shack, later that afternoon, brought to them by factory workers at the government's request. A cot, with blankets and a pillow, squeezed between Chloe and Samantha's double bed and the window facing the beach. A couple pairs of children-sized winter attire, boots, sleeping clothes, and some extra toiletries. A new sketchbook, asked for by Chloe, to replace the first book that had been submitted as police evidence. And a small metal safe, like the kind at the police station. Placed on the dresser, opposite the room from Addie's cot, the safe was filled with Chloe and Samantha's razors, the forks and knives from the kitchen, and a few other sharp objects Addie could utilize as weapons. The officers' pistols and magazines would be stored in the safe as well, before they went to bed. The safe had two keys, worn on string around each of their necks.

"Keep it under your shirt," Chloe said as they put their keys on.

"Why?" Samantha asked.

"So she doesn't try to take one."

"To open the safe?"

"To stab us with."

"I can't tell if that's a joke or not."

—-

—-

THIRTEEN

The sun was setting when they left to get Addie. Chloe carried a bag of clothes for the girl as they stepped through the doorway, the sky grayish-orange, the ocean pushing a freezing breeze of rotted salt across the shoreline. They only made it a couple crunching feet in the gray snow when Chloe heard her name. "Chloe," a man said, quiet with anxiety.

Chloe groaned an orange-white breath, her eyes rolling as she turned to her father. Sean stood at the corner of her and Samantha's shack and the next shack down in the row, his winter gear greasy from work, his head shielded from the wind by a hat, his glass eye shimmering in the orange light, his disfigurements glaring in the dwindling sun, exposing the fright in his expression. "I'll catch up," Chloe said, handing the bag to Samantha, who walked in the direction of the medical center to give them privacy. "Just you today?" Chloe asked, facing her father yet refusing to move towards him.

He closed the gap between them, but only by a few paces. He kept his distance otherwise, struggling to hold eye contact. "Your mom's at home," he told her, his gaze slipping, until he was looking at the snow. "Pregnancy's been making her sick all day."

"She okay?" Chloe said with a spark of concern.

Her father lifted his eye to her, as if reassured by her worry. "Yeah, she's fine." He twisted his head around to make sure nobody was close enough to hear them. "People like you and your mom don't really have problems in pregnancy. Everything works like it should."

"Good." Chloe's anger recommenced after seconds of truce. "You here to talk again?"

"Here to try," Sean said, remorse apparent on his face. "Every day, till you're ready."

"Or just wait for me to come to you." *Whenever the fuck that happens.*

His demeanor turned strict, despite his apprehension. "You know why we can't do that, Chloe." He motioned to her left arm.

Chloe rolled up her sleeve, showing him her unmarked arm. "I told you yesterday, and the day before that, and the day before that, I stopped. I haven't since that night."

"And we told you yesterday, and the day before that, and the day before that, it isn't enough to see no new cuts." Sean tipped his eye to the snow, as if afraid to ask. "The urge still there? Whatever's making you need to do this?"

She rolled her sleeve down and put her arm behind her back as it began to quaver. "I'm ignoring it."

Sean shook his head. "This isn't something you just ignore, Chloe. Is it always that same arm?" He pointed. "It's shaking again."

"Yeah," Chloe responded, rather than lie. "Only took you and mom seven years to notice."

He exhaled a puff of orange-white, shut his eye, as if he agreed with her. Opening his eye, he said, "You know, Chloe, we're not asking you to forgive us. We can't ask you to forgive us when we don't forgive ourselves, but your mom and I have to know you're safe." His mouth curved in a cheerless grin. "You're all that matters, so we need to know what's been making you want to hurt yourself all this time. We're just shooting in the dark till you tell us."

The shaking accelerated in Chloe's arm. She wanted to tell him, him and her mother, like she told Samantha. If she was going to have a chance at quashing her need for release, she knew she had to confess to them. What she said to her parents four days ago prevented her, however. *I wish you never came home.* To say something that despicable and then tell her parents their daughter was a murderer, the consequences were certain to be catastrophic. Like Chloe, her parents had been suffering from reenactment nightmares for years, and their incessant attempts to get her to talk to them only further indicated how close they were to wanting releases of their own. Her parents were assassins, child-killers, liars, yet Chloe had no wish to see them harm themselves with razors or alcohol. "I'm not the only thing that matters anymore," Chloe refuted. "You've got another kid coming. You have to stop worrying about me."

Her father laughed, to her surprise and probably his too. "You know what I learned meeting you that first night in Missio? When you're a parent, all you do is worry."

Chloe glimpsed the western side of north Merenranta, where the medical center waited. "I've got my own shit to worry about today, so you'll have to try again later." She turned away from her father and rounded the corner of the adjacent shack, out of his sight.

"Chloe," her father called, voice straining.

She kept walking, caught up to Samantha, and carried on to the medical center.

Addie was standing at the window, wearing her patient gown, when Chloe and Samantha came to her room. Gunshot wounds mostly repaired, her cast was gone, her left forearm swathed in a bandage, as her left hip likely was, her health monitors removed. Facing north, she scanned the forest she'd come from with her blank eyes, unresponsive to the world outside. "Addie," Chloe said as she and Samantha stood beside the bed. "Addie," she said a second time, when the girl didn't acknowledge them. The child looked over her shoulder, fixed on Chloe yet not snubbing Samantha as she had during the officers' earlier visits. No doubt Addie feared Mayor Darabont's decision, though her expression suppressed any hint. "Mayor's letting you stay," Chloe announced. "He told us this morning. Sam and I are going to take you home. Okay?"

The child gave a nod. She didn't smile, didn't weep with glee, just nodded.

"We brought you some clothes," Samantha said, placing the bag on the bed. "We'll let you..."

Addie reached down and pulled at the bottom of her gown, without care if the officers watched.

"No, no," Chloe yelped, raising her hand as she and Samantha spun around to the door. "Let us step out first. Come out when you're ready." They went into the hall and closed the door.

Addie emerged a couple minutes later, dressed in civilian winter gear, similar to the clothes she had on when Chloe first saw her on the beach, except much cleaner and intact, and also bloodless. Her box of colored pencils was tucked under her arm. "Welcome to Merenranta," Samantha told the child, as the three of them headed for the elevator, Addie walking on her own two legs, as if she'd never been shot.

The trek back was more eventful than Chloe expected, or wanted. The maze of buildings and shacks, the nearby woods and cove, the factories and the wind turbines behind them, the cluttered but living townscape distracted the girl who'd endured so many years in ruins, drew her in several directions, save for the one Chloe and Samantha needed her to go. "Addie," they had to say each time to halt her wanderings. Worse, the crowds of citizens, also on their way home, were swift to contribute to the jumble. Addie cringed at their crunching boots, drooped her head away from their talkative discussions, a physical pain her Second-Gen advantage couldn't pacify. How much of this before Addie's pain turned to panic, panic to her Second-Gen Stage, Chloe had no intention of finding out. "Let's take the beach," she said, diverting the trio to the cove, where traffic was less confining. Easier as the walk became for the child, Addie hunched her shoulders as she moved, as if trying to make herself smaller before bursting with the largeness of her Second-Gen Stage. Fortunately, they made it home without a glow from Addie's irises.

Chloe and Samantha went in ahead of Addie, kicking the snow and sand from their boots. Following through the doorway, Addie trotted past them into the kitchen, leaving a trail of gray boot prints on the floor. She swerved about, surveying the room, the counters and cabinets, the sink and stove, the table and chairs, the doors to the bathroom and bedroom. Flicking on the kitchen light, Chloe said, "Not as nice as your room at the med center, but we have it to ourselves." Samantha shut the door, sealing them off from the icy wind.

With the clang of the door, Addie's attention shifted to the exit, where her provisional guardians stood, and then to each kitchen window, her empty eyes squinting, as if to measure how thick the glass was. She moved to the bathroom door, Chloe and Samantha joining her as she opened and checked the room. Dark and windowless, the bathroom was scrubbed free of the blood from Chloe's last release. Addie turned to the bedroom door.

"You looking for something?" Samantha asked, entering the bedroom behind Chloe and Addie.

The dresser and the safe, the bed and the cot, none of these held Addie's gaze like the windows. Chloe sighed with understanding, her left arm juddering. *You're searching for an escape.* "Here," Chloe said, gesturing to the new sketchbook on the girl's cot. She picked it up and handed it to Addie. "This is yours, to keep this time."

Addie sat at the foot of the bed, the officers standing over her as she opened the book in her lap, set the pencil box next to her. She wrote and flipped the book for Chloe and Samantha to read. "US STAY HERE?"

"Yep," Chloe replied. "You, me, and Sam." She rotated to her partner, tried to smile.

"SLEEP HERE?"

"Yeah, we all do," Samantha said as she turned on the bedroom light. "Chloe and I sleep in the bed." She pointed at the cot. "You sleep there."

"BY MESELF?"

Chloe and Samantha looked at each other, as if deliberating who was going to answer this question. "Yeah," Chloe responded. "Is that okay?"

Addie nodded, turned to the cot as she wrote, "BIG BED FOR JUST ME."

Left arm behind her back, Chloe clutched her shaking wrist.

"You see we're right next to the beach?" Samantha asked, probably at random.

"BEACH SEE YOU FUCKN ON." Addie simpered as Chloe and Samantha read. She might've laughed if she could.

"How about I make dinner?" Chloe suggested, saving herself and Samantha from this conversation.

Addie sat at the kitchen table with her book and pencils, drawing. Samantha sat with her, staring out the window in silent aimlessness, unsteady in her chair as night overtook the ocean and the beach. Now was normally the time she'd be starting her binge at Cheng's. She still wasn't used to eating dinner at home. Chloe took a pot and ration box from the cabinets above the counters. Pot on the stove, box on the counter, she set about cooking, which shouldn't have been so significant, except this was the first time she'd ever made a meal for three people.

The aroma of soup boiling on the stove spread through the kitchen as Chloe noticed Addie standing behind her, sketchbook and dark blue pencil in hand. "WHAT SMELL?"

"Our dinner," Chloe answered. Holding a spoon and stirring with one hand, she waved to Addie with the other. "Come here, I'll show you."

Addie wrote as she joined Chloe in front of the stove. "WHY SMELL LIKE THAT?"

"Because it's cooking," Chloe said, pointing at the mix of broth and vegetables sizzling in the pot. "It's good when you heat it up like this." She held the spoon out for Addie to take, grinning. "You want to stir it?"

"WHY BURN IT?" Addie wrote, ignoring Chloe's offer.

"I'm not," Chloe told her, stirring the pot herself. "Or, I guess I am a bit. You're supposed to do this, so it can cook."

"COOK?"

It occurred to Chloe that everything Addie ate at the Serenity Station and on her journey southeast would've come precooked or would've been eaten without being cooked at all. The girl had never eaten a legit cooked meal, at least none that she could remember. Left arm in her jacket pocket, Chloe said, "Cook means to heat it up, I think. It makes the food taste better." She glanced at the pot. "I think we're just about done, actually. You want to set the table, Sam?"

"Sure," Samantha said, her attention returning to the room as she rose from her chair. "You want to help me, Addie?"

Addie revolved to face Samantha, but kept her eyes on her sketchbook as she wrote. She held the book up for Samantha to read.

"Setting the table," Samantha replied, answering the question Chloe couldn't see.

"I don't think she knows what that means," Chloe said, turning off the stove with her pulsating left hand.

"I'll show you," Samantha said, moving past Chloe and Addie and taking three spoons and napkins from one of the cabinets. Chloe prepared their bowls while Samantha and Addie stood around the table. "You see how I put the spoons in front of each chair?" Samantha said to Addie. There was a pause before Samantha asked, "Why don't you do the same with the napkins? Here."

Another, longer, pause and Chloe heard Addie's pencil jotting in her sketchbook.

"So everyone has a napkin," Samantha responded.

The child scribbled again.

"When people eat at the table, this is how they set up."

Addie wrote more.

Chloe made the last bowl, chortling. *Addie knows how to play question and answer.*

"I don't know why," Samantha said, annoyed. "It's always been done this way. Even before the Reform, I think."

Turning to the table, bowl in her right hand, Chloe watched Addie write a new question and show it to her partner.

Frustration growing in her expression, Samantha said, "I said I don't know why. I guess." She stuttered. "It's so everyone has what they need."

Addie started writing yet again.

Samantha gave up and put the napkins down herself.

Arm resting as she brought their bowls to the table, Chloe laughed and said to her partner, "She asks more questions than I do."

Three bowls, three spoons, three napkins, they were sitting down before Chloe realized she'd forgotten drinks. "Water or vegetable juice?" she asked, going back to the counter.

"Is there alcohol in vegetable juice?"

"How many times are you going to make that joke, Sam?" Chloe placed the juice bottle and a few glasses on the counter.

"Until you stop asking me if I want vegetable juice."

Chloe poured herself a glass. "Water, then?"

"Fine," Samantha mumbled.

Back to the table with one glass of vegetable juice and two glasses of water, Chloe and Samantha started their dinner, only to stop when they both saw how Addie was eating. Spoon and gloves on the table, the child scooped up her food with her hands and filled her mouth to the brim, swallowing with a slurping sound as soup dripped down her chin.

Samantha smacked her face and looked at Chloe. "You want to tell her, or should I?"

"You do it, I made dinner."

After dinner, Samantha sent Addie to the bathroom to wash her hands, while she and Chloe rinsed their dishes in the sink. Somewhere amidst the splashing water and the swishing sponges, Chloe heard the water stop in the bathroom and the patter of Addie's boots as she crossed the kitchen. "Remind me tomorrow," she said to Samantha. "One of us needs to get more food shares."

"Restock?" Samantha asked. Addie's boots tapped next to them, between the sink and the door. The girl was probably getting a look at what they were doing.

"Yeah. I'm used to getting one share. Having you and Addie here is running my cabinets dry."

"I should've warned you," Samantha said, sarcastic. "I eat as much as I drink."

"I doubt that," Chloe quipped in reply. Samantha bumped Chloe with her elbow, laughing. Chloe retaliated in kind, cackling as the front door screeched open, blasting her and Samantha with the nighttime gale. They looked in time to see Addie jog out into the snow, skirting around the corner and vanishing from sight.

"Addie!" Who shouted that Chloe didn't know, because she and Samantha both dashed through the doorway, pursuing the child assigned to their care. Around the corner and the front of the shack, the race of two guardians who'd let their guard down. The girl's silhouette popped up in the dark, like she did that first night, standing in the snow and sand of the beach, her head slanted upwards, her book and pencil in her gloved hands.

"Addie," Chloe shrieked, sliding to a stop beside the child, Samantha on the other side. Addie was static, her eyes disregarding the adults who'd come after her and the freezing drafts that pelted their faces with snow, sand, salt, and decay.

"What're you doing?" Samantha demanded to know. "You can't run off like that!"

"You don't go outside unless we say," Chloe stated, raising her voice so Addie could hear her strictness through the wind. "You understand?"

Addie maintained her elevated stare, not reacting to either of her guardians.

"You listening, Addie?" Samantha said, reaching for Addie's wrist.

Chloe smacked Samantha's hand away, giving her partner a cautionary shake of her head. "What're you doing out here?" she asked the girl.

Finally, Addie replied. Opening her sketchbook, she tapped the flashlight on Chloe's belt, asking for light. Chloe shined her flashlight on Addie's book as she wrote, the pages blowing in the breeze. "WHAT THAT?"

"What's what?" Samantha asked, yellowish-white air puffing through Chloe's flashlight beam.

Addie balanced her book and pencil in one hand, pointed to the grayish-black sky with the other, her eyeballs glued to the waning crescent of white light that glistened in the clouds above the blackened ocean.

"The moon?" Chloe said.

"WHAT MON?"

"She doesn't know what the moon is?" Samantha asked.

"You can't see the moon in Marathon, or anywhere below the overcast," Chloe responded. "I learned about it in school, but I didn't see it till I came south. Neither did my mom."

Addie tapped her sketchbook, asking again. "WHAT MON?"

"Two O's," Chloe corrected. "You tell her, Sam."

"Your turn," Samantha countered. "I taught her how to use a spoon."

Chloe laughed and sat in the snow. "Okay."

Addie and Samantha looked down at her in momentary confusion, and then joined. "WHAT IS MOON?"

Chloe pointed at the waning crescent. "That's the moon. It's like." She paused. This was her first time describing the moon to someone instead of having it described to her. "It's a giant rock in space, I think." She made a spinning motion with her finger. "Every day, it floats around the planet. So wherever you are in the world, you can see it, as long as there's no overcast."

"WHY?" Addie asked, exhaling a puff of yellowish-white over her sketchbook.

Chloe chuckled. "Addie, I have no fucking idea. That's all I remember."

"It makes the tides," Samantha chimed in, gesturing to the sea. The waterline came in and went back out, like it always did. "The moon's gravity pulls at the ocean and makes the tides, I think." She giggled. "I cut class a lot, so don't hold me to that."

"WHAT THOSE?" Addie wrote, waving her pencil at the specks of yellow light that peeked between the clouds in sporadic groups of two or three.

Warming her numb face with a smile, Chloe recalled her and her parents' first night outside the overcast. They'd only been able to see a couple of the yellow dots, yet her mother cried at the sight of them. Subduing the memory and her grin with a few yellowish-white breaths, Chloe said, "Stars. Like suns, but very far away."

"HOW WE GET TO MOON AND STARS?"

The randomness of Addie's question was such that Chloe let Samantha answer. "We don't."

Addie appeared to shiver at Samantha's reply, though that might've just been from the cold. "CAN WE GO OUT THERE AND GET TO THEM?" she wrote, and waved her pencil at the ocean's grayish-black horizon.

"No," Samantha told her, in a reluctant tone, as if she wished there was more beyond the horizon than gray saltwater. "The planet's a sphere, not a plate. You can't go to one side and jump off." She lifted a finger. "You have to go up."

"CAN WE"

"No! No one can go up there anymore," Samantha said, knowing what Addie was writing. She looked at her boots, sunk in the gray snow and sand. "We're all stuck down here."

Addie sat still a moment, as if hoping Samantha would change her answer, and then flipped through the pages of her sketchbook. On a new page, she started drawing, moving on from their conversation.

"Okay, time to go in," Chloe decided.

Samantha stood. "Come on, Addie."

Eyes centered on her book, Addie shook her head and kept drawing.

Chloe stood. "It's cold, Addie." She clicked off her flashlight and put it on her belt. "You can draw inside."

The girl probably couldn't see the paper she was drawing on, yet she continued her sketch.

The child's defiance angered Chloe more than she would've expected, more than was helpful, she knew. "Addie, now, let's go," she said, her left arm quivering.

Addie tensed her arm, pressing her pencil into the paper with greater force, as if she was trying to stab the pencil through the back of the book.

Scowling, Chloe ground her teeth, her left arm about to dislocate itself from her shoulder. She gave Addie one more chance. "Addie."

Nothing. It was as if Chloe was looking at Addie through binoculars and the child was too far away to hear a word she was saying. Addie could hear everything. Chloe knew that.

"Okay," Chloe reached down and snatched the sketchbook from Addie's hand. The child looked at her that time, her expression disordered, as if she'd been asleep and Chloe had shaken her awake. "Time to go," she told the girl, sprinting for the shack with her book. Boots skating in the snow and sand, Samantha ran beside her. If she disagreed with Chloe's strategy, she didn't say. Behind them, Addie leapt to her feet, chasing her guardians up the beach.

Back around the shack, through the open door, without kicking the snow and sand from their boots, Samantha stood by the door, Chloe in front of the stove. Addie followed a couple seconds later, her boots squeaking and sliding on the floor as she came in. Passing Samantha, the girl stopped next to the sink. Samantha shut and locked the door, positioning herself in front of it. Chloe held out the sketchbook. The child concentrated on Chloe, her eyes ignoring the thing she'd run in for.

"Here, we're back inside," Chloe said, keeping the book out as she stepped towards the girl. "You can..."

Addie leaned forward, glaring up at Chloe. Her nostrils wheezed, growled.

"All right?"

The child closed her eyelids. And when she opened them, violet was shining from her irises. There wasn't any of the terrified violet Chloe had seen last week. This violet, this Second-Gen Stage, was drawn solely from rage, a wrath that stretched across Addie's face, inflaming her cheeks.

Addie might've blocked her fright with fury, but Chloe hadn't. Raising her shuddering left hand as she recognized taking the child's sketchbook was a terrible idea, she said, "Sorry, I—-"

The girl's arm came up, her pencil gripped in her hand like a knife. The pencil tip pierced Chloe's glove, pierced the top of her right hand. "Fuck," Chloe shrieked, pain stinging her hand. The pencil snapped and she dropped the book.

"Addie," Samantha yelled, hand on her holster. Addie jumped up at Chloe, noiseless as her fist punched Chloe in the nose.

Chloe was sitting on the floor, her back against the counter, when the blank period after getting hit by Addie ended and her conscious thoughts reactivated. Her nose rang with agony. She could feel hot blood oozing out her nostrils, dripping off her chin. She may've savored the pain Addie brought her, took it as the release she'd been missing for the past four days, were it not for what she saw across the floor. Samantha sat with her back against the door, Addie atop her. Bright red streamed from a gash on her face, no doubt delivered by Addie. The child was grasping at Samantha's holster, going for her pistol. Samantha groaned as she held the girl's wrists, trying to pull her hands away. The effort was inadequate, Samantha's strength minimal compared to the Second-Gen's. The barrel of her pistol slipped out of her holster, Addie's fingers nearing the trigger.

Back on her feet, her Second-Gen Stage igniting to the danger her partner was in, Chloe came behind Addie and tucked her hands underneath the girl's armpits. She curled her arms and spread them, forcing Addie's arms apart. "Enough," she screamed. "That's enough!"

Snarling through her nostrils, Addie tugged her arms back together. But Chloe's Second-Gen Stage was stronger. The child lost her grip on the pistol, her arms separating in Chloe's hold until they were level with her neck. Chloe yanked Addie back, off Samantha. Addie lifted her feet, planting them on the door and pushing off. She and Chloe flung backwards, Chloe slamming on the floor, Addie rolling out of her arms. Chloe rose and turned. A chair was in Addie's hands. The girl swung. The chair cracked against Chloe's ribcage, the pieces scattering on the floor, Chloe among them.

"Fucking," Chloe coughed, lying on her side, clutching her stomach. Her ribs hurt worse than her nose. Panting, catching her breath, she watched Addie leap onto the table. The table wobbled as Addie lay on her back and kicked at the window.

The glass shattered outwards, the freezing night air whistling through the frame. Addie crawled, legs first, into the darkened void, her sketchbook and pencils forgotten in her frenzy. The girl's waist was slipping through the frame when Samantha shot across the room, recovered from Addie's hit, her pistol returned and clasped to her holster. Her hands caught Addie's shoulders, her body braced against the table.

Addie's slide didn't stop. It did slow, enough for Samantha to shout, "Chloe," and for Chloe to stand and come to her partner's aid.

Chloe and Samantha each held a shoulder and heaved, dragging Addie's waist back through the window. They pulled again and Addie's legs followed. A third pull and the table tipped over, sending all three of them to the floor with a crash. Chloe and Addie rose to a crouch at the same moment, facing the bathroom door. Before she could stand, Chloe got her hands beneath Addie's armpits a second time, parting the girl's arms and holding her. Addie thrashed from side to side, her nostrils screaming, her head banging on the wall beside the door, as if she wanted to knock herself unconscious before Chloe did whatever the child believed she was going to do. Samantha squatted at Chloe and Addie's side, reaching for the handcuffs on her belt with one hand and trying to seize Addie's wrist with the other. "Don't," Chloe told her partner.

"Make her stop then," Samantha retorted.

"Addie, stop," Chloe begged. "We're not going to hurt you!"

Addie didn't relax.

"You're safe," Chloe insisted. "Don't keep doing this!"

The girl must've thought Chloe was lying, because her struggle became more ferocious. Samantha took her handcuffs off her belt as Addie and Chloe stomped on the floor.

Chloe made a gamble. They needed to calm Addie down, get her to disengage her Second-Gen Stage, before one of their neighbors or a night officer was alerted to the commotion. "My parents were Dragoons!"

Addie turned her head, looked at Chloe with one violet eye. Chloe hoped she was listening.

"They were partnered together," Chloe told her. "My mom's name is Anna. She's the Second-Gen you heard about."

Addie put her hands down but didn't cease her scuffle. Samantha lowered her handcuffs to her hip, not clipping them to her belt yet not brandishing them either.

"They weren't like the Dragoons you were with. They never hurt me, never would," Chloe said as she clung to the girl. "But they lied, like I'm sure the Dragoons lied to you. I know what it's like to be lied to, and I promise you Addie, Sam and I are not lying to you."

"We're not," Samantha said, supporting Chloe's pledge.

Addie's hands stayed down as Chloe kept her restrained. After a minute, the wailing from the child's nose quieted. Two minutes, and her frame stilled. And after three minutes, the radiance was gone from her irises, her Second-Gen Stage withdrawn.

Chloe turned off her own Second-Gen Stage, freed Addie's arms.

"Officer Armistead, what the fuck's going on?" Sheriff Armistead called over the radio, startling the three of them before they could recuperate. "I'm on the way over with a dozen noise reports. Your neighbors are having a fucking fit."

"Fuck," Samantha mumbled, grabbing her radio.

"Why's the sheriff responding?" Chloe asked. "She's off-duty."

"Copy, Sheriff," Samantha replied into the radio.

The trio treated their wounds in the bathroom. The cut on Chloe's hand, on Samantha's face, and on Addie's head, made when she beat her head against the wall, all cleaned and bandaged. Like the bruises that circled Samantha and Addie's gashes, the side of Chloe's chest was discolored and swelling. This would heal on its own, though, just as her nose had stopped bleeding. The pounding at the front door came as they left the bathroom. "Sheriff Armistead, open the door," Armistead commanded, bellowing from outside. Chloe and Addie went into the bedroom, closing the door as Samantha let her mother in. "What the fuck happened?" Chloe heard the sheriff exclaim. While Chloe stood by the door, eavesdropping as Samantha explained the situation to Armistead, omitting the parts about Chloe and Addie's Second-Gen

Stages, Addie lay down on her cot, tucking herself below the blankets. The broken window made the shack cold enough for their breaths to appear in puffs of yellowish-white, so the girl kept her winter gear on.

"You can take those off," Chloe whispered, so as not to draw the sheriff's attention. "Your boots, I mean."

The child's boots hung off the cot, dirtied with snow and sand. Blankets up to her nose, Addie stared at Chloe, as if unable to comprehend what her guardian proposed.

It took Chloe a moment to realize Addie hadn't gone to bed with her winter clothes and boots on because of the cold; this cold was nothing to her. This was how the girl had gone to sleep every night during the months she'd spent trekking. Temperature and comfort were irrelevant; Addie could fall asleep anywhere. "Never mind."

Addie rolled over, facing the wall, annoyed Chloe was still talking. Chloe switched off the light, though she doubted it mattered to Addie.

"Officer Corday," Armistead said from the kitchen, after Samantha was done with her report.

"Shit," Chloe muttered, her hand slow to grab the doorknob. Glancing to Addie's corner, she said, "Hey."

The child twisted around, the cot squeaking, her undead eyes visible in the moonlight coming through the window.

"I'm going to talk to the sheriff. Don't kill anyone while I'm gone."

Addie nodded, blinking several times.

Chloe laughed, though she knew she shouldn't.

Armistead was standing by the front door, about to leave, when Chloe came out of the bedroom. "So, her first night out didn't go as well as we hoped?" Armistead commented.

You mean as well as the mayor hoped? "No, ma'am," Chloe said, stepping around the overturned table and across the shards of chair and glass. She winced from the ache in her ribs, enjoying the minor release it gave her. "It wasn't all her fault, I—-"

"Officer Armistead told me," Armistead interposed. "I'm still recommending the mayor revoke her citizenship." She grimaced. "Not that he will."

Chloe's left arm tingled. The more Addie acted out, the less confidence in her Mayor Darabont would have, and the less he'd be able to resist Armistead's influence. "Yes, ma'am," Chloe said, without anything else to say.

Armistead gestured to the door. "Step outside a sec."

Left arm quaking behind her back, Chloe glanced to Samantha. "Just me, ma'am?"

"Yes."

Chloe looked again at Samantha, who seemed as bewildered as she was. Whenever Armistead spoke to one of them alone, it was never Chloe.

Dozens of neighbors had amassed in the pathways between the shacks as Chloe and Armistead exited. Unaffected by the glacial squall, the onlookers directed their attention at the officers, their faces concealed in the dark. It was as if the entire oceanfront area of north Merenranta had come to learn what happened at Chloe and Samantha's shack. By tomorrow, everyone in north and south Merenranta, including her parents, would hear of it.

"Clear something up for me," Armistead said, as she and Chloe stood in the snow, heads bent down in the wind.

"Yes, m-ma'am," Chloe stammered, letting her arm shiver at her side with the rest of her body.

"You went to see the kid her first night in recovery, correct?" Armistead asked, her tone routine.

Chloe pressed her gloved fingers into her left palm. This chat wasn't routine. "Yes."

"And the day after I sent you and Officer Armistead to North Creek, that's when she started writing about Marathon and this assassin group?"

"The Black Dragoons," Chloe said, the gust chilling her spine. "Yes, ma'am."

"Just like that?" Armistead queried, her interest leaching through her average manner. "After days of telling you almost nothing?"

Chloe's chest quailed like her arm, sickening her stomach. "I guess it took her a couple days to get used to me," she said, with the same feigned ignorance she'd tried on Samantha, despite knowing it hadn't worked, at least not for long.

"The second night she was in recovery," Armistead said, her head up, eyes staring amid the wind, fixated on Chloe, as if she'd been prepping to ask this question for days. "Guard outside her room said you made a late visit, by yourself, like you did that first night." Sweat moistened Chloe's hair, freezing beneath her hat. "Except this time, you left in a hurry, like you were upset. What was that about?"

"Honestly, ma'am," Chloe coughed, her throat parched, her gaze focused on the snow. She knew Armistead would see her terror if she looked her in the eye. "Sam and I got in a fight, before I met with Addie. I wanted to see if the kid would talk if it was just me, but I was too upset, so I left to go apologize." She swallowed a gulp of frosted decayed air, as if she'd run a mile with her lie.

"What did the girl tell you?" Armistead said, her voice and posture unchanged. "When you were with her?"

Chloe shook her head, blinked. "Nothing worth turning in."

"Is that why you tore those pages out of the kid's sketchbook? Before you submitted the book as evidence?"

The temperature seemed to rise twenty degrees, and then drop forty. Chloe felt her eyelids expand, past the point of surprise to guilt. Looking at the sheriff's forehead, she said, "Ma'am?" as if flabbergasted by the allegation.

Armistead turned her head up and down the walkway, to the neighbors that enclosed them, out of earshot but in sight. She placed her hand on Chloe's shoulder, leaned in close to Chloe's face. To by-

CHLOE: DRAGOON NOVEL #2

standers, it would appear as though the sheriff was consoling one of her officers over the situation with Addie. Hand squeezing, crushing Chloe's shoulder, face ticking, Armistead said, "I don't know why you did it, but I know what you did." White air puffed from each of their mouths, converging and forming a mist between them. "And as soon as I know why, everyone else will know too." She patted Chloe on the shoulder, and walked up the path, leaving the officer alone.

Heart skipping beats, Chloe watched the sheriff enter and be enveloped by the crowd. Chloe rested her side against the shack, flooding her lungs with freezing air, listening as her razor called from inside. She remained outside for a few minutes, fighting the impulse, before returning to the shack, fleeing the observation of her neighbors.

Chloe would've gone right to the safe, pulled the razor out, if the broken window in the kitchen didn't distract her from her release. Someone had already covered the window frame with plastic sheeting, taken from a roll in the cabinets. Taped at the edges, the casing was crude but would keep till tomorrow morning. Below the window, the table was standing upright, the bigger pieces of broken chair grouped under the table. The kitchen itself was empty. "Sam?"

The light was still out in the bedroom. Addie was asleep, or pretending to be, her sketchbook and pencil box in front of her cot. Samantha wasn't in bed or standing by the dresser. Chloe knew where to look this time. Kneeling, she found her partner lying beneath their bed, turned towards Addie's side of the room. Sighing, Chloe cut off the kitchen light and shut the bedroom door, put her pistol and magazines in the safe, where Samantha had stowed hers, and slid underneath the bed. The soreness in her ribs, hand, and nose lingered, yet was mellowed by the same advanced pain tolerance her body deployed after her releases. Setting herself on the dust-coated floor, she lay next to her partner and wrapped Samantha in her quivering left arm. The shakes in Chloe's arm were met by the judders that surged through Samantha's body. "How're you doing?"

Samantha snickered, held Chloe's hand in her own. Hands trembling together, she said, "I need a drink so fucking bad, Chloe."

"I'm sorry," Chloe whispered in her partner's ear, fear in her tone. "I wish what I have to tell you could make it better, but it's probably going to make it worse."

Nodding her head, Samantha said, "What does my mom know?"

Chloe lay silent a moment, impressed with Samantha's intuition. "She found out I went to see Addie, that night. All she had to do was look back through the sketchbook I turned in to figure I ripped those pages out."

Samantha gave a frustrated moan, though she wasn't mad at Chloe. "I fucked up."

"What?"

"At that meeting, after we got back from North Creek. I told the mayor and my mom how Addie only talks to you. I made you the easy suspect."

"No," Chloe rebutted, even as she imagined Samantha was right. She tightened her arm around Samantha, saying, "I'm the one who fucked up. I forgot about the officer on guard. I should've said Addie told me about Marathon and the Black Dragoons that night, not the day after. And just now, I let your mom bait me into admitting Addie and I had a conversation that night, a conversation that's not in the sketchbook. She's just waiting on motive before she makes her case to the mayor, gets Addie tossed out of town, and whatever they decide for me."

"And me too," Samantha was quick to respond.

Chloe shook her head, rubbing her cheeks along the back of Samantha's hat. "She doesn't know you know. And even if she did, she's not going to pin this on her daughter."

"You say that, but she might surprise you."

Chloe looked past Samantha to the legs of Addie's cot, three feet away from them. The girl hadn't stirred, hadn't so much as rolled over.

"The more Addie blows up like she did tonight, the easier it'll be for the sheriff."

"What made her do that?"

"You break free after seven years as a slave; you don't react well to being told what to do again," Chloe speculated.

"So, how do we tell her what to do without telling her what to do?"

"No fucking idea."

"Maybe she could use a diversion, like alcohol for me and, uh, your thing, just less harmful."

Chloe thought on this. "She already has one."

"What's that?"

Shivering, Chloe said, "Killing. She hasn't killed anyone since last week. She's missing her release, like we are."

—-

FOURTEEN

Whether she or Samantha fell asleep first, Chloe didn't know. She awoke in a chilly haze of darkened violet, her left arm twitching as it lay across her partner, her hand still entwined with Samantha's. Dust tickled Chloe's eyes and throat. Violet-white floated from her mouth, clouded the air between her head and the bottom of the bedframe. 2:38 by Chloe's wristwatch and her drowsed senses told her the violet light, illuminating the space beneath the bed, shouldn't have been there. A hand tapped her shoulder and she turned around, almost banging her head on the bed in alarm.

Addie was awake, crouched at Chloe's side of the bed, wielding a red-colored pencil like a blade, her irises shimmering, her face locked on her unarmed guardians.

Chloe's Second-Gen Stage shot from her brain, initiating the alteration process throughout her being. Shaking Samantha with one hand, she grabbed her flashlight off her belt with the other. She wanted to show Addie she had a weapon, even if she didn't intend to use it.

"Huh?" Samantha murmured, rousing.

Chloe's Second-Gen Stage came on, blue light colliding with the violet from Addie's eyeballs.

The child held her index finger to her mouth, and Chloe grasped that Addie's Second-Gen Stage hadn't been activated for her and Samantha.

The shack boomed. Chloe heard the front door crash on the floor in the kitchen. Boots squeaked and stomped on the fallen door.

PHASE 6: EXTINCTION

FIFTEEN

One pair, two pairs, three pairs of boots trotted across the kitchen floor, partnered with the howl of the outside breeze and the clacking of weaponry in the intruders' arms. Addie stood, swerving for the bedroom door. Chloe crawled out from under the bed. Her pistol was locked in the safe, on the dresser above her. The door flung open. A man charged in. Ragged black winter clothes, tattered black backpack, he scanned the room with a black scoped rifle. Red pencil in hand, irises blaring, Addie flew over the bed at the man. She slammed his rifle against his chest as her pencil dug into his eye. A short cry from the man, a hiss from the black suppressor on his rifle, a pop from the wall beside the window, a clang from a shell casing dropping on the floor, and he and Addie fell towards the corner of the room. A second intruder dashed through the doorway, a woman. Her right iris glowed violet, tracking Addie, her rifle following her eye, her gear like the man's. Chloe was up, bouncing off the bed, swinging her flashlight at the Second-Gen's face. The Second-Gen intruder whacked Chloe mid-flight with the side of her rifle. Landing on the floor, flashlight sailing out of her hand, Chloe saw the Second-Gen's rifle aiming down at her, her disoriented limbs and muscles sluggish in their response.

Addie jumped on the woman's backpack, wrapped her arm around the Second-Gen's neck, pulling her body and rifle up and away from Chloe. The woman threw herself and Addie into the wall, cracking the plaster. Hanging onto the backpack, Addie raised a knife, a black switchblade from the first intruder. A third black-clothed intruder, this one a man, appeared from the kitchen, seized Addie's wrist, stopped the tip of the blade millimeters from the Second-Gen's neck. The man tried to yank the knife out of Addie's hand. Holding her rifle in one hand, the woman tugged at Addie's arm around her neck. She or the man could've stabbed Addie with the switchblades clipped to their belts, yet they made no move to. Chloe knew then. These intruders wanted Addie alive.

The child butted the man with the back of her skull; he lost his grip on her wrist. Addie unstrung her arm from the woman's neck. She swung the knife back, driving the blade into the man's shoulder, until the handle met the fabric of his jacket. They tumbled atop the body of the first intruder, the man hollering in pain. Recovered from her hit, Chloe swept the Second-Gen's feet with her leg. The woman dropped on her side. Chloe sprawled herself over her, pushed and held her rifle on the floor. The man's shouts reverted to a gurgling sound. Red misted from his slashed throat, soaked Addie's switchblade. The Second-Gen drew her knife, Chloe reached for it. The woman thrust it at her. A yellow flash lit the room, hammered in Chloe's ears.

"Drop your weapon!" Samantha stood by the dresser, the safe open, her pistol, or maybe Chloe's pistol, clutched in her hands, barrel smoking, a hole in the ceiling. Her weapon was trained on the Second-Gen, though Chloe was in her line of fire. "Drop your fucking weapon! Now!"

With an irritated groan, the woman let her knife clatter on the floor, didn't fight as Chloe took the blade to cut her rifle's black strap. Rifle in one hand, switchblade in the other, Chloe rose to a squat against the wall, pointing the rifle at the woman.

Samantha skimmed the windows and the bedroom, wheezing panicked breaths of white, bracing for more black-clad intruders. When none appeared, she said, "How many more are there?"

"None you'll meet tonight," the Second-Gen intruder replied, lying on the floor, her hands raised in front of her. Her voice was composed, thick with age. Chloe noted then that this Second-Gen was much older than she and Samantha, as many as fifty years older, a child of the Previous Civilization. Grayish-brunette hair sticking out of her hat, expression wrinkled and filthy, she had an old red scar on the left side of her face, a pre-Awakening wound, exempt from Second-Gen healing capabilities, just as Addie's vocal cords were. Her left iris didn't shine like her right, because the eye was false, made of glass, like Chloe's father's.

Even in her Second-Gen Stage, Chloe was dazed by horrific recognition as she recalled Addie's drawing of the Serenity Station. She turned to the corner, where the bodies of the first and third intruder lay in a puddle of dark red. Addie sat on her knees in this puddle, switchblade at the ready, as if she worried the men might resurrect themselves. The three intruders had the same clothing, the same suppressor-equipped T-05 Snipers, the same switchblades and backpacks, all black, adhering to one of Marathon's two sacred colors. These three intruders were Black Dragoons.

"Chloe, you okay?" Samantha asked.

Chloe didn't reply. *They must've followed her, all those months. She was too far ahead to know, but now they've caught up to her, in Merenranta.*

"Chloe?" Samantha asked again.

Chloe nodded, the only response she could summon.

"You okay, Addie?" Samantha said next.

Addie didn't nod or shake her head. The child kept her back to Chloe, Samantha, and the Second-Gen Dragoon, as if it were just her and the two dead Dragoons in the room. Chloe gathered that Addie couldn't face the leader of her enslavement, the woman. Trying to kill the woman, Addie could handle. But she probably didn't want to make another attempt while Chloe and Samantha were holding firearms. What little trust the girl placed in them couldn't account for this.

"Chloe?" It wasn't Samantha speaking that time. Chloe curved her head back to the woman, and felt as if she was being thrown through the wall. This intruder, this elderly Second-Gen, this commander of the Black Dragoons Addie drew in her picture, was gazing at Chloe with amazement. "Your name's Chloe?" the woman asked, studying Chloe's blue Second-Gen irises, as though she'd forgotten Chloe and Samantha were training weapons on her. Chloe tightened her hold on the woman's T-05 and switchblade, curled her index finger at the rifle's trigger. The Dragoon commander smirked. Glancing at Addie and the

Dragoons the child killed, the woman said, "Bad move, checking the window before we came in. Woke Addie up. But now, I get to meet you, Chloe."

Killing the Dragoon commander, before Samantha could handcuff her, was the safest choice, Chloe knew. In her old age, the Dragoon commander must've had decades upon decades of experience as an Awakened Second-Gen, possibly stretching as far back as the Previous Civilization. And yet, Chloe couldn't execute her. The black and red Marathon knife, the same switchblade the Dragoons carried, that Chloe held right now, was in her mind, with the soldier and the soldier's son. *Wake up, wake up!* If murdering the soldier in Marathon didn't make Chloe like her parents, then murdering an unarmed prisoner would. *Might as well call me a Dragoon.*

Samantha's radio croaked. "Officer Armistead, come in," Sheriff Armistead called, strict and alert, as if she'd never gone to sleep that night.

Hands fused to her pistol, eyes on the Dragoon commander, Samantha didn't dare reach for her radio.

"Officer Armistead, come in! What's your situation?" the sheriff asked. A pause, then she said, "Night patrol's reporting a gunshot. We're trailing three unknowns inside the perimeter. Boot prints heading your—-"

"Fuck! Their fucking door's down," another officer yelled, his voice catching on the radio and echoing through the breached front entrance. The yellow beam of a flashlight flickered in the window. Armistead and the night patrol officers were approaching the shack.

"Chloe, your eyes," Samantha warned. "You too, Addie!"

The order for retreat was made in Chloe's mind, made and ignored. Twice more she gave the command, twice more her Second-Gen Stage remained active, her eyeballs shining with criminality, unable to switch off, her parents' concerns confirmed. This would've petrified her, if the Dragoons and their Second-Gen commander, who was acting as if she knew Chloe, hadn't already done that. In the corner of the room, Addie's violet irises reflected in the dark red, her Second-Gen Stage frozen in place also.

"Officer Armistead?" Armistead shouted from the front doorway, over the wind, voice stern yet uneven with what Chloe hoped was fear for her daughter. Yellow light cut through the bedroom. Boots tapped into the kitchen, one pair, two pairs, three pairs, weapons clicking with every guarded step.

"Chloe," Samantha beseeched, terrified for her partner and the child in her care.

"Officer Armistead?" Armistead answered.

The Dragoon commander chuckled, amused.

Chloe could only shake her head at her partner. Even if she shot the Dragoon commander, her Second-Gen Stage would still be on. The Black Dragoons had come to Merenranta, come to her and Samantha's shack, for Addie. Her alternative state wasn't going away fast. Neither was Addie's. She and the girl were caught. That realization was arriving on Samantha's face as their fellow officers entered the room.

They crowded the doorframe, between Chloe and Addie, armed with pistols and flashlights, missing none of the evidence the room provided. Armistead was on point, the first to speak after a ten-second delay that silenced her and the two night patrol officers with incredulity. "Put your weapons down, Chloe," she roared, her expression building from bewilderment to ferocity, as she faced two and a half pairs of glowing Second-Gen eyes. Her pistol centered on Chloe. The other two officers pointed their weapons at Addie and the Dragoon commander. Fingers clung to triggers, waiting for the smallest unauthorized move from the Second-Gens, one of whom was somehow Awakened as a child. Chloe set the T-05 rifle and Marathon switchblade down, half-expecting the sheriff to put a round in both her eyes.

"Kid, drop that knife," one of the night officers instructed. Addie didn't.

"Ma'am," Samantha said, attempting to intercede, her pistol still on the Dragoon commander.

"Hands on your head," the other night officer told the elderly Second-Gen. The Dragoon commander obeyed.

"Hands on your head, Chloe," Armistead copied. Chloe lifted both hands, intertwined her gloved fingers at the back of her hat.

"Drop the knife!" Again, Addie disregarded the officer. She hadn't acknowledged the officers in any form. Chloe wondered if the girl knew they were here at all.

"Ma'am, they're not—-" Samantha began.

"Don't, Sam," Chloe interrupted.

"I didn't fucking say you could talk," the sheriff snapped. She motioned to the Dragoon commander. "Officer Armistead, cuff this one!"

"Drop the fucking knife," the officer shrieked. "I'm not telling you again!"

"Let me take it from her," Chloe pleaded. "Addie will listen to me!" *I hope.*

"Shut the fuck up, Second-Gen!" Armistead angled her pistol closer to Chloe's head.

"Listen to her, mom," Samantha bellowed.

"How the fuck is this kid Awakened?" asked the officer with his pistol on Addie.

"Addie will kill all of you," Samantha claimed. "Let Chloe disarm her!"

"You'll have to cuff her too," the Dragoon commander laughed.

"Keep quiet! I'll fucking shoot you," the other officer said.

"Cuff the old Second-Gen, Officer Armistead," Armistead ordered. "I'm taking Chloe!"

"The fuck you are!" Samantha advanced on Chloe.

"Samantha," the sheriff said to her daughter with infuriated surprise.

"Sam, stop," Chloe screamed.

One hand on her pistol, Samantha gripped Chloe by her jacket collar. Chloe stood with Samantha's tug, followed her partner through the officers to the corner, their boots splashing on the dark red floor. "Cuff her, before she kills us!" Chloe dropped to her knees, beside Addie, her pants sopping in the Dragoons' blood.

"Samantha! What the fuck?" Armistead snarled. The other officers were so distracted, Chloe was concerned they might forget about the Dragoon commander. The woman observed from the floor, smiling at the scene.

Both hands on her pistol, barrel lowered towards the floor, Samantha rotated to her mother and colleagues. Standing between the officers and Chloe and Addie, she declared, "Chloe's going to disarm Addie and put the cuffs on her. She's the only one who can. You try to stop her, this kid will lay you out next to these two fuckers behind me." Samantha's speech juddered, her weapon shaking in her arms. She had to know what she was doing to herself. Yet she persevered. "When Chloe's done, you can cuff us both, take us to lockup."

"Us?" Armistead asked, though her dismay made it seem like she already knew.

Samantha nodded. "Chloe told me five days ago, about her and Addie."

"Sam?" Chloe said in bafflement. Addie's Awakening at age three made more sense to her than Samantha's confession. Nothing her partner had done for her and Addie over the last five days was reasonable.

"Hurry up, Chloe," Samantha replied without turning from her mother's line of vision, as if she feared her mother might raise her pistol at them first chance she gave her. "Sheriff Armistead's got arrests to make."

The Dragoon commander was handcuffed and taken to the kitchen, her backpack, rifle, and knife confiscated. As the officers worked, Chloe turned to Addie. Immobile, the child held the exact same position, switchblade in her hand, oblivious to the dark red she and Chloe sat in and the activity a mere couple feet behind them. Splotches of blood glimmered on Addie's jacket, gloves, pants, and cheeks, lit by the violet from her irises. Her eyes were more alive than Chloe had ever seen them, even if the rest of the girl seemed as dead as the two Dragoons before them. Arm out, to block an attack if there was one, Chloe whispered, "Addie?"

No shift in the child's attention. It was as if the Dragoons' reappearance had robbed her of her hearing and vision, just as her voice had been stolen pre-birth.

Chloe thought to give Addie her sketchbook and pencils, hoping those items would be comforting enough to get her to cooperate. The book and pencil box were drowned in dark red at the front of Addie's cot, useless. "Addie." Chloe took her handcuffs off her belt, held them up so the girl could see. "I need to put these on you, okay? The cops will shoot you if you don't let me."

Addie didn't nod or shake her head, didn't drop the knife. Perhaps she wanted the officers to kill her, to save her from the Black Dragoons.

Developing a new tactic with such speed it could only have come from her Second-Gen Stage, Chloe asked, "Do you remember what I said, that first night I came to see you in the med center?"

No reply.

"How you and I are safe and everything is going to be all right?"

At last, a slight nod, as if Addie didn't want the officers to notice.

Chloe nodded back. "Okay, well I'm sorry, Addie. I was wrong. But do you remember what Sam and I told you? In the kitchen?"

The child nodded.

"Sam and I aren't lying to you. I'm not lying to you, Addie. If you keep Sam and me safe while we're prisoners, we'll—-"

Addie looked at Chloe, violet and blue merging in the dark red pool, as if to tell her she better understand what she was saying.

Chloe reiterated without hesitation. "You keep us safe, we'll keep you safe. Agreed?"

The nod came first. Then, Addie set the blade on the dark red floor, put her wrists together in front of her to receive Chloe's handcuffs.

"All Merenranta officers, all Merenranta officers, this is Sheriff Armistead," Armistead broadcasted on her radio, watching from the bedroom doorway as Samantha removed the magazine and chambered-round from her pistol, placed the weapon and ammo on the bed. "Be advised, we have a breach in the perimeter. I say again, we have a breach in the perimeter." With one officer guarding the Dragoon commander in the kitchen, the other officer handcuffed Chloe and Samantha. "One Second-Gen bandit in custody, two bandits dead at Samantha Armistead and Chloe Corday's shack in north Merenranta. More bandits potentially at large. Black clothing and gear. Heavily armed and highly dangerous."

"They're Black Dragoons," Chloe said, as the officer confiscated her and Samantha's police wristwatches, keys, and the equipment from their belts.

"Don't talk," the officer told her.

Armistead turned to the kitchen, discounting Chloe's warning. "Additionally, all Merenranta officers, be advised..." The sheriff hesitated, before resuming with a tone of saddened animosity. "Chloe Corday and the nomad known as Addie are Second-Gens. Once again, Chloe Corday and the nomad known as Addie are Second-Gens. Samantha Armistead has confessed to colluding with them. All three are in custody as of this time. We're moving to lockup. Civilians and nonessential government personnel are to remain indoors. Wake Mayor Darabont and inform him of the situation. Over."

While one of the night officers stayed to secure the crime scene, the group left the shack in a line, Armistead at the lead, Samantha second, Addie, Chloe, the Dragoon commander, and the other night officer in the rear. Pistols and flashlights out, the officers took the prisoners to the cove, walked them along the high-tide beach, away from the community perimeter. Boots sinking in snow, ice, and sand, white breaths swirling in the putrid windstorm, Chloe followed the sheriff to the western side of north Merenranta. The moon was veiled by clouds, the officers' flashlights and the Second-Gens' irises beacons in the gray-ish-black, though that wasn't the only light. Half the shacks in north Merenranta and a quarter across the cove in south Merenranta were lit, the citizens becoming aware something was happening. By dawn, every household, every parent and child, every human would hear the news. More than six years of goodwill, extinguished the second Armistead saw Chloe's glowing eyes. This was Chloe's last night in Merenranta, as it was for Addie and maybe Samantha too. Exile or death would come with sunrise.

Lockup sat opposite the town hall lobby from the police station behind a single door, opened with Armistead's master key. The entrance felt more like another office than the town prison. Even lockup itself lacked the reputation the Detention Center once had in Marathon. Six iron-bar cells, three on each side, three lamps suspended from the ceiling, windowless walls, and a concrete floor encrusted with dust. The room wasn't used often enough to warrant regular cleaning, but at least it was warm like the rest of the building. The Dragoon commander went to the first cell on one side, Chloe, Samantha, and Addie to the first cell on the other, sharing the cell at Armistead's command. Four prisoners in four cells were four targets. Four prisoners in two cells were two targets. Doors locked, hands unshackled, Addie went to the back of the cell, sat on her dark red-stained knees, facing the corner so she didn't have to see the Dragoon commander. Chloe stood at the bars, Samantha joining her, blocking the Dragoon commander's view of her former child slave and assassin. Armistead and the night officer stood at the exit, silent.

A knock and Armistead opened the door for the mayor. Stride slow, joints and limbs tense, clothes creased and hair astray, Darabont looked as if Armistead had forced him to come. He cringed at the sight of the Dragoon commander, her violet iris, her glass eye and scar, her excellent physique despite her age, and her unafraid demeanor, even as she stood imprisoned. Then, Darabont turned to Chloe and Samantha, their bloody boots and pants, Chloe's blue irises, and caught himself on the wall before he could faint. "Fuck," he gasped.

"Sorry, sir," Chloe said. She wished she could've told him herself, after what he'd told her and Samantha yesterday.

"Don't talk," Armistead barked.

"Fuck," Darabont muttered. His vocabulary was narrowed by what he was seeing.

"Excuse me, sir," another night patrol officer said, bringing a couple more prisoners into the room.

"Shit," Chloe yelled, startled, though she shouldn't have been. The Dragoon commander cackled, as if she just heard her first joke ever.

Sean Halley came in, garbed in civilian winter gear, handcuffed, yellow light glittering in his glass eye. Anna Corday was with him, dressed the same, her prosthetic arm tied to her live arm. *Sheriff Armistead must've ordered their arrest when we were on our way here.*

The parents surveyed their daughter and their daughter's partner, expressions shifting to horror as they noticed the blood. They both said, "Chloe—-"

"Been a long time, Vanguard One, Vanguard Two." The Dragoon commander snickered, body pressed against her cell bars, violet iris glaring at Anna and Sean, smile growing until Chloe thought it might rip through her cheeks.

Chloe's parents halted at the Dragoon commander's cell, voiceless. It was as if they were falling down a hole in the floor, hopeless to retain control of their lives. That didn't last for her mother. "Darius, you fuck," Anna screeched, irises glowing blue, left hand pulling at her handcuffs, wanting to strike the elderly woman. "The fuck did you do to my daughter?"

Sean stepped between his life partner and the Dragoon commander. "Not here," he told her, as Armistead and the night patrol officers put their hands on their holsters.

"I'd listen to him," the Dragoon commander jested.

"Fuck you, Darius! Fuck you," Anna countered, shoving her life partner out of the way. "Why the fuck are you still alive?"

The name Darius prodded Chloe's memory. *Addie wasn't writing about a regular unit commander, she was writing about Commander Darius! One of Marathon's three elite Commanders was a Second-Gen, has been a Second-Gen this entire fucking time!*

"Anna," Chloe's father blared, unfaltering as Chloe's mother directed her shimmering irises at him, turning his glass eye blue. "Not here!"

Darius chortled. "Nice to see you two are still together."

"Fuck yourself, Commander," Sean retorted.

Second-Gen Stage still on, like the other three Second-Gens in lockup, Anna went with Sean into the second cell on Darius's side. Their cell was locked, their hands freed, their cuffs unnecessary behind bars that even Second-Gens couldn't easily force open. Armistead sent the night patrol officers back to their posts, called on the radio for one of the remaining daytime officers to head to the crime scene, the other to come and guard the lockup entrance. Left alone with the prisoners, the sheriff stood in the hallway amid the cells, the mayor by the exit, either collecting himself or attempting to hide. Holster unsnapped, hand tight at her pistol, Armistead turned from Darius to Chloe to Chloe's parents. "You all know each other?"

"Oh, we can talk now?" Samantha said, snarky, as if she was outside the cells with her mother.

"Not you!" Armistead pointed at her daughter to be quiet.

"Sheriff," Darius said, getting Armistead's attention.

"You got something to say?"

Darius sneered. "If it'll get us out of these cells faster, then yes."

Armistead nodded. "Who the fuck are you?"

Eye widening, as if she was surprised, Darius said, "You mean none of them told you? That's disappointing."

"Sean, who the fuck is she?" Armistead asked, irate.

A moment of hesitancy and Chloe's father said, "Commander Darius, one of three Marathon Commanders. Dead in the civil war, we thought."

"And how is it you and Anna know this Commander Darius?" the sheriff said.

Their family lies exposed, Chloe's father explained to Armistead and Darabont that he and Chloe's mother were Black Dragoons under Darius's command, fifteen years ago, and eight years before the civil war. "Chloe didn't know until a few days ago," he added. "We lied to her, same way we lied to you all." This only made Armistead angrier, however.

"I would've recruited Chloe, if not for the civil war," Darius commented. The Commander looked at Chloe. "She seems usable, even if she's as unreliable as you were, Anna."

"Eat shit, Darius," Anna shouted.

"You and Sean were happy eating my shit the last time we were together," Darius responded. "Addie too."

"Shut the fuck up, whatever the fuck your name is," Chloe wailed, shaking the bars of her cell, her rage powered by the sound of Addie's wheezing nostrils. The child had closed her eyes, covered her ears, and tilted her head against the corner wall. No doubt, her mind was spiraling with each word from Darius. "Addie killed two of your precious Dragoons and all she needed was a fucking pencil! She'll kill you—-"

"Enough," Armistead interjected. "How did you get through our perimeter?" she said to Darius.

Darius laughed. "We fucked up with Addie once we got in, but getting in wasn't a problem, especially with a perimeter as lightly defended as yours."

"How many of you are left?" Armistead asked, unyielding.

"Myself, three in the woods." Darius grinned. "And Addie."

"Where in the woods?" Armistead inquired, scraping her pistol with her fingers.

"North of town," Darius disclosed, though not because she was threatened. "They're on standby till I return or till daybreak. I wouldn't try moving on them. Pistols versus sniper rifles isn't much of a fight."

"What happens at daybreak, if you don't come back?"

"Your people learn just how defenseless your perimeter is."

Armistead paused a second to consider Darius's warning. "How'd you find us? This town?"

Darius nodded to Chloe and Samantha. "We saw those two patrolling a creek, several miles north. Thought of neutralizing them on the spot. Followed them back instead. You're welcome."

Chloe thought of North Creek and the two dead nomads she and Samantha found, nomads who'd been shot with high-caliber rounds and robbed for their supplies. *Dragoons have suppressors on their rifles. That's why we didn't hear the shots.*

"Fucking shit, mom," Samantha scolded. "That was your fucking pointless patrol!" Chloe knew the Dragoons likely would've discovered Merenranta on their own, with how long they'd been chasing Addie, but she shared her partner's anger.

Armistead ignored her daughter. "What'd you come here for?"

Expression stiffening, her smile vanishing, Darius said, "Addie, just Addie."

A sniffling noise came from Addie's nose, as if her nostrils were stuffed.

"Why?" Chloe said.

Darius focused her eye on Chloe. "Because as Second-Gens, we belong to something bigger than us."

"What the fuck does that even mean, Darius?" Anna said, as if she'd heard that proclamation before.

"We're a correction," Darius replied, iris still on Chloe, though she may've been trying to see Addie. "For humanity."

Silence spread amongst the Second-Gens and humans, a hush of such hollow magnitude that Chloe could hear boots tapping outside lockup, probably one of the daytime officers coming to guard the entrance. After a minute, Darius spoke again, her eye on Armistead. "Somewhere inside, you all know. Humans have known since the first Second-Gen, back in the Previous Civilization. Hate us all you want, but we're your replacements."

"Replacements?" Samantha asked.

Darius turned to Samantha. "Our species is evolving, yours isn't. Our species is growing, yours isn't. The Reform sped things up, but the process was underway long before the end of the Previous Civilization. Someday soon, humanity will be extinct, and Second-Gens like Addie will have their universe."

The desire to sit down reached Chloe in her Second-Gen Stage, the heft of Darius's prediction pressing on her being. She took a breath and kept standing, for Addie. The same unnerved gulps came from her parents and Samantha. Armistead and Darabont were worse. Nothing in the past week, from Martin Donnelly's murder of Sarah Murphy to the last half-hour, equated to the gaping looks of disaster that appeared on their faces. It was as if they'd just watched the entirety of Merenranta, five and a half decades of history and almost five hundred human inhabitants, evaporate in an instant. The Commander's words were only theory, but Chloe recognized the rationale. To Darius, Addie was an improvement, a milestone on a beach leading down the coast. And at the end of that coast was a curve, where a race of Second-Gens absorbed the remnants of the human species.

"We've been scoping you out for days, bypassing your patrols and searching for Addie," Darius stated with a sullen tone, empty of the humor she'd employed a few minutes ago. It was as if the Commander had no true personality and instead cycled between them. "Just give me Addie and there will be no conflict. We'll take her and never come back."

Chloe turned to find Addie shaking her head and rubbing her hatted hair with her hands, as if she was trying to disconnect her brain and shut down her awareness of what Darius was offering.

"And getting the kid back," Armistead said, voice quavering, reeling from the Commander's belief that her species was doomed. "That's all your three Dragoons in the woods want?"

Samantha shouted, "Mom—-" Armistead's hand came up again.

Nodding, Darius told Armistead and the others, "They want her back as much as I do." Chloe witnessed it then, in the Commander's violet eye and the expression around her scar, like the fear that hid below Addie's fury. "We've taken a lot of weapons from the rubble of Marathon since the war." Desperation. Darius's behavioral transitions were a façade, a ruse to shield her desperation. "But none of them have been as valuable as Addie." The Commander was trying to reclaim what she'd lost, Marathon. And to do that, she needed a weapon like Addie, the future of Second-Gens.

Armistead perused the room, the cells and the prisoners in them. "You think the Dragoons will take these people too?"

"What?" Chloe and Samantha bellowed in shocked unison.

"What is this, Sheriff?" Chloe's father supplemented.

"You're out of your mind, Dylan," Chloe's mother yelled.

"Sheriff, I..." Darabont said, finally attempting to join the uproar.

Darius's grin returned. Iris fixated on Armistead, she said, "We are in need of a couple new Dragoons. Can't say we have use for all your prisoners, though."

"Don't do this, Sheriff," Chloe pleaded.

"Please, mom," Samantha said, placing emphasis on the word "mom," as if to tell her the final thread was about to break between them.

"However many you take," Armistead responded, adamant. "As long as we give up the Second-Gen kid, the Dragoons will leave?"

The Commander nodded, showing her teeth with her smile. "Leave and never come back."

"Okay," Armistead said. A yellow flash and Chloe heard the bang, a crack from the pistol that was now in the sheriff's hand. A cloud of bright red and pink ejected from Darius's violet eyeball, dousing the bars of her cell. A shell casing dinged on the floor, smoke flowed at the pistol tip. Commander Darius collapsed, head thumping against the bars, and didn't move from the floor, didn't speak. Commander Darius was dead.

Chloe, Samantha, Anna, Sean, and Darabont, they all took a step back as Armistead holstered her weapon. Nobody spoke. Chloe doubted any of them could. She certainly couldn't. The lockup door squeaked open. The officer on guard raced in, pistol drawn. "Sheriff," she called.

"Prisoner went for my gun," Armistead lied, staring at Darius's body and the red puddle expanding around it.

"Shit," the officer said, as the puddle leaked into the hall. "Anybody hurt? Besides her I mean."

"No," Armistead reported. "Scene's secure, resume your post."

"What?"

Armistead turned and patted the officer on the shoulder, as if to calm her. "Resume your post. Radio the med center and tell them to send a team for the body."

"Yes, m-ma'am." The officer moved back to the exit.

"And holster your weapon."

"Yes, ma'am. Sorry," the officer replied, closing the door.

"Jesus Christ," Sean hollered, though Chloe didn't understand what he was saying.

Anna spit through her and Sean's cell bars, saliva landing, floating in the red hallway slick. "Good fucking riddance!"

"Dylan, what are you doing?" Darabont asked, cowering against the wall by the exit.

The sheriff shifted to the mayor, rolled her eyes. "You're still here?"

"What are—?" Darabont stuttered, his body trembling. "What're your intentions, Sheriff Armistead?"

"My intentions?" Armistead said, tipping her head forward, edging the mayor on.

Chloe thought Darabont might run for the door, but he stayed. "Are you going to execute all these prisoners?"

"Not till I give that Second-Gen kid to the Dragoons," Armistead vowed, as inflexible as she'd been with Darius.

"Mom," Samantha whimpered, more in despair than ire. Chloe saw water filling her partner's eyelids. In the corner, Addie rose from the floor.

"You still want to make this deal?" Darabont said, staggered.

"The Dragoons have been watching us for days without us knowing! They broke through the perimeter like it wasn't there! My department can't take these people head-on," Armistead asserted. "I have to offer the girl and whoever else they want in exchange for a pledge not to attack Merenranta!"

"The Dragoons are mass murderers," Chloe countered. Addie's boots tapped behind her.

"They'll kill you and the rest of us outright," Anna agreed.

"Then invade Merenranta and kill till they're out of ammo," Sean insisted.

"Losing their commander and half their unit will make them more willing to negotiate," Armistead said, unmoved by the former Dragoons' warnings. Before tonight, she was never one to advocate negotiating with criminals. Even if she wasn't showing it, the sheriff must've been terrified of the Black Dragoons, and basing her unfounded decisions on that terror.

Chloe shook her head in dread. "We should fortify! Barricade everyone in the industrial neighborhood! They'll be less vulnerable when the Dragoons assault the perimeter!" Addie pushed through Chloe and Samantha, got a look at Darius's corpse.

"I," Darabont said, stammering again. "I agree."

"You agree?" Armistead replied, wide-eyed, as if offended.

Darabont hesitated, craning his neck to the ceiling as he admitted to his mistake. "Yes."

"You agree with the Second-Gen?" Armistead shrieked.

The mayor flinched. "This is my…" He paused, dipped his head to the floor. "You answer to—-"

"No," Armistead roared. Darabont lifted his hands to his face, as if afraid Armistead would shoot him too. "Your fucking office just ran short of chances! Your fucking predecessors let in Martin Donnelly, let in Chloe and her parents, granted citizenship to fucking Second-Gens! And now you've gone and done the exact same fucking thing with this kid! Let her bring a gang of fucking assassins to Merenranta! You trusted a murderer over your own sheriff, completely missed the clear fucking fact she and Chloe were manipulating you!" Sheriff Armistead pointed at Mayor Darabont. "You fucking brought this to Merenranta, Amin! Every fucking citizen, every fucking child in this town is in danger because of you!"

"And you fucking murdered an unarmed prisoner," Samantha shouted, coming to the mayor's and, by extension, their defense.

"She was a Second-Gen," Armistead rejoined. "Second-Gens are always armed! For fuck's sake, Samantha, I never thought you'd forget that!"

Samantha punched the cell bars. "Go fuck yourself, Sheriff!"

Addie looked up at her.

It wasn't just fear of the Dragoons guiding Armistead, Chloe saw now; it was Darius's forecast of extinction for humankind, extinction and replacement by Second-Gens. She couldn't be reasoned out of her judgement, for she believed her judgement was reasonable. "My mom's pregnant," Chloe said, making a last attempt at sympathy.

"I know," Armistead said, unbothered. "All the more reason to get rid of her before she gives Merenranta another fucking Second-Gen!"

"What about your daughter?" Chloe responded. Her partner shook her head, as if telling her not to try.

"She's not my daughter anymore!"

"And you're not my mother," Samantha retorted.

Armistead turned back to Darabont. "And you're not in charge!" The mayor jumped to the side, and then followed with his head down, as the sheriff marched to the exit. "I won't be long." The door opened, shut, and locked from the outside, leaving Chloe to wonder if she, Samantha, Addie, Anna, and Sean would soon join Darius or join what was left of Darius's people.

PHASE 7: BEACHFRONT

SIXTEEN

The wait was longer than Sheriff Armistead had implied. Three hours by Chloe's estimation, and the sheriff still hadn't returned for the prisoners. The Dragoons' deadline had to be close, an hour at best until daybreak. Chloe worried that Armistead might've chosen instead to evacuate the town to the industrial neighborhood, intentionally abandoning her and the other prisoners in the process. But she reminded herself that Armistead was too resolute in her stance to change her mind. Most likely, her plan and her subversion of Mayor Darabont's authority was meeting opposition from the mayoral staff, as well as anybody else in the government who valued the mayor over the sheriff. This was only a delay, Chloe suspected: Darabont didn't have the fortitude to take his leadership back from Armistead, and even if he did, he would also sentence the Second-Gens and their human allies to some form of punishment. The possible outcomes were the same whoever came for them, death or exile.

Hungry and thirsty, Chloe and Samantha sat on the floor of their cell, backs against the bars. Second-Gen Stage turned off, Chloe didn't bother to hide the tremors that seemed to be trying to tear her left arm away from her body. Her wounds from her fight with Addie were painless, healing quick, much to her irritation. The bandaged gash on Samantha's face was still bruised, yet that was probably the least of her concerns. She shook as if her nerves were taking commands from Chloe's arm. Addie stood next to them, gazing through the bars, just as she'd been doing since Armistead and Darabont left and Darius's body was removed from lockup. She gazed at the stains of dried brownish-red, on the floor and the adjacent cell bars, the last bits of her abductor. Her irises still shined with her Second-Gen Stage, but her bloodied expression was neutral. *Killing them isn't enough for her, just like releasing isn't enough for Sam and me.*

"Can I ask you something?" Samantha said, breaking the defeated quiet of lockup.

Chloe glanced around the cell and shrugged. "I don't have any-where else to be."

"When you...when you're in your?" Samantha pointed at her eyes.

"When I'm in my Second-Gen Stage?" Chloe asked, piecing to-gether her partner's clumsy mumble.

Samantha nodded. "What's it like?"

No human, not even her father, ever asked Chloe this. Somewhat discomfited, she looked across the hall. Her parents sat alongside the bars of their cell, facing one another. The talk between cells had been sparse, mostly Chloe catching her parents up on Addie's situation, but Anna was swift to take notice of her daughter. With a light smile and nod, as if she'd overheard Samantha's query, Chloe's mother gave ap-proval. *Mom must've told dad plenty about our kind. He doesn't need to ask me.*

"I don't know if it's different for each Second-Gen," Chloe said to Samantha. "But in my Second-Gen Stage, it's like..." The answer eluded her; it was difficult for her mind to hold on to. "It's like, everything I want to know about myself is right there in front of me. I don't need my release anymore. I have everything I need." She paused, her arm tin-gling with remorse. "But then, my Stage goes off. I come back and I, I hate myself."

Samantha seemed confused by Chloe's entire response, yet it was the last part that got her to say, "Why? Because of the civil war? That soldier and—-"

"Because," Chloe interrupted, before her parents heard about the Marathon soldier and her son. "When I'm in my Second-Gen Stage, and sometimes when I'm not, I'm looking down at your kind, Sam."

"You're looking down at us?"

"Humans, yeah." Chloe would've wavered on this, if she believed she and Samantha would survive the morning. "You can't do what I can, what Addie and my mom can do. I don't want it to, but that difference makes me look at humans as inferior." She gestured to Darius's vacant cell. "Just like Darius with her fucking prophecy."

Even in their present circumstance, Samantha's reply surprised Chloe. "Maybe it's time my kind went extinct. The Reform was humanity's doing." She snickered. "We've killed far more people, yet we think Second-Gens are more dangerous."

"I'm sorry, Sam. I'm sorry you're here."

"That's not your fault. I chose to be here."

Chloe grabbed her left wrist, out of habit. "Why? You could've said you didn't know we were Second-Gens, didn't know I was helping Addie."

Samantha inhaled, then gave her first real smile since the previous day. Smacking her face, she giggled and said, "Chloe, how are you so smart when you're this stupid? We betray everything we're taught to stand for, for the people we love."

Chloe swore the shakes stopped in her arm, if only for a second. She leaned in, held Samantha's cheek, and kissed her. "I love you, Sam," she said, as her partner reciprocated. "I mean, I love you too." Lips together, they chuckled, their partnership enduring for the limited time they had left.

Addie's boots tapped around Chloe and Samantha. They parted lips as the child sat in front of them, her violet irises diverted away from Darius's blood to her guardians. "What is it?" Chloe asked, concerned Addie was on the brink of another fear-induced tantrum.

No sketchbook or pen to communicate with, the girl pointed at Chloe, then Samantha, puffed her lips, mimicking a kiss.

Samantha laughed. "Kissing?"

Addie nodded, continued her imaginary kiss, rubbed her hands together.

"What's that mean?" Samantha said, glancing at Chloe in confusion.

Addie made a circle with her index finger and thumb, kissed the air and stuck her other index finger through the circle, jabbed her finger in and out of the hole.

"That's not what we were doing," Chloe blurted out. She lifted her quivering left hand, signaled for Addie to stop.

The girl pointed at them again, puffed her lips, as if puzzled.

"We were kissing, that's all," Samantha told the child.

Addie must think kissing's just a precursor for sex. "Kissing isn't...isn't just..." Chloe stuttered. "Isn't just for that!"

Addie shrugged her shoulders, seeming to ask them to explain.

"Chloe and I were kissing to say we care about each other. We're a couple."

Addie shrugged again, bemused still.

"She doesn't know what that means," Chloe told her partner.

"Couples?"

"Caring." *Addie can't care about someone if she doesn't have empathy.*

Samantha shivered, daunted by something so essential and so seemingly instinctive. "Caring is, uh, caring for someone, you know."

Addie shook her head, as if she thought Samantha was asking a question.

"I guess it means, watching out for someone, protecting someone." Samantha turned to Chloe, then Addie. "Not because you agreed to protect them if they protect you, not because you made a deal." Chloe's head seemed to rotate without her consent, her eyes settling on her parents' cell. Anna and Sean stared back through the bars. Three irises, none gleaming, concentrated on Chloe. "You're honest with them. You support them when they can't support themselves, and when they can." Her parents smiled at her, but Chloe saw the shame behind those smiles, a disgrace that doubled in her.

I wish you never came home. I actually told my parents that, told them I wish they'd stayed Dragoons, slaves to Darius, like Addie.

"Chloe and I kissed so we didn't have to repeat all that." Samantha tittered. "But sometimes you say it anyway, like when Chloe and I said we love each other."

"Chloe," her father began, voice cracking with guilt. Trapped together in lockup, the talk he and her mother wanted to have with her for the past five days was going to happen. Arm quaking, razor shouting, Chloe shut her eyes and turned back to her cell.

"You don't know what love is either, Addie," Samantha said with abrupt sadness. Chloe lifted her eyelids. Addie was looking at Chloe, attention zeroed on her and discounting Samantha, as if they were back in the medical center on the girl's first day in Merenranta. "Do you?" The child didn't nod or shake her head, didn't blink. She appeared to be waiting, as though she expected Chloe to answer.

The lockup entrance opened, impeding further conversation from Chloe or her parents.

The prisoners stood up in their cells as Mayor Darabont entered, alone, letting the door close behind him. The mayor—-if he could still be called that—-walked forward a foot or two, then stopped, staying near the door. Samantha said what Chloe and probably her parents were thinking. "Surprised you came back here, sir."

"So am I," Darabont replied, facing the center of the hall to evade direct eye contact with the Second-Gens.

"Why did you?"

Inhaling, as if the act required physical exertion, Darabont shifted his head to Samantha's cell and the two Second-Gens contained within. "I came. I wanted to talk to, to, to your partner, Sam."

Chloe moved to the end of the cell closest to the exit, Darabont approaching the bars yet maintaining a few feet of separation. Samantha and Addie kept to the other side of the cell, observing as Chloe's parents did from their cell. Though Darabont had come to Chloe, she was the first to speak. "It's almost dawn. Is the sheriff coming back or not?"

Darabont swallowed and coughed. "Dylan's got a lot of people in disagreement, my staff in particular. Even some of her officers are unsure, but the police department's following her and that's all she needs. She'll be here in a minute."

"Why're you talking to me then?" Chloe responded, hands on the bars, one of which vibrated with her left hand.

Darabont glanced at his boots, either frightened or embarrassed by his oncoming words. "I just want to know."

"Know what?" Chloe asked. She had an inkling.

"Why you lied," Darabont said, eyes on the floor, as if he didn't believe Chloe deserved to be in his eye line. "When you and your parents stumbled upon Merenranta, asked for citizenship, you told us you and your mom were human." Offense pricked at his tone. "You spent all those years lying, lying while I, we, told you the truth. Why?"

In one maddening second, the years of regret Chloe felt for lying to Darabont, to Armistead, to everybody in Merenranta, were swept up, compiled, and disposed of by fury. Or perhaps, regret was working in cooperation with her frenzy. Hands squeezing the metal, face pushing on the bars, she said, "Merenranta prides itself as a fucking sanctuary, but bans Second-Gens and acts fucking shocked when they lie to live." Darabont's eyeballs rose, granting her a glimpse. "Either you people are that fucking idiotic or Second-Gens aren't the only liars in this town."

Darabont didn't get a chance to reply before the door unlocked and Armistead returned to lockup. Two officers at her back, the sheriff surveyed the room and told its occupants, "Time to take a walk."

Hands cuffed, Chloe and the other prisoners were taken from their cells and gathered in a line, Addie at the head, followed by Chloe, Samantha, Sean, and Anna. The child made a fleeting look to Darius's cell, to the dried blood of the Dragoons she was about to rejoin, then stepped forward at Armistead's order. Out of lockup and into the lobby, the prisoners found a crowd waiting.

The employees of Merenranta's government jammed the space from the west to east exits, winter clothes and hair in varying stages of dishevelment, depending on how fast they got ready upon hearing the news. Jaw-dropped gawks abound, shock at Addie, Awakened before the age of thirteen, horror at Samantha, the daughter of Sheriff Armistead, a traitor to her hometown, and hatred at Chloe and her parents, who lied to everyone in this room. Their audience was quiet, as if Sheriff Armistead forbade them from speaking and no one wanted to risk challenging her. Chloe's left arm quavered with her walk, her handcuffs rattling with her wrist, though of course that didn't surprise her. What did surprise her was Darabont.

As Armistead and the officers led them to the east exit, the mayor didn't part ways with the prisoners, didn't flee and disappear in the crowd to lessen his association with the condemned. Instead, he trailed the group, five feet behind Chloe's mother. *Mayor wants to see us off, make sure we actually leave Merenranta, or he's pretending it's still his job.*

Dawn was moving in from the sea as the group departed town hall, a horizon of grayish-orange coming ashore to lighten the grayish-black above them. The wind was down; gray snowflakes fell in the calm frozen rot of the air, as if the weather was busy spectating on the prisoners, as the whole of Merenranta appeared to be doing. Like the lobby of town hall, the pathways between the buildings of north Merenranta were strewn with disarrayed and sleepy onlookers. Non-essential government employees, civilians from south Merenranta, parents and children from both sides of the cove, all apparently aware, all disobeying Armistead's shelter-in-place order, all braving predawn cold and Dragoons to watch the sheriff escort the Second-Gens and human traitors from their community. Bearing witness wasn't sufficient for them, however. This crowd spoke, in whispers and mumbles, in screams and exclamations, their white-puffed voices amplified in the windless early morning.

"Daddy, why're that girl's eyes glowing?" one young child asked his father.

"Fucking Second-Gen," a civilian man blared.

"How?" a government employee said. "How is she Awakened that young?"

"That's Sam Armistead! Why's she being exiled, mom?" a teenager asked her mother.

"She's a criminal," the mother replied. "She helped the Second-Gens."

"But she's a police officer."

"Not anymore."

"Fucking Chloe and her parents must've tricked Sam into helping them," another civilian man ventured.

"They lied to all of us! They must've lied to Sam too," a civilian woman agreed.

"Last week it was Martin. Now it's Chloe and Anna?"

"That fucking nomad kid too!"

"How many Second-Gens are there?"

"Why do Second-Gens keep coming here?"

The words of her once-welcoming neighbors sliced through Chloe, jerking her limbs and torso. The judders ricocheted down the line, like a wave flowing towards shore, shaking Samantha and her parents all the same. And it wasn't just the prisoners. Darabont quivered with them, his face souring, not with ire or fright, but grief. It was as if Darius's prediction was playing out for him to see, the town he knew a mere few hours ago evolving into someplace he couldn't recognize.

Addie was the only one who didn't respond to the mob, didn't shift her attention or alter her expression, and didn't withdraw her Second-Gen Stage. For most of their slog among the neighborhood structures and distraught citizens, Chloe assumed the girl just didn't care. Addie had spent most of her week in Merenranta in the medical center. She had no connection to these people. Nearing the beachfront of north

Merenranta, where the light from the horizon was more prominent, Chloe noticed it. Addie wasn't blinking, not even to clear the snow out of her eyes. The child had been frightened since the night she met Chloe and Samantha on the beach, since her Awakening on the last day of the Marathon Civil War. Fear was her life as much as murder was. But today, as she walked towards a reunion with the Black Dragoons, Addie's terror was such that what little sync she still had with the universe was fading. If anything, the child had lived in her own universe from the beginning. Anyone who tried to cross over and join her did so at great peril. Chloe wasn't done trying, though.

Past the beachfront shacks, past Chloe and Samantha's home, the door-less front entrance roped off with police tape, the prisoners were herded onto the beach, away from the relative cover of the neighborhood. To the north, the woods sat in a darkened snowy haze of grayish-brown lines, concealing the last of Marathon's Black Dragoons. Likely armed with the same T-05 Snipers Darius and the other two Dragoons used in their invasion, the Dragoons could be glassing the prisoners, officers, and the mayor right this moment, debating whether to open fire to retrieve Addie. The crowd must've realized the danger as well, because they congregated between the beachfront shacks, spectating without stepping out into the snow and sand. The beaches of Merenranta were now hostile territory.

A fourth officer joined their party as they traversed the beach to the waterline. The tide was low but returning, the water as flat as the wind, a plate of unreflective gray connecting the land to the sea's growing grayish-orange wave. Snowflakes collected on the ground and in the ocean, gray dots dropping from one gray plain to another. Armistead halted the group and positioned the prisoners parallel to the beach and sea, facing north, boots angled against the rotten edge of the current. Addie ahead of Chloe, Samantha, her father and mother behind her, all of them had a view of where they were going. *Sheriff Armistead's going*

*to walk us up the beach till the Dragoons show themselves, or just ambush
us and take Addie without a discussion.*

Armistead ordered Chloe and the prisoners to look straight ahead,
assigned the fourth officer to guard them, and moved to the back of
the line with the other two officers, Darabont tagging along like a child
trying to play with their older sibling's friends. Out of eyesight yet
not earshot, Chloe heard the sheriff addressing her subordinates, heard
the stress in her voice. Armistead might've ignored the risks of leaving
Merenranta when she sent her daughter and Chloe to North Creek.
Not this morning though. As illogical as she was acting, she saw at least
some of the hazards of her plan. "I'm taking them from here. The rest
of you will stay, guard the perimeter. You hear shots, you get everybody
back inside, don't wait for word from me."

"Ma'am?" the officers replied, sounding concerned for their sheriff
and relieved for themselves at the same time.

"Understood?" Armistead asked, firm in the responsibility she'd es-
tablished for herself, only herself.

"Yes, ma'am."

Armistead's radio screeched on as she transmitted her intentions to
Merenranta, giving Chloe an opportunity.

"Addie," Chloe whispered to the top and back of the child's head.
"Don't turn, just listen. Okay?" The girl didn't acknowledge with motion, so Chloe only had time to assume Addie heard her. Left hand
gripping the chain of her handcuffs in an attempt to placate its trembling, she said, "What we agreed last night, the deal we made, before
they took us to lockup." Addie stood in the snare of the northbound
beach, from which she'd come a week ago. The people who'd come to
reclaim her waited somewhere in those trees. It was possible the child
believed she already belonged to them again. An even split deal wasn't
enough for her, not even enough for a nod in confirmation. Clutching
the chain until the metal poked her palm through her glove, Chloe told
the child, "I'm making a change." Chloe thought she saw Addie con-

vulse, heard her nostrils wheezing. A white cloud rose from her face, as if the girl had the air punched from her lungs. "It's not I protect you and you protect me anymore. When we're out there, it's you protect you and I protect you." Samantha's handcuffs clattered from behind and Chloe felt a tap on her hip. Brief as it was, she smiled and said, "You protect you, I protect you, and Sam protects you. You keep yourself safe and we'll keep you safe."

Addie swerved around, facing south in defiance of Armistead's instruction. Her violet eyes flamed at Chloe and Samantha with a demand for sincerity, ready to pounce at the slightest sign of deception.

"Hey, turn around," the officer on guard barked.

In the margin of her left eye, Chloe saw the officer's hand drop to his holster. That didn't discourage her from calling down to her alternate state and responding to Addie. "Whatever becomes of this."

"No talking."

Second-Gen Stage galvanized, left arm subdued, Chloe knew Addie could see her blue shining irises. "Whatever happens."

The officer drew his weapon, the pistol clicking as it rose to Chloe and Addie. "I said no talking."

Neither Second-Gen faltered. The officer cocked the hammer on his pistol. "Fuck yourself," Chloe's mother said. Chloe glanced back as the officer redirected his weapon to her mother. Anna was facing north, but her irises glowed blue, her Second-Gen Stage on.

"The fuck you say?" the officer retorted.

"You heard her," Sean said, winking his live eye at his daughter.

"You hear this?" The officer cocked his pistol again.

Chloe turned to Addie. Unblinking, she avowed, "You won't go back to the Dragoons."

The child glared back, unemotional, then nodded.

"Holster your weapon," Armistead snarled, drawing her own pistol as she and her entourage returned to the prisoners.

"Yes, ma'am." The officer complied without waiting for an explanation, as if he was more afraid of the sheriff than the Second-Gen and human prisoners. Addie turned north again. Chloe heard Samantha and her parents' boots crackle in the snow and sand as they straightened themselves.

Darabont and the officers kept to the west of the prisoners as Armistead stepped to the front of the line. Pistol held in both hands yet aimed at the snow, the sheriff scanned the prisoners she was offering to the Dragoons and declared, "We're moving up the beach. We keep moving till I say stop. Anybody stops before I say, anybody walks out of line, anybody so much as talks will be shot."

"That's your plan, really?" Samantha said, challenging the person who was once her mother. "Take us on a fucking walk till the Dragoons decide to join? You honestly think they won't just shoot you and—-"

Armistead raised her pistol to the sky. A flash and bang shushed Samantha's lambast of the sheriff's farce, rebounded against the beachfront shacks, skipped across the water. Darabont and the officers balked. Chloe and Addie didn't. Amid the startled shouts from the citizens at the end of the beach, Armistead roared, "Anybody who talks will be shot! That was your only warning!" Samantha didn't contest further.

Barrel smoking, the sheriff lowered her pistol and shifted herself to the east, on the prisoners' right. Boots splashing in the tidewater, her back to the ocean, she stood at Chloe and Addie's flank. *The Dragoons won't risk shooting Sheriff Armistead if Addie's in their line of fire.*

"Sheriff," Darabont said, his voice so low the inch high waves almost muffled him.

"What now?"

Recoiling, Darabont told her, "I'd like to come, too. I don't agree, but it's my job. It's my job to see that this deal takes place."

Chloe couldn't tell if she was more shocked that Darabont wanted to come, or that Armistead said, "Fine." As he circled the line and joined them at Chloe and Samantha's side, shoulders and head curved downwards, she assessed why Armistead was letting him go.

Something goes wrong, it'll be easier for her to maintain control.

"Let's move," Armistead commanded, her pistol clicking as she gestured north. Addie hesitated a second, and then walked forward, Chloe sticking close behind, stomping her boots deep into the snow and sand, so the child would know from the crunch that she was with her. Samantha and her parents followed, Armistead and Darabont keeping pace. Separating themselves from the officers and the mob, the group of seven, five prisoners, one usurped mayor, and one pistol-wielding sheriff, marched up the coast, towards the perimeter of Merenranta and Marathon's last surviving Dragoons.

Snow crunching, sticking to their clothes, wet sand squishing, the group stamped across the community perimeter, cornering themselves on the coverless beach, in the funnel of the trees and ocean. Chloe half-expected the Dragoons to emerge from the thickets or attack the instant she and the others stepped onto the open beach. Neither occurred. Boot step by boot step, minute by minute, Merenranta and its people shrunk behind Chloe, the beach lengthening in front of her, and the edge of the sea brightening with grayish-orange, daybreak imminent. And yet, the Dragoons remained unseen. Addie's fright didn't diminish with the lack of Dragoons. A quarter mile from Merenranta, the child's tread and thereby the group's slowed until she wasn't moving at all, her nostrils panting, her head and back twitching, even in her Second-Gen Stage. "I didn't fucking say stop, keep walking," Armistead shouted, violating her pledge to shoot anyone who stopped. Addie obeyed, but paused again, a quarter and then a half-mile later, her unhinged breathing and shaking unremitted. The sheriff ordered the girl to continue each time, her pistol never elevating, even as her tone rasped with accruing anxiety. Addie was too important for Armistead's threats. That reassurance was a grain of salt in the ocean for Chloe, however. Were it not for her own Second-Gen Stage, Chloe's left wrist would be smacking against her handcuffs, her razor stalking her up the coast.

Addie's next terrified standstill came a mile from Merenranta, the town a couple distant dots in the dawning light, the orange-yellow rim of the sun peering over the gray ocean. Martin Donnelly's execution spot was up alongside the tree line, his body out of sight though sure to still be in the woods. The child's fourth stop was sudden, so much so Chloe almost bumped into her, Samantha into Chloe, and so on. In the second, smaller, line, Darabont stumbled to prevent himself from hitting Armistead, who groaned and rotated to the girl. "For fuck's sake! Did the Dragoons not teach you what 'keep moving till I say' means?"

"Dylan?" Darabont muttered.

The sheriff's pistol clicked in her hands. "Or should I put this to your temple and tell you again?"

Chloe winced, her boots jolting in the slush of snow, sand, and salt-water. Only the danger of being shot by Armistead held her tongue.

"Dylan!"

Chloe, Armistead, Samantha, Sean, and Anna all turned with Darabont's unexpected yell. The mayor with no jurisdiction stared past them, expression and frame taut with alarm. Addie was looking in the same direction, across the beach, towards the forest, eyes wide and violet. Spinning with the rest of the group, Chloe saw what made Addie freeze.

The figure stood in the mounting sunlight, in the thick snow and sand just outside the trees. Black winter gear, black backpack, and a black T-05 Sniper rifle, black scope and suppressor incorporated, this person's allegiance was clear. "That's a Dragoon," Anna said with knowing dread.

Addie coughed, white air puffing from her face, her head rocking up and down. Two more Dragoons stepped from the woods, their gear and weapons identical to the first. Three altogether, the Dragoons faced the prisoners and officials from Merenranta, soundless as the snow that fell between the two groups. They appeared to glance to one another, nod. Chloe couldn't be certain in the dim light. Then, the Black Dragoons advanced.

The assassins walked in a horizontal line, their rifles down but clutched tight, Addie and the others centered in their unified gaze. Addie sniffled. A white cloud hiccupped from her mouth and she lifted her cuffed hands in front of her, as if making a plea with the Dragoons.

"Addie," Chloe began. What she was going to say wasn't yet assembled. She didn't get to finish anyway.

"Hold your ground," Armistead commanded her prisoners, as if they were soldiers. The sheriff's pistol, a weapon inferior against even one T-05 Sniper, stayed at equal level to the Dragoons' weapons, clicking as her fingers constricted at the grip and trigger. Darabont moved behind Armistead, his boots squishing in the sand, plopping as the water came in. He ducked his head, using the sheriff as a shield.

"Chloe," Samantha said, imploring, as if hoping her partner had an idea. Chloe's parents looked at their daughter and at each other.

Addie kept her hands up. She shook her head. Her boots twisted with her legs, sucking into the slush and sand, attempting to tunnel away. "Addie," Chloe and Samantha uttered in unison.

"Hold your ground," Armistead repeated. "Nobody fucking move! Let them come to us!"

When the Dragoons were close enough Chloe could tell they were two men and one woman, Addie dropped to her knees. Pants wet in the snow, sand, and saltwater, she put her head in her hands and cuffs, sheltering her eyes from the Dragoons. The Marathon assassins took notice of the child's distress, their heads dipping to track the girl, their gait quickening for half a second before slowing back to a walk.

Chloe knelt beside Addie. Samantha knelt beside Chloe. The seawater came in waves, soaking their boots and pants. Even Chloe's Second-Gen Stage couldn't spare her from the icy pain of the ocean's deadly temperature. Dragoons or not, Chloe needed to get Addie standing before hypothermia floated in to meet them. She almost made the mistake of patting Addie's shoulder with her hands as she said, "You have to stand, Addie. I'll help you."

"I have Addie," Armistead shouted to the Dragoons, as if they couldn't see that. "She's unharmed!" None of the Dragoons replied. Their wordless approach continued.

Addie shuddered, wheezed, her head tipping lower, until it was just above the snow and sand, water splashing her face. "Let me help you," Chloe insisted. *I should just pull her up; my Second-Gen Stage is stronger than hers. She'll fight you; get Sheriff Armistead and the Dragoons shooting.*

"She killed your commander, Darius, and the other two," Armistead lied, unease evident in her voice. "I'm sorry," she added, another lie. The Dragoons looked at each other but pressed on without a single word.

"The fuck?" Samantha mumbled in fearful confusion.

"Chloe," Sean said in warning.

"Addie, please," Chloe pled, as the crunch of the Dragoons' boots became audible.

The sheriff's boots stamped behind Chloe, her weapon clicking as she shifted positions. Leaving Darabont in the comparative safety of Addie's shadow, Armistead came forward and stood ahead of the prisoners' line, directly in front of Samantha.

"Addie, I'm here," Chloe told this child who'd been entrusted to her less than twenty-four hours ago. "I'm right here. Sam and I are right here."

"You aren't going back to these fucking people," Samantha averred, not seeming to care if her mother heard her. "The sheriff can trade us all she wants, but you won't be a Dragoon again."

Chloe nodded in concurrence. "Not today, not tomorrow, never. We won't let anything happen to you."

Addie elevated her head, revealed her wet and blood-stained face, her bruised forehead, to the beach. And as soon as she did, Armistead yelled to the Dragoons, "You can have Addie back!" Her tone quaked with her pistol, as if someone was shaking the sand beneath her. "And these other prisoners! Two of them are Dragoons!" Armistead cringed, shook her head as she corrected herself. "Fuck, Second-Gens! Two are Second-Gens!"

Two Dragoons, the two male Dragoons, beamed. Their smiles of insidious excitement went to Addie, right to Addie, not meant for anyone else, smiles of lust for the child. One of them winked and Addie bent away again, snorting, convulsing. Last night's dinner spattered in the slush. The girl plunged her gloved hands and cuffs in the submerged snow and sand as she vomited. "Fuck," Chloe said. She wished she had time to cry for the child.

"Addie," Samantha sighed, sounding closer to weeping than Chloe.

"You can have them," Armistead promised. Sputtering, she said, "If you agree not, as long as, if you don't attack Merenranta, our town, again."

No reply from the Dragoons and the trio passed within thirty feet of the Merenranta party, they and their clicking rifles threatening to overtake the sheriff and her prisoners. Chloe's father stepped to the side, placed himself in front of Chloe's mother. Hands, real and plastic, tied together, Anna wrapped her left arm and her prosthetic around Sean's chest, as if the limbs were bullet resistant. As Chloe's parents braced, unable to reach their daughter without chancing a shot, Darabont sank to his knees, surrendering to the Dragoons just as he'd surrendered to the sheriff. "Shit," Armistead said, speech and expression clenched in panic, at last seeing the corner she'd boxed herself into. She had a pistol, loaded and primed, and yet she was unarmed.

Chloe had seconds for another try. "You protect you, Addie," she reminded the child. "You protect you, I protect you, and Sam protects you."

"That's good there," Armistead besought.

The Dragoons narrowed the gap to twenty feet and snubbed the sheriff's request.

"Dragoons or no Dragoons," Chloe told Addie. "You protect you and we protect you."

Addie's hands resurfaced from the slush, rose with her head and back. Shivering like her guardians, white clouds panting from her nostrils, she turned to Chloe and Samantha. Violet tears sparkled in her eyelids, snowflakes shined as they fell past her irises. The eyes of a child, not a killer, nor a Second-Gen, but of a child. Armistead and the Dragoons neglected to factor that. Addie shook her head, sprinkling Chloe with violet water.

"That's too close," Armistead begged.

"You keep yourself safe and we'll keep you safe," Chloe reaffirmed. Unbowed, even as the Dragoons closed in the periphery of her blue Second-Gen eyes, she said it once more. "You keep yourself safe and we'll keep you safe."

"Time to go, Addie," said one of the male Dragoons.

Inhaling and unblinking, Addie shook her head at Chloe.

"Addie—-"

The child gritted her cheeks, bounced to her feet, knocked Chloe into the slush as she ran.

"Fucking," Armistead yelped, startled, as Addie darted south, boots splashing between Samantha and the ocean. One step, two steps.

With speed only fear and prejudice could supply, the sheriff flipped around. Her back to the woods, the Dragoons forgotten for a reactionary moment, she raised her pistol. Chloe pushed on the snow and sand with her elbows, about to leap and reach for the weapon. One yellow flash, one boom, and a shell casing struck Chloe between her right eye and her eyebrow, a light burning sensation to reward her futile effort. Bright red tore from Addie's jacket, from her ribcage. The impact jerked her body towards the sea, twisted her waist and legs until her back was to the sheriff. A second flash, a second boom, and then a third. Four, five, six, seven, eight flashes and booms in a max of three seconds. Bright red misted from seven holes in Addie's back, erupted from the rear of Armistead's skull, her neck, and her back with the hiss of three T-05 Snipers. Like buildings with shattered foundations, child and sheriff collapsed, Addie on her stomach in the watered slush, Armistead atop her daughter. Orange-yellowish-red and orange-yellowish-pink fogged the air, tainted the snowflakes caught in its spread, showered Chloe and Darabont, and sent Chloe's parents scrambling for cover on the ground.

"Addie! Addie!" Chloe thought her cries could rip apart the universe, until the humans of the Previous Civilization and the Second-Gens of Darius's proposed future were covering their ears at the sound. But the noise only appeared to accelerate the rate at which the snow, sand, and saltwater were turning dark red around the unmoving girl.

"Addie, fuck," one of the Dragoons bellowed. They sprinted the last fifteen or so feet, boots crunching, rifles clacking, suppressors smoking at the tip. The Marathon assassins hadn't anticipated this.

"Addie!" Chloe rose from the slush, about to stand. One of the Dragoons thumped her in the back with the butt of their T-05. She landed on her stomach, her cuffed hands wedging in her chest, the slush, dark red with Armistead's blood, saturating the few still-dry parts of her clothes.

"Stay down," the Dragoon woman shouted as she and the other two Dragoons passed over Chloe. "All of you! Stay on the fucking ground!" Sitting in the snow, Anna and Sean didn't challenge. Samantha lay underneath her mother's lifeless body, blood and skull fragments coating her face, probably too stunned to register the Dragoon's command.

The two men ran to Addie. Rifles hanging from straps, they knelt beside her, inspecting the damage to their most treasured weapon and slave. The woman stopped next to Chloe, her boots splashing Chloe with snow and water. "Shit! Shit," one of the men squealed, grim as he shook his head.

One hand on her rifle, the woman bent over and seized Armistead's pistol. "What's her status?"

"Addie," Chloe screeched, eyes wetting.

"Shut the fuck up!" The woman kicked Chloe in the side of the head, though it felt like a slap at most. "What's her status?"

"She's fucking lit up! You can fucking see that yourself," the man snapped back, pressing his hands on Addie's back, his black gloves turning dark red.

The woman chucked the sheriff's weapon into the ocean. "One of you get your med-kit!"

"Fuck, I think one of them went in her heart!"

"Help her," Chloe cried, more at the sea than the Dragoons.

"I told you to shut the fuck up!" Free hand back on her rifle, the woman aimed the tip of her T-05's suppressor at Chloe's face. Chloe's tears dried, not with terror but anger, a swift billowing rage, like the ocean under a storm.

"Please," Darabont said, screaming louder than Chloe ever thought his vocal cords would allow. "Help her!" The sight of Addie, shot and bleeding in the sand before him, was overriding his petrification. The woman turned her rifle on him and he dipped his head, put his hands in front of his face. "Please!"

Chloe's storm came crashing ashore, a kind of second Second-Gen Stage reserved specifically for hatred, hatred of being Second-Gen. She sprang upwards.

Shrieking, snarling, Chloe tackled the woman before she could pull the trigger. They splatted in the slush, Chloe's locked hands pinning the woman's chest, T-05 lodged between the Dragoon's side and the sand. The men gripped their weapons and revolved towards Chloe.

Addie moved.

Like the bullets she'd been downed with, Addie shot from the slush. Mid-jump, she kicked the man to Chloe's right, knocked him and his rifle into the snow, vaulted off him and upon the other man, rolled over his shoulders onto his backpack, strung her handcuff chain across his neck, pressed on his pack with her boots, and yanked at the chain. It was as if she didn't have eight bullets in her body, didn't have two rounds surgically removed a week ago.

The woman drew her black Marathon switchblade, snapped it open in her free hand. Chloe couldn't reach for it without releasing her hold. The woman lunged at Chloe's gut. Samantha caught the knife handle in her bloodied hands, tugged it back. Breaking from the stupor of her mother's death and squatting beside Chloe and the woman, Samantha planted her boots in the watery snow, steadying herself as she fought to pry the blade from the Dragoon's hand. But the woman clung to her knife, groaning with white puffs, a melody of exertion to match the desperate gasps from the man in Addie's chokehold. White clouds howled from the child's nose, blowing over her red wetted face and the sparks of violet from her eyeballs.

The second man rose to one knee, readjusting his slush-drenched rifle. A shout and Sean rushed into Chloe's view, dove on the man, splashing them both in the freezing micro-tidal waves. Another screech and Anna slid into the men, the Dragoon and the former Dragoon. Mouth wide, eyes glowing blue, Chloe's mother bent her head, sank her teeth in the lump at the front of the man's neck as Chloe's father held him down. The man wailed, then coughed as Anna arched up, tore off a chunk of his neck. Bright red spouted, sprayed the former Dragoons, turned the slush dark red around them. Thrashing, the man pushed back against Sean, blood burbling in his mouth. Anna spit in his eyes, blinding him with his own blood and skin, and brought her bright red teeth back down, biting his lips. She twisted her head to the side and ripped the flesh above and below his mouth away. The man's resistance weakened.

What the fuck, mom? Seeing her mother devour the Dragoon's face distracted Chloe. The woman freed her T-05, curled her wrist, angled the rifle suppressor towards Chloe and Samantha. Darabont grasped the rifle and dragged the barrel up, attempting to snatch the weapon. The Dragoon woman was stronger than Samantha and Darabont combined. Hands cuffed, Chloe couldn't seize the Dragoon's weapons, couldn't restrain her, couldn't arrest her.

The black and red Marathon switchblade of seven years ago reemerged, dripping, stabbing Chloe's mind.

"Wake up, wake up!"

Chloe heard the boy weeping for his mother, for the Marathon soldier she killed. The longing for her razor arrived, slipped through the buffer of her Second-Gen Stage, not by force but with her permission. She wanted the need to be there, wanted its pain. That ache stayed with her as she glanced at Darabont, at Samantha, at her parents, and at Addie, all fighting, all dependent on her now.

Sorry.

Chloe raised her hands, released the Dragoon from her clasp. Exhaling, the woman pitched up, pulled the knife from Samantha's grip, swung the blade at Chloe again. Chloe caught the handle as her partner had, tugged the knife down, and drove the blade into the side of the woman's neck as far as it would go.

The woman's eye sockets expanded, then slackened, her head resting in the snow. Chloe let go of the knife, stared with Samantha and Darabont as blood drained from the Dragoon's mouth. Looking back at them, the woman blinked repeatedly, as if asking them not to watch. She stopped blinking right as the gurgling ceased from the man without lips and just as a pop came from the neck of the man in Addie's chain. The Black Dragoons extinct, Chloe's Second-Gen Stage withdrew and the shaking started, in her left arm and her right as well.

The bodies of Sheriff Armistead and the Dragoons rocked in the tide, slush and seawater reddening. Samantha and Darabont sat refilling their lungs with multiple quick gulps of white air. Anna splashed her lips, cheeks, chin, neck, and chest with water, scooped some in her mouth with her left hand, rinsed, and spit. Saltwater apparently tasted better than the Dragoon. Sean sat shivering, scanning his daughter with his left eye, either waiting for her to speak or making sure she was unharmed. Eight gunshot wounds in her back and ribcage, Addie stood, walked around the Dragoon she killed, and faced Chloe. "Addie?" Chloe whispered, scared of what a higher volume might do. Arms shuddering, handcuffs clanging, she rose before the child. The others remained yet were ignored. This was Chloe and Addie's conference. The blood on the girl's face glinted in the light of the sun that now levitated in a complete orange-yellow circle above the ocean horizon. Addie's nostrils were quiet, her body still, not shaking. Even the few snowflakes that continued to fall did so with an extra shush, a calm the morning demanded. The violet glow hung in Addie's irises for several seconds, then went out. Blood trickled from the child's mouth and nose like red saliva and snot. The quivering intensified in Chloe's arms, nausea curling in her stomach. The blood in the slush was getting darker and thicker behind the girl's boots, pouring down her legs from her back. "Addie." Addie's legs buckled and she tilted to one side. "Fuck!" Chloe ran to the girl as she collapsed in the shallow dark red water.

Chloe crouched at Addie's side, put her hands under the child's torso and elevated her back. Addie was awake, cognizant. That didn't reduce Chloe's revulsion. The girl's lack of frightened reaction to being touched and the overflow of blood and slush on her back that saturated Chloe's already soaked gloves told Chloe what was happening. Still, she said, "I'm going to take you to the med center, Addie. Get you a doctor."

Trembling in Chloe's hands, Addie squinted one eye, shook her head in stern refutation. The suggestion of doctors and medical treatment was insane to the girl. She'd used the last swell of her Second-Gen

Stage to kill that Dragoon. She knew just as well that she wasn't leaving this beach.

"Why did you run?" Chloe knew the answer and knew Addie couldn't reply. *You were too scared to believe me.* The question was a desperate one, without reason.

But Addie replied. Lifting her cuffed hands, she caressed Chloe's blood-strewn police uniform, the burn mark between Chloe's eye and eyebrow, and the bump on the side of Chloe's head. Chloe thought the child was delirious, her hands moving at the order of her diminishing mind, until she saw it below the bright red on Addie's face. Worry. Not worry for herself, however, worry for another person, worry for Chloe.

The astonishment of seeing Addie fear for someone else's wellbeing was almost as unbalancing as witnessing the child's Second-Gen Stage for the first time. Chloe's brain juddered like her arms, frantic to decipher how. Then, she reevaluated what Addie did right before she ran, the headshake she gave. "You were trying to get the Dragoons to chase you? That's why you ran?"

Addie lowered her hands, nodded.

The queasiness in Chloe's stomach converted to a bulge in her chest. "You wanted to get the Dragoons away from us? Away from me and Sam?"

The girl nodded.

Rock in her throat, Chloe said, "Even though you knew the sheriff might shoot you?"

Addie shrugged.

Tears rolled through the blood on Chloe's cheeks, fell in red drops as the awareness flattened her with its agonizing mass. Addie shook her head because she trusted that Chloe and Samantha would fight and potentially die to keep her from the Dragoons. Addie ran so they wouldn't die or, worse, become slaves like she'd been. Addie had empathy, had it before she met Chloe and Samantha, before she found Merenranta. The child had disguised it beneath layers of fear, rage, and comfort for killing, defensive coatings nobody saw through. *She warned me before the Dragoons came in last night. I'd written her off by then, a killer.* "I'm sorry, Addie. I'm so sorry, dear."

Addie blinked, made a slow tip of her head from one side to the other. Chloe hoped the girl wasn't trying to absolve her of wrongdoing. Boots stamped behind Chloe. Darabont leaned beside her, holding out his hand. In his glove, Armistead's master key, taken from her belt. Chloe understood what the mayor intended when she noticed he was crying too, as were Samantha and her parents.

As gentle as her arms permitted, Chloe set Addie down, unlocked and removed her own handcuffs. Then, she gave the key to Addie. After some effort, the child liberated herself, dropped her handcuffs in the slush. Chloe gave the key back to Darabont, nodded a thank you. The mayor walked back and rejoined Samantha at the body of the Dragoon they'd helped Chloe kill.

Hands free, Chloe held Addie by her back and legs. The girl was shaking more than Chloe now, her breath sporadic, rapid puffs of red and white gaped by terrified airless stares. "Thank you, Addie. Thank you. You saved us."

Addie smiled.

Whimpering, Chloe raised Addie in her arms, embraced her, and rested the child's head on her shoulder. Her arms hung limp between them, but Chloe wrapped them around her back one at a time, so the girl had someone to hold onto. This might've been Addie's first and only hug, the only affection without sinister motive she'd ever received. "You're safe, you and I are safe and everything is going to be all right." Addie's chest enlarged, a red and white breath iced the side of Chloe's neck. Chloe exhaled a white puff and said it again. "You and I are safe and everything is going to be all right." Addie coughed, inhaled and respired, chilled Chloe's neck with another red and white cloud. "You and I are safe and everything—-" Red and white air brushed Chloe's face. The child's chest expanded and didn't contract again. Addie left for her own universe.

PHASE 8: RELEASE

SEVENTEEN

It was after sunrise when the survivors returned to the Merenranta perimeter. The handcuffs were removed at the mayor's request. Soaked in dark red slush and sand, all shivered with hypothermia. The snow had ceased falling yet the air dropped several degrees. Mayor Amin Darabont walked at the head, leading them. Samantha, daughter of the now-deceased Sheriff Dylan Armistead followed a couple crunching paces behind. Chloe's parents were in the back, Sean leaning his head on Anna's shoulder, sobbing from his left eye. Anna stroked his hair with her left hand, whispered attempts at comfort even as she wept. Out of all of them, they were the only two whose tears hadn't been stilled by shock and cold. Chloe thought it might've been her mother's pregnancy, the increased prevalence of children on their minds magnifying their anguish. As they neared the first row of shacks, however, Chloe remembered her parents' confession to her five days ago and realized they continued to cry because the death of children was something they'd caused, not once, not twice, but thrice as Black Dragoons. Sean Halley and Anna Corday were child-killers, just like Dylan Armistead.

None of their party was armed. Chloe was the only one who carried anything at all. That made little difference to Merenranta. As the group came upon the shacks, three officers swarmed, pistols drawn and level, movements quick and alarmed. To this town, Second-Gens and their human collaborators were always armed.

"Mr. Mayor," one of the officers called, as if he believed Amin Darabont didn't know Chloe and the other unrestrained prisoners were behind him.

"You all right, sir?" another officer asked.

"What happened?" said the third. "Where's Sheriff Armistead?" All three officers noted the body in Chloe's arms, but the mayor and the remaining prisoners were their prime concern.

Darabont paused, raised his palm to the officers. The prisoners and officers stopped at the same instant, the mayor between them.

"Are you hurt, sir?"

"Where's Sheriff Armistead?"

"Should I call the med center?"

One officer brandished his weapon past Darabont, at Chloe and the other prisoners. "The fuck they do out there?"

"Lower, lower your weapon, weapons," Darabont said, slurring with the daze of what he and the people behind him experienced on the beach.

"Should we take them back into custody?" one officer asked, missing or mishearing Darabont's order.

"Sheriff wanted them out of town! We need to ask her!"

"Holster your——" Darabont started to say.

"Mr. Mayor, where's the sheriff?"

"What happened to their cuffs?"

"Get Sheriff Armistead on the radio," one officer instructed, centering his pistol on Chloe. Chloe faced the weapon's barrel, inert except for her arms. "On your knees, all of you! Mr. Mayor, please step away! We're——"

"Stand down!" The mayor's yell was more militaristic than governmental. Chloe shuddered, as did her fellow prisoners and her former colleagues. This wasn't a command made to convince people Amin Darabont had authority. This was a command made per Mayor Amin Darabont's authority, an authority regained in the void left by Dylan Armistead and no doubt driven by sorrow for what he'd allowed her to do, what he'd allowed to happen. A child shot to death, much like his family. "Stand down and holster your weapons!"

The officers glanced at one another. "Sir?"

"Sheriff Armistead's dead, the Dragoons too," Darabont informed them. "It's over. We're safe now."

"The sheriff's——?"

"Get a patrol going to recover her body, bring it back for memorial preparations." Before the officers could be sidetracked by disbelief, he continued, "She's a mile or so up the beach. Make sure you collect the Dragoons' weapons and gear as well, before any bandits come along."

The officers looked at each other again, and then holstered their pistols. "Yes, sir."

"Thank you. Watch out for each other." Darabont moved forward, motioning for Chloe and the others to follow. "Been enough losses today."

"What about these prisoners, sir?" an officer asked.

Darabont didn't waver, didn't avert his glare. "I said we're safe now. They're not prisoners, they're citizens." Samantha, Chloe, Sean, and Anna passed the officers without incident. Their citizenship restored, pending Darabont's removal of the law on Second-Gens from the town charter, the four reentered their community with their mayor.

The citizens flocked onto the walkways once more, those who'd gone home rejoining those who'd stayed, north and south Merenranta reunited in confusion. Darabont led Chloe and the others west towards the medical center in unhidden view of the crowds, vulnerable to their words. But the words didn't come. The sight of the dead child in Chloe's arms muted their outrage.

Addie's lifeless arms, legs, and head dangled from Chloe's own shaking arms. Dots of dark red trailed Chloe's boot prints. The girl's eyes were closed, shut by Chloe, yet her eyelids scowled at the gathered populace. Addie had departed Merenranta as a supposed danger to every human still in existence, a danger the town would never have to see again. But now she was back, and the humans of Merenranta were seeing the person that Second-Gen had been, seeing what had become of this child. With each turn Chloe and Addie took on the path, the sound of crying children—-assumed-human children—-heightened, even when their parents tried to shush them.

Chloe didn't comprehend that Samantha had separated from their group until they reached the medical center. Boots squeaking through the eastern lobby doors, the same doors Chloe carried Addie through a week ago under similar yet crucially different circumstances, she recalled witnessing Samantha veer off and merge with the crowd somewhere on the trek across north Merenranta. Exhausted and overcome by the child in her arms, she hadn't asked her partner for an explanation, and Samantha hadn't given one. Where her partner went, Chloe wanted to know, but she could only address so much with the energy she had.

In the lobby of the medical center, staff converged on Mayor Darabont, who promptly told them to aid the people with him. Uneased and reluctant, the staff nevertheless agreed. Just as it'd been done a week ago, a gurney was brought for Addie. Today, though, it was to take the girl to the morgue, not an operating room. Half a dozen requests from the staff and assistance from her parents were required to get Chloe to lay Addie on the gurney, let go of the child, stand by as her body was wheeled away to be stored in the same room as Darius and two other Black Dragoons. *Sheriff Armistead will be there too before the morning is over.*

Chloe, Anna, Sean, and Darabont were taken to an exam room. Wrapped in blankets to reverse hypothermia, they were each checked by a nurse, then a doctor. When their conditions were found to be stable and satisfactory, Darabont said to Chloe's parents, "Go home. Get some rest if you can."

"Thank you, Amin," Sean said, tears still running from his eye.

"Yeah," the mayor replied. "I'm sorry we're not better."

"I'm going to the bathroom," Chloe lied. Knowing her parents would insist she come back to their shack with them, she exited the exam room and instead of going to the bathroom, returned to the lobby, walked out of the medical center, and out into the bitter air.

Brain and body numb, she hobbled her way back towards the beachfront. The walk wasn't anywhere near as quiet this time. Without Mayor Darabont as escort and Addie in her arms, there were numerous Merenranta citizens who had no qualms about heckling her.

"Where the fuck you going, Second-Gen?" one man shrieked.

"Drowning yourself in the ocean I hope," the woman with the man added, earning a laugh from him and their teenage daughter. Only their son, seven or eight years old, didn't join.

A woman Chloe's age eyed her blood-coated jacket and declared, "You fucking killed Dylan, didn't you?" When Chloe didn't stop or reply she said, "Fucking admit it! You fucking murdered her! She spent her entire fucking life protecting this town and you people fucking murdered her for it!"

Each verbal assault strengthened the urge, lengthened the razor's call, until release was the sole goal of Chloe's life. Everything between her releases was unimportant, a period of imprisoning irrelevance she was condemned to after every freeing trip with the razor. And this most recent sentence had gone on for much too long.

White puffs panted from her mouth as she arrived at her and Samantha's shack. "Go back to Marathon you fucking traitor fuck," an elderly man, a child of the Previous Civilization, shouted from the pathway as Chloe ducked through the police tape at the door-less entrance. Lights out, air equal in temperature and salted decay to outside, she crossed the kitchen to the bedroom. The police had already removed the bodies, weapons, and equipment of the Dragoons, as Chloe expected. The corner of the room was brownish-red with dry blood that extended underneath Addie's cot and the bed. Grayish-yellow sunlight seeped through the windows and the bullet holes in the wall and ceiling. To Chloe's worsening hyperventilation, she saw that the safe she'd put her razor and other sharp objects in had been taken by the police as well. The tool of her release was locked in evidence at the police station. Darabont had let her come back to Merenranta, but he'd said nothing of her status as a police officer. And even if she did have access, the clenching in her chest and throat that made her work for each white breath mixed with fatigue to make another march in the hail of her fellow citizens' vocal attacks quite undesirable. She would have to improvise again, just as she did in the bathroom at Cheng's.

She bent down to grab Addie's bloody pencil box, but ended up sitting on the girl's cot, holding her brownish-red stained notebook, as if the child was lingering about and intended to write a message via Chloe's hand. Chloe flipped the blood-sodden pages back and forth, Addie's written voice lost in that brownish-red haze. On the fourth or fifth pass between covers, she landed on a page speckled with blood yet still predominately clear, its markings visible. It wasn't writing, however. It was a drawing. Of what, Chloe took a minute to grasp, because the whole picture was drawn in one color, dark blue. The book vibrated with her hands.

The dark blue snow and sand of the Merenranta coastline, the dark blue waves of the sea, the child had drawn the beach. Not just the beach, the dark blue crescent that stuck out of the dark blue clouds, which tapered off at the brownish-red edge of the page, incomplete. A few dark blue dots surrounded the crescent. *HOW WE GET TO MOON AND STARS?* The last sketch Addie ever did was of the moon and stars, where she wanted to go, where she might've been trying to go from the moment she escaped the Serenity Station. Her entire journey southeast could've been an effort to get off the planet, an attempt to ensure she never saw the Black Dragoons again. Chloe dropped the book, her hands quivering, breaking her grip.

The tears came back, drenching Chloe's sore eyes on the first wave. *I stole Addie's notebook.* The water overflowed on the banks of her eyelids, rained down her grime and sand-laden face. *Addie couldn't speak, but she had a voice.* Chloe seized her hat-covered head with her turbulent hands. *A voice I stole!* She squeezed her skull, hoped she crushed it. *Just like the Dragoons! Just like Sheriff Armistead!* Coughing white clouds, she picked up the pencil box. *But I didn't get hurt for it.* Pencils clattering, she opened the box and tried to take a pencil. Her fingers wouldn't grasp. "Fuck!" Another attempt; she got the pencil halfway out, only for it to slip through her fingertips. "Fucking! Fuck you!" She smacked her hand down on the pencils, thinking the tips would puncture her skin like when Addie stabbed her. Every tip snapped. None of them even ripped through her glove. She threw the box at the cracked wall. "Fuck!" The box clanged, the pencils scattering as she stood. "Fuck!" Chloe kicked Addie's cot, kicked it again and knocked it on its side against the wall. "Fuck me!" She slammed her knees on the floor, punched the brownish-red. "Fuck me!" Her knuckles screamed with the pain she demanded, and she pounded the floor a second time. "Fuck!" Three times. "Fuck!" Four. "Fuck!" Five. "Fuck!" Six. "Fuck!" Seven. "Fuck!" Eight "Fuck!" The floor fissured, yet the shaking in her arms didn't slow. Lacking the strength to raise her fist again, Chloe slumped on the floor, curled up with the brownish-red. She closed her draining eyes, wished the cold would keep them that way.

"Wake up. Wake up, dear."

She recognized her parents' touch, felt them lifting her off the floor. The inside of her right glove was warm. Her knuckles ached. If she'd been asleep, she didn't know for how long. She thrust herself back onto the floor, kept her watering eyes shut.

"Can you open your eyes for us?" she heard her father ask, a hand rubbing her shoulder and trembling upper arm.

A hand pulled at Chloe's right glove, removed it. "Shit," Anna muttered.

Chloe shook her head, longing for the ocean to rise and sink her shack.

"Let us help you, Chloe," her mother said.

The pain in her hand powered the anger in her response. "How the fuck can you help me?"

Her mother sighed. Chloe heard her parents' boots squeaking on the floor. For a second, she thought they might actually be leaving. Then, she was encircled in their embrace, their cold breath on her face and neck. "We've lost people too," Sean stated. There was a scraping sound. Chloe guessed he was brushing his scars with his hand. "People we loved."

That word got Chloe to open her eyes. Sean was lying next to her on the brownish-red floor, hand on his disfigured cheeks, his left eye red. Anna lay in front of her daughter's head, holding Chloe's twitching and bloodied hand, pressing the red gashes in her knuckles. Eyelids red like her life partner's, Anna's teeth were soiled with lasting dabs of blood, bits of skin wedged in the gaps. The sight of her parents made it easier for Chloe to twist her head and say, "I didn't love her. Addie didn't love me either."

"Yes, you did," Sean asserted. He reached over and moved a loose strand of hair out of Chloe's wet eye. "And Addie loved you."

Before Chloe could refute, Anna looked at her stomach and said, "She was a sister you didn't know you had."

Chloe moaned. A white puff from her mouth cooled the water that came from her eyes. "If I loved her," she replied with skepticism, "it's because she was more alone than me, loved that she was more alone than me. I used her to feel better about myself. And then." Chloe blinked, her eyelids splashing in a new surge of tears. "Then, I did nothing to help her." Amid her cries, she told her parents how she stole Addie's notebook the previous night, sparked a fight between them. To her displeasure, her parents didn't concede.

"Siblings fuck up," Sean responded with a sympathetic grin. "I'd tell you how many times my brother and I fought, but I can't count to infinity."

Anna raised her hand to Chloe's quavering wrist, said, "You loved her because you saw she was more alone than you, and you didn't want anyone to be more alone than you. I think that's why you became a cop, even with the risk. You wanted to help people more alone than you." Tears renewed in her mother's eyes. "But you're not alone, Chloe. We should've done more to help you realize that. We were." Anna wiped her eyes on her shoulder. "We were too caught up by our own shit to see what was happening to our own daughter."

Sean joined, Anna's tears reigniting his own. "I'm sorry we lied, all those years we lied. Fuck, I'm sorry we didn't even say fucking sorry that night you found out."

"I abandoned you," Anna wept. "Left you alone in Missio an entire fucking..." She coughed, a white cloud of icy tears sprinkled Chloe's face. "An entire fucking year. When I got back you." Anna let go of Chloe's wrist, seeming too ashamed to believe herself worthy of her daughter's touch. "You asked me if I left because of you. I said it was my fault, but that's where it started for you." Anna closed and opened her water-filled eyes. "We don't deserve you."

Chloe was silent. Even at the height of her parents' worst reenactment nightmares, the memories of Carthage and their service with the Black Dragoons ricocheting in their minds, she'd never seen them this exposed, this disjointed. The truth now might keep them down on that floor forever. But Chloe didn't think she could endure another day without them knowing. "I don't deserve you either, or anybody else."

"What?" her parents said in unison.

"I lied to you, too, to both of you." Chloe couldn't say it all in one burst. Her lungs didn't have the capacity. "The day we left Marathon, the day the civil war ended, I killed someone."

"After we were separated?" her father inquired. His voice seemed to be diminishing, as if he was talking to her as he and Anna left, left her to die alone in her freezing shack.

Tongue dry, eyeballs prepared to watch her parents stand and leave, defeated by their daughter's confession, Chloe answered. "That was my Awakening, where the blood on my clothes came from. Soldier tried to rob me, get the supplies we took from Ignis. She, she had her kid with her. His mom puts a T-05 in my face. My Awakening goes off. I take her knife and I. I murdered a parent, in front of her own fucking kid."

"No," Anna rejoined. Chloe's parents drew closer, not back, hugging her tight. "No, dear. You listen to us. You listening?" Chloe nodded, surprised by their immediacy. "That soldier attacked you, in a war that by then was so fucked it's a wonder she didn't shoot you outright."

"She told me to give her the fucking bag," Chloe objected. "She didn't want to kill me. She just, just wanted the supplies for her and her kid, wanted to live outside Marathon. Like we did."

"Someone draws a rifle, the burden's not on you to decide if they really intend to use it or not," her father said.

Anna patted Chloe's quaking arm. "You aren't like me and your dad. You didn't choose to make a killer out of yourself, a killer was made out of you."

Chloe shook her head. "The kid was crying, trying to wake his mom up and I fucking left him on Broad Street! That was my choice."

"Your only choice," her father replied. "Besides dying."

"I lied," Chloe said again, perplexed by her parents' continued stubbornness. "And fuck, I didn't tell you about my arm. That's when it started."

To Chloe's genuine shock, Anna chuckled under her breath and tears. "You think you're the first person to hide what they don't know how to say?"

But Chloe's tears only multiplied. "I said, 'I wish you never came home.'"

"It was our fault you said that," her father responded.

Chloe elevated her bright red hand. "I could've made you like me," she blared through her sobs.

Her parents didn't so much as wince. "You thought we'd start hurting ourselves?" Anna asked. "Because of what you said?"

As her mother said it, Chloe heard its ridiculousness. "All your reenactments. What I said, what I told you. It's not too much for—-"

"No," her parents said, kissing her forehead.

"There's enough out there already that could destroy you," Sean whispered. "Don't do that to yourself."

"You are our entire universe, an unending, indestructible universe," Anna seconded. "Whatever you do or tell us or however many kids me and your dad have, you'll be the same person you've always been, always our daughter, always Chloe."

Finally, Chloe's cries began to wane. But the shudders in her arms subsided. "It's been seven years. What if I'm locked?"

Anna inhaled a nervous breath. "I wanted to kill myself once. I was a Dragoon and I thought I'd lost you, so I tried cutting my wrist. But here I am. You're not locked. Just don't expect to get out by yourself."

It took Chloe perhaps a minute to refocus her mind. When she did, the shaking waned in her arms, her fear shifting. *Sam.*

"I'm sorry, Chloe," Sean reiterated. "About everything. But more than that I'm so proud of you."

"For what?" Chloe's right arm relaxed at the sight of her father's smile.

"Staying you."

Chloe giggled with a release more potent than any provided by her razor. The last tear dropped, her eyes damp though beginning to dry. She stretched her arms around her mother and father, hugged them as they all lay on the floor, hugged them as if she hadn't in seven years, hugged them for what felt like seven hours.

"We're going to tell you everything," Anna said, calming with her daughter. "Everything we haven't yet."

Chloe's left arm stilled, not forever she knew, but long enough. "And I'll listen to all of it." She deciphered then where her partner must've gone. "Soon. Right now I need to find Sam. Dinner tonight?"

Knuckles washed and bandaged, hand wrapped in gauze and shrouded in her dark red and black glove, eyeballs aching though un-flooded, Chloe circled the cove to the edge of south Merenranta. Exhausted as she was, her concern for her partner pushed her on, pushed her to Cheng's Bar and Restaurant. Still dressed in her blood-stained police uniform, she kicked the snow from her boots outside the entrance and went in.

At once they were staring, an older couple eating a meal at one of the window tables. They didn't speak or shout like the people she passed outside, yet their shoulders hunched and faces gritted with simultaneous glares of fright and anger, as if they were yelling so loud in their heads they didn't realize they weren't screaming at all. These looks would continue throughout Chloe's life, and not just hers.

Samantha Armistead—-traitor to her hometown, tied with Chloe's father as the most hated human being in Merenranta, wearing the dark red blood of her mother—-was right where Chloe worried she'd be, sitting on a stool at the bar. Empty shot glasses were grouped in a line on the bar, as if she desired some organization to her drinking. She held a full glass in her hand, downed its contents. *Cheng's hoping she'll drink herself to death. Why the fuck else would he let her in?*

Chloe cut between the table rows to the bar. "Sam." Samantha set the glass on the counter, didn't look at Chloe as she tried to slide the glass into alignment with the others, her drunken hands overshooting and then undershooting. "Sam?"

"Was wondering when you'd get here." Chloe stopped at the voice of the bar's owner.

Cheng stood in the corner of the kitchen, several feet back from the bar, new tray of shot glasses in hand, green work shirt on. The tray joggled in his hand, his expression illegible, as if his thoughts were unsure what route to take.

A few feet from the bar and her binge-drinking partner, Chloe recalled the older couple at the window, counted the people in the building in case the simple presence of a Second-Gen elicited a hostile response. Addie's death and Chloe's own lethargy would likely delay her

Second-Gen Stage if she had to activate it. She gestured at Samantha, to explain herself to Cheng, and said, "You letting me in?"

Cheng glanced past Chloe, to the couple that was certainly observing. Then, he looked at Samantha, walked to the bar. Placing the tray on the counter, he asked Samantha's partner, "You buying?"

"Yes," Chloe said.

Samantha reached for the shot glasses on the tray, taking one in each hand before Cheng could give them to her.

"Stay as long as you have the ration slips," Cheng said, removing each glass from the tray.

The couple gasped, as amazed as Chloe was. "I don't have any on me," Chloe responded. "I can go back and—-"

Cheng shrugged, carried the tray back to the kitchen. "We'll call it an extended tab."

She had to smile. *Guess alcohol doesn't discriminate.*

Samantha gulped a shot as Chloe sat at the stool beside her, nostrils tingling with the scent of liquor. "How many of those you having?"

"Every one." Samantha's face was somehow both flushed and barren, like a rock in sunlight. She lined the finished glass up with the others, scraping the bottom of it on the glossed counter.

"On the bar? Or in the restaurant?"

"Till my liver quits on me."

"Well," Chloe said. "You've been worse. So..."

Facing forward, as if attempting to limit Chloe to the periphery of her eyesight, Samantha chugged another shot. "Think I should go faster?"

"I want you to stop." Chloe clutched Samantha's gloved hand before she could do the next shot. Pulling off her glove and Samantha's, Chloe interlocked their fingers, kissed Samantha's freezing hand. "Please."

"Why? You hate me, right?"

Mystified, Chloe put her other hand around Samantha's shoulders, scooted closer. Samantha reached for another shot with her free hand. "What's making you think that, Sam?"

Hand hanging over the glass but not grasping, Samantha's cheeks brightened, her eyelids condensing with ire. "My mom killed Addie." Rage traveled down to her tone, strapped itself to each word. "I'm her family and she killed a kid and I couldn't fucking protect either of them! Then I...fucking came here! As soon as we got back I fucking came here! I can't even fucking stop myself!" Samantha balled her free hand into a fist, beat her forehead. "Sheriff Armistead couldn't stop herself. Neither can I."

Tightening her hold on Samantha's hand and her shoulders, Chloe set her chin on Samantha's shoulder blade. "My parents killed kids too. I haven't." Samantha stopped hitting herself, but still didn't turn to look at Chloe. "The Dragoons raised Addie to be an assassin. She left them." Her partner groaned, shook her head. "We learn from our parents, we don't become them." Samantha closed her eyes, gripped her hatted head. "Look at my hand, Sam."

Her partner's eyes opened and expanded, gazing at the bandages and gauze that covered Chloe's knuckles. She lowered her hand, curved her head. "Chloe..."

Chloe lifted her arm, curled her hand around Samantha's head, and connected their lips, her kiss almost pushing Samantha off her stool. As they parted, Chloe told her, "We can't stop ourselves every time, but we can try again. Addie would if she could."

Samantha planted her face on Chloe's shoulder, liberated herself in tears. Her cries were soft, though Chloe felt the water moistening her jacket. "It's going to be okay, it's all going to be okay," she told her partner, smiling, choosing to believe that claim. Samantha nodded into Chloe's shoulder, trusting her partner.

"You going off alcohol again?" Cheng asked from the kitchen, standing at the door to the main seating area, probably on his way to check on the older couple.

Samantha giggled in Chloe's shoulder. "Afraid so."

Cheng smirked. "You know, the place is called Cheng's Bar and Restaurant. I sell food here, too."

Chloe and Samantha held each other in a laughing embrace, much to the clear disdain of the older couple who gawked at them from across the room.

"My parents are making dinner tonight. You want to go with me?"

"Okay."

—-

EIGHTEEN

Nine months after Addie arrived in Merenranta, Chloe sat alone in the lobby of the medical center, in the shimmer of grayish-orange that crept in as the sun began to set outside. Wounds long past healed, she was dressed in a civilian winter jacket, pants, boots, and gloves. She hadn't worn her uniform since the day after Addie's death, when she turned it in to the police station at Mayor Darabont's behest, officially ending her employment with the Merenranta police department. "I'd keep you on if I could, Chloe," Darabont had said. "But a Second-Gen police officer, the town might riot at that, try to exile you and your parents on their own, or worse." Chloe would've liked the opportunity to resign, make the decision for herself, or at least pretend to. However, she understood Darabont had to terminate her, in hopes of appeasing the strong majority of the townspeople angry at him for letting her, her parents, and Samantha return. Chloe's renewed citizenship was akin to that of her Marathon citizenship, following her mother's Awakening: granted by her government yet unwanted by her neighbors.

"I bet that fucking Second-Gen gets called before we do," a man sitting a few chairs away whispered to his life partner, not quiet enough. "The fuck she here about anyway?"

"You didn't hear?" his life partner replied, with the same false murmur. It occurred to Chloe that they wanted her to hear what they were saying, just to make her obsess over how often people must talk about her and her family. "Her mom went into labor. There's a whole new Second-Gen taking up space here."

"Fucking ye, couldn't she just push the fucking thing out at home? Rinse it off in the shower? Second-Gens never get sick, the fuck do they need to come here for?" The child sitting between the man and his life partner coughed multiple times, her tiny body convulsing and bouncing in her chair. "I'm sorry, dear," the man said, gentle, fear in his expression as he rubbed his daughter's back.

"We'll see the doctor soon, okay?"

"They're ready for you upstairs," one of the clerks called to Chloe, frowning.

Chloe took a short, anxious breath and rose. "Thank you." The clerk stared down at his desk, as if humiliated at having to speak to her. Walking to the stairs, Chloe listened to the girl's unrelenting coughs. *Better to live open and give them someone to blame than lie about who you are.*

The recovery room was an exact replica of the room Addie stayed in, except on the east side of the building, so the setup was backwards. Out the window, north Merenranta stood in gray snow, the blackening ocean behind it. Chloe's parents lay together in the bed, Anna in a patient gown, Sean in scrubs. And lying on her mother's chest, wrapped in blankets and snug in her mother's left arm, was Chloe's baby sister. A doctor had told Chloe the sex when he came to the lobby to update her on the birth. Elation enveloped her muscles and nerves, the sight of her sister's bald head and plump cheeks producing something like a Second-Gen Stage but better. "Hey," she mumbled, beaming at her family.

"Hey," her parents said, smiling back, their eyes red from tears. The baby made a noise, a sort of sneeze-hiccup, and Sean blinked, as if he might cry again.

"How'd it go?" Chloe asked, taking a seat beside the bed.

"Sucked," Anna giggled. "I thought being an Awakened Second-Gen this go-round would numb the pain some." She chuckled again, Chloe with her. "Nope. But that's okay, she's a hundred percent."

The baby hiccupped, reached her little hand out of the blankets. "I think someone wants to meet her big sister," Sean laughed. With slow, careful movements, he sat up on the bed and lifted the newborn in his arms, rotating to Chloe.

Chloe tipped her head to her sister. The baby kept her eyelids closed for the most part, but in brief moments, she opened them and Chloe saw two blue irises, the same blue irises she and their mother had. Smile straining her mouth, she wondered how she'd ever been afraid this girl would take their parents away, steal all the time they had for their first daughter. "What's her name?"

Sean turned to his life partner, as if for final clarification.

"Addie," Anna said. "Addie Corday-Halley."

Chloe's left arm started to tingle as she kept her gaze on her sister, the second Addie, and remembered Darius's prediction. *If Second-Gens are evolving, replacing humans, will my sister's Awakening come before she's thirteen, like Addie's?*

"I like that name," she told her parents. Her arm was shaking, but it shook true.

Leaving Addie and her parents to rest for the night, Chloe departed the medical center into the orange glare of the evening sun and headed west to visit her other sister. Boots crunching in the gray snow of early winter, orange-white misting from her mouth, she went around the industrial neighborhood as the factories emptied out for the evening, around the wind turbines and their unchanged activity, to the tree line on Merenranta's western perimeter. The trees were gray with snow, their branches leafless, as they were every winter, though a sweet smell still wafted from a few of them, the scent peeking out from beneath the veil of salted rot and decay. The cemetery was just inside the woods, the gravestones strewn about the stalks in no precise pattern. Upon a citizen's death, space was found, a grave dug, and the casket buried, usually in the warmer months when the ground wasn't frozen. Those who died in winter lay in the morgue until the cold lifted.

Rectangle-shaped with rounded tops and colored gray, the gravestones were like hardened piles of snow, packed together and built up from the ground. Light was dimmer below the trees, but Chloe could still read the names etched to each stone. Many names she didn't recognize, names of people who lived here before she and her parents found Merenranta, before she was born even, all the way back to the Reform. Some she did know. The largest stone in the cemetery, twice the size of the others, was marked:

"SHERIFF DYLAN ARMISTEAD. PROTECTOR OF MERENRANTA. SACRIFICED HER LIFE IN DEFENSE OF HER COMMUNITY. 5th YEAR-55th YEAR."

The tremors in Chloe's arm worsened the farther into the cemetery she walked. By the time she got to the grave—-a lone stone at the absolute edge of the perimeter, where a single step more was a step out of town—-her shoulder was sore from her flailing limb. Her release couldn't wait any longer.

She sat in the snow, sat in front of the grave and its inscription:

"ADDIE. FRIEND. SISTER. FIGHTER. 55th YEAR."

Digging into her jacket pockets, Chloe took out a notebook and pencil. She set the book in her lap and turned to a blank page, began her release.

"I met our baby sister today," she said to the stone, drawing. "She's got my eyes." Chloe chortled to herself. "My eyes and your name." She drew the walls and window first, then the chairs and medical supplies, recreating the surroundings of the recovery room before moving on to the bed. As she sketched, the shakes declined in her arm, the pain lessening in her shoulder. And as she finished the rough outline of her parents and the bundle of blankets and baby on her mother's chest, her arm settled, her release gratified. "Don't laugh, but I think I'm getting better." The stone didn't laugh. Chloe gave her parents and infant sister some additional details: mouths, noses, ears, five eyes total, hair for her parents. "Wish we could've done this together while you were here." She scribbled some scars on her father's face. "I'm sure you'd be happy to tell me how shitty my drawing is."

"I think it's great."

Chloe jumped. Samantha laughed, standing over her. "Fuck," Chloe jested, slapping Samantha's leg. "You sneaking up on me?"

Teeth glowing in the orange sunlight, mouth wide with a mischievous grin, Samantha shrugged her shoulders and said, "Just trying to be quiet. People aren't supposed to make noise over here."

"Yeah, okay," Chloe giggled. Her life partner sat beside her. "What are you doing out here actually? Patrol?"

Clothed in her police uniform, Samantha nodded and said, "Last check on the perimeter before I clock out for the day." She skimmed Chloe's drawing, seeming to take closer note of the image. "What'd they have?"

"Girl. Named her Addie."

Samantha tittered, slanted her head onto Chloe's shoulder. "Addie and them all good?"

"Yeah, everything went fine." Chloe put her arm around Samantha's back and set her hand on her life partner's shoulder.

"Sorry I wasn't there. Asshole kids tried to steal a couple liquor bottles from Cheng's."

"That's all right, Sheriff."

Samantha made a grumbling sound.

"Still don't like the name?"

"Mayor's out of his fucking mind thinking this will work out because of my last name." Samantha scoffed. "Half the town doesn't even qualify me as human. Maybe I should start agreeing with them, see if that calms them down."

Chloe dipped her eyes to the notebook in her lap, to the family in her drawing. Two parents, Anna Corday and Sean Halley, a Second-Gen and a human, partnered together for almost sixteen years, one Second-Gen child born, another Second-Gen child grown and partnered with a human. Chloe raised her head to Addie's grave. She thought of Darius's prediction again, but not as she had prior to now. "No, you're the same, and you're not...humans are not going extinct, even if what Darius said is real. The Previous Civilization said we're separate species and nobody questioned that. But when you found out what I am, you kissed me and said, 'feels the same to me.'" Chloe Corday hesitated, turned and saw Sheriff Samantha Armistead smiling at her, reassuring her. "We'll start there."

ACKNOWLEDGEMENTS

To my readers, friends, and extended family, thank you for the support you've continued to show me as I move from my first book to my second.

To Jamie Fueglein, Maggie Peyton, and Abbey Elliott (Elliot), thank you for working with my books and helping to make them what they are.

To Wanda Fisher and Ethan Ratke, thank you for the encouragement you've given me since well before I was a writer. I love you both and I hope I've been able to give you the same reinforcement.

To my parents, I would not be a writer without the two of you. I would not be myself without the two of you. I owe every book I write to the two of you. Thank you and I love you.

ABOUT THE WRITER

Evan Ratke was born and raised in the suburbs of Richmond, Virginia. He graduated from Longwood University with a Bachelor of Science in Sociology in the spring of 2016. Somewhere between exams, papers, and an awkward attempt at a social life, he started work on what would eventually become his first novel, Dragoon, released in 2018. His sequel novel, Chloe, followed in 2019. Ratke is an active runner and continues to live in the Richmond area. He is currently pursuing new writing efforts, including his third novel.

Made in the USA
Middletown, DE
21 January 2020